"Broadfoot is the real deal. A s[illegible]
CRIMESQUAD.COM

"It's hard to believe [this] is a deb[illegible] a certainty of purpose, a clarity of voice and a real sense of danger leaking from the pages of this politically charged crime drama… Broadfoot is here, and he's ready to sit at the table with some of the finest crime writers Scottish fiction has to offer." RUSSEL D. MCLEAN

"Gritty with a strong identity. Broadfoot is destined for crime success." DUNDEE INTERNATIONAL BOOK PRIZE JUDGES

FALLING FAST

NEIL BROADFOOT

CONTRABAND

Contraband is an imprint of Saraband

Published by Saraband
Suite 202, 98 Woodlands Road
Glasgow, G3 6HB, Scotland

www.saraband.net

ISBN: 9781908643537
ebook: 9781908643544

Printed in the EU on sustainably sourced paper.

1 3 5 7 9 10 8 6 4 2

Editor: Craig Hillsley
Text design by Laura Jones

Almost twenty-five years ago, I made a promise to a very special woman. So this one has to be for my Gran, Edna Wright, who probably would have needed a whisky and lemonade ('Though just a wee one, John') after reading about all the daft buggers I've dreamed up, but would have been proud of me anyway.

1

For an instant she believed she had become the angel he always told her she was. Suspended there – time congealing as the city unfolded towards the horizon, the cold air searing her lungs – she felt as though she could reach into the flawless blue of the November sky and touch Heaven itself.

Up here, away from the arguments, the fear, the hatred, she had finally found the peace that had escaped her for so long. She smiled, realising he had been right all along. At the time, she had thought him naive, but now she realised what he had said was true; all you needed was the strength to believe.

Faith.

But instead of Heaven, it was Hell that claimed her. Her stomach lurched as gravity yanked her brutally to earth, the ground hurtling towards her. The howling wind tore at her eyes and pinned them open as it roared in her ears, drowning out all other sounds, including her own rising scream.

• • •

Brian Edwards slipped into East Princes Street Gardens at the entrance next to the Scott Monument, dodging people without really being aware of it, eyes already scouting out a good spot where he could take a seat, eat his lunch and admire the view as he tried not to think about the job he was quickly coming to despise; the computer screen and customer service calls he would have to return to in just an hour. He had spotted a few suits on the way here, all with the same anaesthetised look he noticed every time he looked in the mirror at work. Was this really it? Was this what he had become at twenty-four, just another wage slave staggering around Edinburgh's financial services sector? Clinging to whatever shitty job was available like it was a chunk of wreckage from the Titanic after the recession iceberg hit, too scared to let go, spending the days punching in numbers and giving customers your best 'here to help' voice, while filling your notepads with doodles of chairs hooked up to car batteries and computer screens exploding in a spray of glass and smoke?

Spotting a potential seat on the grass beside the Monument, Brian made his way forward. He got about two steps when the first scream rang out, freezing him. His head darted around, heart hammering from the fright as he tried to see who had screamed and wh…

A dull whump rang out to his left, shock juddering through his body as though God had clapped His hands next to his ear. Something warm splashed onto his side and his left cheek. Brian instinctively flinched away, losing his footing and falling heavily to the ground. More screams now, drowning out the steady drone of buses and cars on Princes Street. Gasps of panic and fear; choked, thick gargling as someone was violently sick; hysterical sobbing: all crowding in on Brian's shock-addled senses.

'Aw Christ, no, no.'

A baby mewling, quickly rising to a high, keening wail like a dentist's drill.

'…call an ambulance…'

'…no help…'

'…be sick…'

He reached up, trying to wipe at whatever had splashed onto his face. His hand came away bloody. Brian felt all heat drain from his body.

SHOT! his mind screamed. A few days ago, he had read in the *Capital Tribune* about groups of neds running around the city, taking pot-shots with BB guns at anyone that took their fancy. He'd walked with hunched shoulders ever since.

You've been shot. Some stupid little fuck with an airgun's got off a lucky shot and...

'Help!' Brian cried in a high, wavering voice that was almost a scream. 'Help me please, someo...'

His voice died in his throat as he looked at where the thumping sound had come from. To his left...

Oh Jesus, Jesus, Jesus, please no. Don'tlookdon'tlook.

But he had to look. And when he did, he saw the entire scene with such horrific clarity he thought it would drive him insane.

A body lay in the grass about a foot from him, twisted and broken. Bone peeked out from several places like a hedgehog's spines – driven through flesh and clothing by the force of the impact and glinting a hellishly brilliant white in the heatless early afternoon sun. With the terror and adrenalin, it was like looking at the scene with a microscope. He could see tiny flecks of fabric, blood and ruptured skin hanging like bloody streamers from some of the bones.

All he wanted was to look away, but he couldn't. He could feel the images branding themselves into his mind, knew he would be revisiting them for the rest of his life. But then his eyes moved towards the head, and Brian felt his mind give a sickening wrench that made him want to die.

Don'tlookdon'tlookohsweetjesusbriandon'tLOOKatthe...

...head that had crumpled open on impact. Brian tried to suppress the growing scream clamouring in his mind and looked at the mangled mess of dark, almost black blood and oozing grey brain matter...

Porridge and blackcurrant jam, he thought, and cackled.

...which, in the sunlight, winked and sparkled from between clotted masses of what looked like blonde hair. He wiped his hand across his face again...

Bloodandbrainbloodandbrainbloodandbrain.

...knowing what he would find. A siren wailed somewhere in the distance; Brian could just hear it over the roaring in his ears. He began to wipe and claw frantically at himself, trying to get the blood...

AndbrainsbloodandBRAINS.

...off.

Tears slid down Brian's cheeks as he finally began to scream, his own blood – from the welts he had dug into his face and hands – mingling with that of whoever it was that had just jumped off the Scott Monument and landed just a few inches away from him.

2

Doug McGregor was just settling down to his first pint when the phone rang. He glanced over to the bar, where the Halfway House's owner, Mike Granger, gave him a scowl sour enough to curdle the head on his Guinness. As the cracked burgundy leather booth seats, sanded floors and sepia-toned pictures that dotted the bar's walls showed, Mike was a traditionalist who believed everything that came after the Sixties was either a waste of time or a complete fuck-up. It wasn't hard to guess which category mobile phones fell in.

Doug shrugged his shoulders and gave Mike what he hoped was an apologetic smile as he dug the phone out of his pocket and read the screen. 'WALTER – Office', it flashed. Doug's finger hovered over the answer key as the thought of just switching the damn thing off flitted across his mind.

He could sell it, too. After all, he was in the sticks, all the way out in Prestonview on the outer edge of East Lothian to be exact, and everyone knew that mobile phone reception could get patchy this far out of town.

Sighing, he pressed answer and clamped the phone to his ear.

'Walter, lovely to hear from you,' he hissed into the phone, painfully aware that he, Mike and a flea-bitten mutt called Denver were the only living things in Prestonview's most popular social venue at that moment. 'How's my favourite news editor today?'

'All the better for hearing your sweet voice,' came the gruff, Glasgow-tinged response. 'Where ur ye?'

Doug glanced up at Mike, who was busying himself restocking juice bottles behind the bar and trying his hardest not to make it so obvious he was listening intently to every word Doug said.

'You know, the usual,' Doug said. 'Just checking out a few things.'

'A few things that come in pint glasses, I'll fuckin' bet,' Walter grunted down the phone. 'You getting anywhere with that yet? Any lines on McGinty?'

'No,' Doug replied slowly, dropping his voice and clamping the phone closer to his ear. 'And to be honest, this isn't the best time to talk about it, Walter.'

'Awww,' Walter replied, 'did I call at a bad time?'

'Well...'

'Tough shit. You may be able to persuade the boss that sitting in a pub is cutting-edge investigative journalism, but no' me. I need you to check something out for me.'

Doug sighed and pushed his pint across the table and out of reach. It wasn't as if he really wanted it anyway. Too early in the day. But sitting in a small-town pub, asking delicate questions and ordering an orange juice was just asking for trouble. He knew answering the phone had been a bad idea. 'What's up?'

'Had a jumper about an hour and a bit ago,' Walter said, trying – and failing – to keep the edge of relish out of his voice. 'Someone took a dive off the Scott Monument. Made a hell of a mess, by all accounts.'

Doug sat forward, suddenly interested. He glanced at his watch. Just after 1.30pm. 'I take it you managed to get something for second edition?' he asked cautiously. The last thing he needed to hear right now was Walter telling him that the paper was waiting to run a third edition and he was up to write the story. Hitting the newsstands at 5pm, the copy deadline would be 2.30pm to get the new pages to the printers in time. Tight turnaround. Ah, the happy life of the crime reporter.

'Yeah,' Walter grunted, clearly unhappy with what the paper had managed to get on the story so far. 'It was sketchy though. Unidentified suicide victim, witnesses said this, body declared dead at scene, all the usual boring shit.'

'So what do you need from me?'

'Details,' Walter replied in a you-know-better-than-that tone. 'The cops are playing this one very close to their chests, and I thought that with your contacts, you could get us the inside track on what happened and who this person was.'

'Aw, come on, Walter,' Doug said, reaching for his pint again, raising it slightly as Mike glanced over. 'Someone else can do that, surely? You know what I'm trying to do here.'

'Skive as much as possible?' He paused for a moment, his voice becoming softer and more serious. Doug could almost see Walter back at the *Capital Tribune*'s offices, slouched in his chair, a meaty paw engulfing the phone's receiver, clamping it conspiratorially close to his mouth.

'Yeah, Doug, I know. And I know you'll get something. But this won't take long. And it's a splash on a day when fuck-all else is looking like a contender. So get on it, okay?'

'Yeah,' Doug sighed, glancing at his watch again. 'I'll get back to you as soon as.'

'I can hardly wait,' Walter replied, then cut the line.

3

Sam McGinty stood in the middle of his living room, listening to the phone's shrill ring as it cut through the silence. He glanced up nervously at the front window, checking again that the heavy curtains Rita had pleaded for him to put up that morning were drawn tight against the afternoon sun and the army of reporters that had laid siege to their home.

Fucking vultures.

It has started again last week, just as he and Rita were starting to fool themselves into believing it *wouldn't* start again. It began as it always did: a polite phone call first, asking for a quote on the latest development. When this was greeted with the usual response – which, depending on how stubborn the reporter was and how many calls Sam had already taken that day, ranged from polite to 'fuck off' – they started knocking on the door.

Always in pairs these days though, and always with a photographer at the end of the garden path, camera eagerly trained on Sam, ready to capture him if he lost his temper again. He had only done that once, after a particularly bad spell that had reduced Rita to a whimpering wreck of a woman, scared of her own shadow; a crude parody of the woman Sam had met and fallen in love with all those years ago at the Newtongrange Pit dance. After a fortnight of constant calls and door knocks, Sam had finally answered his door.

The journalist who had been knocking was some zit-faced little shit, apparently from one of the bigger Glasgow-based tabloids if his nasal drone was anything to go by. He had forgotten all his questions as soon as the door opened and he caught sight of the axe Sam was holding.

The memory of the look on the little bastard's face still brought a smile to Sam's face.

'Sam? Sam, you down there?' Rita's voice, calling down from the top of the stairs.

'Yeah, love. I'm here. You okay?'

'What do you think?' she replied, trying for levity and failing. He could hear the tension in her voice, the anxiety. She tried to hide it from him, tried to be strong, but they both knew how much this took out of them. The passing of the years didn't make it any easier.

And all because of their one and only son; the apple of their eye, their precious gift from God.

The little cunt who had made their lives a misery.

'You want a cup of tea, love?'

'Yes, please,' Rita called back. 'But pull the phone out of the wall first, will you? The ringing's bringing my headache back.'

'No problem.' Sam made for the phone. He meant to simply pull it out of the wall, but as he reached out, anger scalded through him. This was no way to live, held a virtual prisoner in your own home by a bunch of slimy hacks who thought nothing of hounding an old man and woman out of their minds in search of a juicy quote to feed a scandal-hungry public. He thought of the pack of journalists camped across the road right now, camera lenses hanging out of saloon car windows as they tried to blend in and not look suspicious. He had counted four cars this morning, knew there would be more by the end of the day. There were no TV camera crews yet, but it was early and they would turn up sooner or later. After all, Derek McGinty was the biggest story of the day.

Sam snatched up the phone, the arthritis in his knuckles moaning as he clenched the handset as hard as he could and tried to ignore the stinging heat behind his eyes.

'Listen,' he hissed, 'I don't know who you are, and I don't care who you work for. We haven't heard anything from Derek, and we won't. You think he'd come within fifty miles of this place with you parasites hanging around?'

Silence on the other end of the line. No, not quite silence; Sam could faintly hear breathing through the static and distortion. Whoever was calling, they were on a crap line.

'Fine,' Sam snarled, his vision jumping with his heartbeat as his blood roared through his ears. 'Whoever you are, fuck you. You're nothing more than a fucking coward, a fuc...'

'Dad.'

Sam jumped as though the phone had been electrified. The rage and frustration drained out of him, replaced by a numbing cold that twisted around his stomach and up his spine. He heard himself gasp as though he had just been punched in the guts. When he spoke, his voice was a rasping whisper. No surprise. It was hard to talk properly when it felt as though your lungs had been filled with concrete.

'D... Derek? Derek, that you?'

'Yeah, Dad, it's me.' The voice was flat, hard, full of the old Derek defiance. Sam had first heard that tone when Derek was about sixteen, just at the point things started to get really bad. Derek had stolen his old air rifle, taken it into the woods that sprawled across the hills behind Prestonview for a bit of hunting. It was an asthmatic old .77, not powerful enough to kill anything he shot. But Sam knew Derek didn't care about that. He was more interested in watching things suffer.

After finding the gun missing from the shed, Sam had headed into the woods, which was Derek's favourite place to play. He found his son crouched over a rabbit he had shot, watching its chest rising and falling rapidly, mouth snapping for air, blood oozing slowly from the pellet holes peppering its body.

He had snatched the rifle from Derek, knocked the little shit off his feet with one heavy-handed slap to the back of the head. Sam hesitated over the rabbit, swallowed back the bile rising in his throat, then caved its head in with the butt of the rifle. Better that than a slow, lingering death with Derek leering over it.

'What the fuck you thinking, you wee shit?' Sam had roared, barely resisting the urge to deal with Derek the way he had with the rabbit. 'Why the fuck would you do something like this?'

'Dunno,' Derek had grunted, rubbing the back of his neck, dark eyes (so like his mother's, Sam had thought) glaring back. 'Wanted to see what it was like firing it, is all.' The voice the same as the one on the other end of the phone now; disconnected, cold. Defiant.

'Dad? You still there?'

Sam took a deep breath, blinked away the past. 'Where the fuck are you? It's like a bloody circus here. There're cameras and reporters everywhere. Your mother's up to ninety.'

'What the fuck you want me to do about it?' Derek snapped. 'I didnae ask for this, did I? You want me to say sorry? I'm sorry, okay?'

'Bit late for that, isn't it?' Sam winced as he spoke, but he couldn't help it. He could feel the anger starting to glow again, hot coals being fanned.

On the other end of the line, Derek sighed, impatient. 'Look, is there any way you can get away from the house without being seen?'

Sam's stomach gave an oily lurch. Here it came. He fought the urge to just slam the phone down, leave his son hanging. After everything, no one would blame him, least of all Rita, but...

But...

'Dad?'

'Yeah,' he replied, voice dropping to a whisper as he glanced at the stairs, praying Rita hadn't heard. 'Where?'

'They've not built on the old railway yet, have they?'

'No,' Sam replied. The old railway was the former East Coast line that ran along the spine of Prestonview on its way through East Lothian and into Edinburgh. It was once the main way of getting both people and coal from the pits into the capital city. Now it was a tarmacked walkway intended for and mostly ignored by pedestrians, cyclists and all those who thought they could put a little distance between themselves and the inevitable hole in the ground by wheezing their way through a run.

'Great. Remember where you caught me smoking that time?'

Sam nodded, recalling a gnarled old tree at the side of a railway bridge. It was when Derek was about eleven: Johnny Evans, who'd worked at the pit years ago and now ran the local newsagents, had called Sam and told him he'd seen Derek with a few other kids who had bought a packet of Regal for a fly puff.

'The kid I sold them to was old enough,' Johnny said, voice sharp with guilt. 'But when I saw Derek, I thought you'd want to know.'

Sam had wanted to know. And it hadn't been hard to figure out where Derek would be. He had loved to climb that tree. Loved to do other things there, too.

Other things…

'Yeah,' Sam said, suddenly exhausted. The phone was getting heavy. 'When?'

'It'll take me a while to get there. Tomorrow, say about eight o'clock?'

'In the morning?'

Derek's laughter grated down the phone. It sounded like the background static that crackled on the line. 'No, Dad,' he said slowly, as though talking to a dim child. 'At night. It'll be dark then. And quiet.'

'Oh, silly me. Of course.' Sam's voice hardened. He'd almost forgotten Derek's casual cruelty. Almost.

He was vaguely aware of Derek hissing down the phone. '…fer fuck's sake, Dad, it's not as if…'

But Sam had already slammed the phone down. His whole body shook as he fought back the tears. He looked around at the room forced into gloom on a bright autumn day, cursing his son for bringing this on them, and himself for not being able to shut that son out of his life.

4

After hanging up on Walter, Doug's first move had been to finish his pint. He didn't want it, sure as hell didn't need it, especially if he was driving. But it was the job. After all, it wouldn't help to be seen as the type of guy who dropped everything the moment his boss tugged at his leash.

He drained the Guinness deliberately, just slowly enough to look casual, then returned the glass to bar as he got up to leave.

'That you away, then?' Mike asked. It never failed to amaze Doug how stating the blatantly obvious could be passed off as conversation.

'Yeah, that's me, no rest for the wicked.' He gave a heavy sigh, hoping Mike would understand that leaving his pub was the last thing he wanted to do. 'Listen, Mike, if you happen to hear anything about...'

Mike waved the rest of Doug's words away with a large, pale hand. 'No problem,' he said softly, eyes straying to where Denver lay, a pile of matted fur snoring loudly on the floor. 'If I hear anything about McGinty, I'll let you know. Don't think there's a chance in hell that he'll come back to Prestonview though.'

Doug nodded his thanks and headed for the door. In truth, he agreed with Mike – family ties or no, the man would have to be either a complete fuckhead or totally suicidal to return to his home town. But still, there was always the chance. The press pack camped outside his mum and dad's front door wouldn't help, but if there was even a sniff of the bastard in Prestonview, Mike would hear about it.

It was the nature of small towns. As a talking shop and confessional, the local – and in Prestonview's case, only – pub did more trade than a church. And thanks to a month of afternoon pints, nightly visits and conversations about the state of the local Under 16's football team, which just happened to have Mike's grandson Kenny playing centre forward – a fact Doug had been very careful to give prominence when he wrote up a match report on them for the *Tribune*'s weekend round-up – Doug was now seen as a member of the congregation. An occasional member who always turned up late and sang out of tune maybe, but at least they were talking to him. If Mike heard anything, he'd tell him.

Outside, the sky's earlier brightness had given way to a smear of bruised cloud and anaemic sunlight. There was a smell of rain in the air. Doug unlocked his car (which, save Mike's battered old Cortina, was the only visitor to the car park), got in and dug his phone out of his pocket. He punched a pre-programmed hot key and listened as the phone dialled and began to ring.

'Hello, CID. Detective Sergeant Drummond speaking.'

'Hiya, Susie. How's tricks?'

A sigh at the other end of the line. She'd been expecting him to call for most of the morning. 'Doug. What a surprise. Can't think why you'd be calling me today.'

'You know me, I love to be unpredictable. Listen, Walter wants me to get something on the Scott Monument diver. Any chance you can fill in some of the blanks for me?'

A pause on the other end of the line. Then Susie's voice, quieter than before, more aware of those around her and who could be listening in.

'You must be psychic,' she said. 'I'm heading down to the lock-up just now about that. If you're around the Cowgate in about half an hour, we could maybe meet up after that?'

'Love to,' Doug replied brightly. 'Give me a call when you get free and I'll meet you.'

'You could always come in for a tour if you wanted,' Susie teased, knowing there wasn't a chance in hell that Doug would ever set foot inside the city mortuary, known by police officers throughout Edinburgh as 'the lock-up'.

'Nice to see you're still working on that sense of humour, Susie.'

'Isn't it, though?' she shot back. 'See you soon.'

Doug clicked his phone off and started his car, enjoying the throaty growl as he over-revved the engine. His parents were right, he knew it deep down. The car, a low-slung roadster with a ridiculously large engine, was painfully expensive to insure and an invitation to rack up even more points on his already colourful licence. But fuck it, it was fun. At thirty-three, the boy racer in him wasn't quite dead yet.

He drove out of the car park, took a left and crawled along the main street, which was a long, grey downhill of newsagents, bakeries and betting shops that gave way to about a dozen old-style granite homes with huge lawns, heavy double doors and white-painted window frames; one of the few lingering signs that Prestonview was once a town with money and success.

Doug stayed on the 30 mph limit until the road widened and he saw the national speed limit sign. 'You are now leaving Prestonview,' the East Lothian Council sign read. Some comedian had scrawled '*Away tae' Fuck*' over the sign in spray-paint. Smiling, Doug dropped down into second and hammered the accelerator. The car leapt forward, almost as eager as he was for the narrow, winding roads that would take him along the coast and back to Edinburgh.

5

Doug pulled into a space on High School Wynd, a narrow cobbled lane just off the Cowgate and next to the city mortuary. The car's engine seemed to sigh a little when he pulled the key from the ignition. He wasn't surprised; after hurtling around hairpin corners on single-track roads at what felt like 90 mph, Doug felt a little like sighing himself.

He double-checked his phone to make sure he hadn't missed a call from Susie, then went to retrieve his notes from the boot. With nothing else to do but wait, he decided to go over what he had on Derek McGinty on the off-chance he had missed something – some clue as to what his next move would be – in the first hundred or so times he had picked his way through the rubble that was McGinty's life.

In 1990, at the tender age of sixteen, Derek McGinty had been a typical example of the small-town thug. With no real education behind him and little chance of work in Prestonview – now that the mining industry had more or less ceased to exist throughout the Lothians, transforming once-prosperous communities into virtual ghost towns at a stroke – he got to work creating an alternative record of achievement. Breaking and entering, reselling stolen goods, GBH, casual cruelty to animals: all the usual fun activities that made a young man's parents so proud.

His record, a copy of which Susie had given Doug on the quiet after a lot of pestering and the promise of work on her car, was peppered with appearances in front of the youth panel and snippets of reports from social workers. Phrases such as 'chronically demotivated', 'socially ill-adjusted' and 'set in a cycle of boredom and frustration through which criminal activity is his only release' kept popping up like rust blisters on old bodywork. To Doug, they all amounted to the same thing: what his own dad would have called a 'bad little bugger'.

Two years later, Derek got bored with life in Prestonview and made his way to Edinburgh. He quickly became involved in working on the doors of some of the city's less fashionable nightclubs. It made sense; cash in hand, no questions asked and a job snarling at people to discourage trouble, or stepping in with fists flying if anything ever kicked off. McGinty's name appeared a few times in police reports about drug dealing and assaults in those clubs, but there was never enough evidence to prosecute. For some reason, witnesses didn't seem too eager to talk about him.

But then, on September 14, 1992, Derek McGinty graduated from small-time thug to Edinburgh's most wanted man in one sickening leap.

Her name was Bethany Miller, a twenty-one-year-old originally from Derby who was in Edinburgh to study English literature and history at the university. She was, according to the friends and family who talked to the police and the press later, a bright, vivacious girl who loved Edinburgh and the social life that went with it. She was outgoing, they said, the type of person who lit up a room and made a party.

Looking at the pictures he'd culled from the *Tribune*'s library, Doug could see the appeal. Bethany was your typical early-twenties bombshell: tall and athletic, but still with a figure, and an open, inviting face you never got tired of looking at framed by long, dark hair. But, according to her tutors, her most attractive feature was her mind. She was sharp, they all said, always asking questions and ready to challenge established ideas. Her eyes said as much to Doug. In the photograph he had, a hand-out from the family at the time of the court case, she was frozen in mid-stride, a birthday cake in hand. She was smiling from ear to ear, showing off small, white teeth and the type of dimples models killed for. Happiness and confidence seemed to radiate from her eyes, the deepest, purest blue Doug had ever seen. *I have my whole life ahead of me,* those eyes said. *I'm happy here and now. I know what I am and who I am and I'm happy.*

I'm happy.

Which only made what McGinty did all the worse.

According to what was reported at the time, Bethany had been on a night out with a few of her friends. They had visited a few student haunts in and around the Old Town, including a club in the Cowgate.

Doug glanced up from his notes for a moment, staring down the lane. He knew the place, had been in there a few times himself at the tail-end of a night out.

Naturally enough, Bethany had attracted more than her fair share of attention that night. But one of the people watching her happened to be Derek McGinty. When Bethany and her friends left, McGinty had followed. Doug wondered what was in his mind then, if he had already planned what he was going to do and how far he was going to go. If he did, then the bastard was even more dangerous than he had first thought.

Bethany's friends, who lived in the university's halls of residence overlooking Arthur's Seat, made sure she got home safely as she lived in a flat in Marchmont that her parents – a doctor and a teacher – were renting for her during her studies. The friends shared a taxi from the club, swinging by Bethany's flat to drop her off on the way back to the halls.

'She got home safely,' one of her friends was quoted as saying in the *Tribune*'s report on the trial. 'We always made sure we all got home safely. I mean, that's what you're meant to do, isn't it? Make sure your friends are safe?'

Not safe enough.

Police reports and forensics – again supplied off the record by Susie – showed that McGinty didn't have much trouble getting in; the lock on the door to Bethany's tenement was broken, meaning all he had to do was jog up the stair to her flat on the third floor. Once there, he simply knocked on the door. Doug closed his eyes and saw Bethany, mind addled by booze, ears ringing from the pulsing bass of the club, swinging the door open to see who was there. One of her friends who had forgotten something, maybe? Had she left something in the taxi? He saw her trying to slam the door shut as McGinty pushed his way into the flat, saw her trying to scream as he clamped a hand over her face, suffocating, choking…

The full extent of what happened next wasn't reported in the *Tribune* or any other newspaper – it was deemed too disturbing. Reading through the police reports, Doug wasn't surprised.

McGinty had manhandled Bethany into her bedroom, giving her a few hard knocks when she struggled, and had tied her to her bed, gagging her with a pair of her own stockings as he did so. He stripped her and sexually assaulted her for more than three hours. During this ordeal he had taken his time, pausing to consider what torment he could inflict upon her next.

McGinty ransacked Bethany's room and found a vibrator, which he used both vaginally and anally. He also forced Bethany to give him oral sex. Repeatedly. And, just to make sure he had a memento of the event, McGinty used Bethany's own camera to take photographs. Doug skipped a few pages ahead to a transcript of Bethany's interview. She mentioned the camera repeatedly, and he imagined he could hear her voice rising in panic as she remembered. The flash burning her skin, the harsh snap and click as he circled her, recording every moment of her degradation. Searches of McGinty's flat – a shithole tenement in the rougher end of Leith – failed to uncover the camera, and he refused to tell police where it was in subsequent interviews.

Another torment for Bethany to endure. She would have to rebuild her life knowing that somewhere, somewhere, there were pictures of her. Naked and exposed, McGinty's hands on her, legs forced open, her face a frozen cry of pain and shame.

Doug paused, eyes wandering across the street in front of him. There was something about the attack that bothered him; something beyond the obvious, that is. He re-read the relevant paragraphs, eyes seeking out the key words and phrases: 'forced penetration with a foreign object', 'oral rape', 'condoms found in several locations', 'victim reports being photographed repeatedly by assailant'. He chewed his lip, considering, then shrugged. Nothing.

McGinty finally left Bethany at a little before 7am. Doug wondered what had made him leave. After all, he had his victim completely subdued and a flat that was totally sealed off from the rest of the world. At the trial, police and psychologists believed the breaking of the day panicked McGinty, who would have wanted to make his escape when the stairwell was quiet and the streets were empty. Doug could understand this, but part of him knew it was simpler than that. Nightmares and monsters lost their power in daylight. And that was what McGinty was. A monster. And a coward.

Bethany was found just after noon that day by her friends, who had gone to her flat after she missed her morning lectures and failed to answer her phone. They found her as McGinty had left her – bound to her bed, bleeding and broken.

But despite this, Bethany was able to give the police a full description of McGinty. She even waived her right to anonymity and made a public appeal through the police to help track down her attacker and help other women avoid the same ordeal. This, coupled with the statement of one of her friends who said she had seen 'some creepy doorman' eying Bethany up in the club, and a media baying for blood over such an outrage against an attractive, middle-class girl with 'her whole life ahead of her', meant McGinty didn't remain at large for long. He was arrested three days later, police crashing through the door of his council flat with sledgehammers in hand and the image of Bethany fresh in their minds.

Three months later he was put on trial. Someone on the prosecution team was very smart, very lucky or very connected, as they managed to push the charges all the way up to attempted murder. And, after no more than a week – during which Bethany was forced by both the prosecution and defence to relive what had happened in front of a room full of strangers – McGinty was sentenced to fifteen years in prison.

After the trial, Bethany quit her university course and returned home to her parents. Doug couldn't find any mention of her after that, but he hoped she had found a little peace. She deserved it.

McGinty, meanwhile, served six years before appealing against his sentence in 1998. A bleeding-heart judge, who Doug could only assume was a woman-hating fuckwit whose brains had long since turned to mush beneath his wig, heard the appeal, which hinged on diminished responsibility and a 'febrile atmosphere at the time of the case due to media interest'. The judge ruled that McGinty's sentence was overly severe, and promptly slashed it to eight years, including time already served.

Derek McGinty walked free of Edinburgh's Saughton jail on January 26, 2001. The story was a national sensation, with reformers, right-wingers and human rights activists all chipping in to the debate over sentencing and rehabilitation. Bethany was only mentioned in passing. Not surprising. Why dwell on yesterday's news?

At the time, speculation was rife as to what McGinty's next move would be. As he had attacked Bethany before the introduction of the Sex Offender Register, he was free to go wherever in the UK he chose, and the police couldn't do a thing – officially. Unofficially, a close eye was to be kept on him. But not too close, the human rights groups made sure of that. The last thing the police needed was some injury-claims-rent-a-lawyer suggesting McGinty should sue them for harassment.

The reports Susie had provided showed that McGinty initially headed west, working his way from Glasgow up to Greenock on the west coast and then back inland and east towards Fife. He had appeared to settle in Cairneyhill, a small village outside Dunfermline, and take work in a local pub as a barman. That had lasted until about a month ago, when a TV news and current affairs show aired a programme about Scotland's relationship with the UK and the European Union. One section examined human rights law – including how it had influenced the slashing of Derek McGinty's jail term.

The show used file footage of him being led away after being sentenced at his trial, footage that was seen by more than one resident of Cairneyhill. Ugly scenes followed, and officers from the Fife arm of Police Scotland were called to escort McGinty from his home to avoid a public lynching of 'that perverted bastard'.

McGinty had been offered protective custody, which he blankly refused. The police could do nothing but let him go and he promptly vanished.

But, asked the media, where would anyone, even a 'sick sex pervert', go when they had no job, no place to stay and no money?

Everyone came up with the same answer. Home. After all, it was known that, despite everything, he had kept in touch with his mother and father.

And so a game of cat and mouse began. Doug had written several pieces connected to the story, from feature stories about a town 'living in fear of its most infamous son' to hard-edged news and political pieces calling for reform of the legal system and retroactive listing of anyone in Scottish prisons for a sexually-related crime. The stories gave him a headache every time he sat at his keyboard, as he was running along a legal knife-edge with every sentence he wrote, but it was a great story, and the deeper Doug looked, the more he wanted to know what would happen next.

But so far, McGinty had failed to appear.

Doug shuffled through his papers, finding a shot of McGinty

taken from his trial. About 5ft 8ins tall, thick set with the beginnings of a beer gut, severely cut dark brown hair with a sharp widow's peak. Thin lips, a nose that was obviously no stranger to knuckles. Police reports described McGinty's eyes as brown, but to Doug they looked black. In the picture, he was glaring straight into the lens, unashamed. *Come and get me, fucker*, those eyes said. *Come and get me.*

Doug was startled out of his thoughts by his phone. He flicked answer.

'Hello?'

'Doug, it's me.' The voice was flat, almost atonal.

'Susie? That you? You sound awful.'

'Yeah, fuck you very much, Doug.' A pause, then a heavy, body-shaking sigh echoed down the line. 'Shit. Sorry, bad day. You still want to meet?'

'You still up to it?'

'As long as it's in a pub,' Susie replied. 'After what I've just seen, I need a drink. And you're buying.'

'No problem. Where do you want to meet?'

'You know the Mitre?'

Doug mumbled a response. It was a pub in the middle of the Royal Mile, close to its junction with North Bridge. 'How long?'

'Say about ten minutes?'

No problem,' Doug said. 'I'll have a drink waiting for you.'

'Make it a double, will you?'

'No problem, Susie. See you in a bit.'

Doug hung up and began gathering his notes on McGinty. As he did, he came across the photo he had been studying when Susie called.

Black eyes boring into him, full of hatred and arrogance. *Come and get me, motherfucker. Come and get me.*

Doug intended to do just that. If not for him or his readers, then for Bethany. She deserved that much at least.

6

Susie paused on the steps of the morgue and waved at a couple of uniforms she knew who were sitting in a patrol car at the entrance, waiting for the security barrier to rise. They had offered her a lift back to the CID room at Gayfield Place but she made her excuses, saying she needed to chase up a few leads while she was in the centre of town.

The sky was now dull and heavy with the threat of rain. She wished it would. Maybe it would wash away the cloying sting of chemicals and the rotten, bitter-iron tang of blood and dead, mangled flesh that clung to the back of her throat.

The morgue was at the top of a slight hill overlooking the Cowgate. She watched as cars droned past, drivers blissfully unaware of the horrors contained in the building she had just emerged from. The stench of blood and chemicals and decay, bodies that had been burnt or stabbed or beaten, or the decayed husks of those who just closed their eyes and never woke up. All framed in harsh florescent light and cold glinting metal, making sure you saw every detail. Susie envied the passers-by their ignorance. She closed her eyes, took a few deep, greedy breaths of the damp fresh air. She ran a hand around her neck inside the open-necked collar of her blouse. It wasn't tight, but she felt stifled.

She glanced to her right, down the hill towards the Pleasance. When she was a student at Edinburgh, the Pleasance – and the gym there – had been her refuge. She supposed it was natural enough as she had always been interested in sports. Tall and willowy as a child growing up in Clydebank, her long lean frame made her perfect for athletics. The male-dominated school teams suited her; with her slight build and natural auburn hair singling her out amongst her female peers, she preferred being with her male friends.

While many of her classmates set their sights on bagging a man and a couple of pregnancies before they hit their twenties, Susie took an English degree, head filled with her parents' encouragement to be a teacher. After all, it was a good enough career for them, so why not her as well?

She knew the stories of life in university and she expected to become just another student cliché: overindulging in her new freedom in a haze of drinking and random shagging; books left unopened, essays left unwritten. But it never happened. She made friends in her halls, mostly studious girls from single-sex boarding schools in the Home Counties. Girls whose career ambitions were matched only by their desire to snag a posh heir playing student until Daddy organised that first job in the City.

She went for the nights out, had a couple of not-overly-serious boyfriends, and settled into a quiet routine. She devoured the classics and found a taste for Dickens, but the lectures infuriated her. Sitting for what felt like hours, listening to some tweed-jacketed academic or too-cool cord-wearer trying to dazzle with his intellect. All the while pretending he wasn't leering at the tight-jeaned crotch and bulging pecs of the second year in the front row. She felt a burning need to be active. To move, just as she had done as a child, running as fast as she could with the taunts of the bullies ringing in her ears.

Looking for some way to burn off her frustrations – finding the student staples of sex and drinking insufficient – she turned to the gym after seeing a flyer on the hall wall, and fell in love. The repetition of the treadmill provided a sense of relief from the mental strain of studying, and a brief romance with a member of the hockey Second XI introduced her to weight training. She loved the feel of physical strength; nothing bodybuilder-like, but enough to allow her to easily carry her own shopping and lift heavy boxes when moving halls. While other girls simpered and made shopping look even heavier to lure men to their rescue, Susie resented the implication of inherent female weakness.

Maybe that was what attracted her to the police stand at a career fair in the students' union, the chance to prove herself in a 'man's' job. Her parents were disappointed – 'Such a dangerous job for a girl,' her dad had muttered, while her mother despaired of 'that uniform', which was 'so unflattering on the hips' – but they supported her anyway, especially when they heard about the accelerated promotion scheme for graduates.

She signed up as a cadet as soon as she graduated, found she took to the training easily. But what she loved most of all was pounding the streets on dark winter nights, especially when the rain cleared the pavements. Mile after mile, the rhythm of stride after stride drowning out her restless thoughts.

Susie felt the first tickle of adrenalin as she imagined her dry-lunged rasp as she powered up a hill, losing the images of shattered bone, torn, bloodied flesh and congealed, pulverised brain in the pounding rhythm of her stride. Tonight. She would get home, pull on her running gear and hit the streets. A 10k would do it, just long enough to build up a bit of heat, clear her thoughts.

She walked away from the morgue and towards the pub, mentally skipping through tracks on her iPod running playlist, drowning out the morgue memories with ever-increasing volume whenever they threatened to surface.

• • •

The Mitre was late-afternoon busy; caught in the twilight zone between the end of lunch hour and the end of the working day for the businesses nearby. A few workers from those offices, who had either knocked off early or just decided to call it quits after lunch, were scattered around the bar, nursing pints or shorts as they made themselves busy with smatterings of paperwork or the evening paper; the quiet acts of desperation underlining the fact they were putting on a show for the world, trying to make it look like the drink wasn't the only reason they were there. They were joined by a handful of tourists – standing out from the herd by virtue of their bomber jackets, baseball caps and oversized video cameras. It occurred to Doug that tourists never looked like they were on holiday any more, never looked like they were having fun. With their cameras, maps and incessant questions, they looked to Doug more like fact-finders.

Or the advance party.

He ordered at the bar – a pint for him, a double vodka and lemonade for Susie –then took the drinks up to the back of the pub where there were about half a dozen tables set for lunches and dinners and a few corner booths. He slid into one of the booths, taking the bench that faced back down into the bar and the saloon-style double doors leading into it, and waited for Susie.

She appeared about five minutes later. At first glance, she looked like just another office worker; conservative charcoal suit (about half a size too big for her, Doug thought), long, auburn hair pulled back in a loose pony tail draped over her left shoulder. Light make-up that accentuated her high cheekbones and gave some extra volume to her thin lips, making her look about five years younger than her thirty-four years. She even carried the standard-issue briefcase of the middle-management executive. But it was her eyes that broke the illusion. They strobed across the pub as she walked through the bar area to where Doug was waiting for her, that piercing, grey-green gaze flitting from one face to another as she searched for recognition and sized up potential trouble. Doug had seen the look and the subtle, almost bird-like motions of the head a million times before. To him, it said 'police' louder than a uniform or warrant card ever could.

'Hiya, Susie,' he said as she slid into the seat opposite him. 'How's your day going?'

'Shit,' Susie said, her voice still affected by the flat, almost apathetic tone he had heard on the phone. When she reached for her drink, Doug noticed her hand wasn't quite steady. He watched as she took a large gulp, grimacing as the vodka bit into her taste buds. She tilted the glass slightly towards him in thanks.

'No problem,' he said. 'Rough day?'

'You have no idea.' Her glass was back on the table now, but she hadn't let it go yet. Doug didn't think she would until her drink was finished. He was itching to get down to questions, to find out what she knew and how it could be built into a story, but he knew better than to push. She would talk to him in her own time. She always did.

'Right,' she said after a moment, more to herself than anyone else. 'You better get a notepad in front of you, Doug, you're going to want to write this down.'

Doug produced a notepad and pen from his jacket pocket, theatrically pulling the cap off the pen as he did so. Ready when you are, the move said.

Susie fixed Doug with her hardest stare. He felt the urge to look away or busy himself with his pint, but resisted it. Christ though, she could be intimidating when she wanted to be. *I'm the boss*, her look said. Doug wasn't about to argue.

Susie's voice dropped to little more than a whisper as she leaned across the table, cupping her hands around her glass. 'Before we go any further, this is anonymous, Doug. I don't need my name attached to this shit right now, okay?'

'Okay,' Doug said. 'But surely it won't take them too long to figure out who's been talking?'

'I'll worry about that. Trust me, there's going to be press coverage on this one anyway, a lot of it. At least this way, we can control the story for a little longer, make it work for us.'

Doug bristled slightly, forced himself to swallow his pride. He knew most coppers only talked to reporters when they needed or wanted something, but he didn't like to be reminded of the fact so bluntly, especially by Susie, who he also considered a friend.

'So, what's the story, then?' he asked.

Susie exhaled, as though blowing out smoke from a cigarette. She swallowed back the itch at the back of her throat for one. Just one.

If she caught the edge in Doug's voice, she'd ignored it. 'Most of it, you already know. Just after noon today, a young woman fell from the top of the Scott Monument. She died on impact and managed to give the poor sod unlucky enough to be close to where she landed enough material for a lifetime of nightmares.'

'Any sign she was pushed, or does it look like a suicide?'

Susie's mouth twitched in what could have been mistaken for a smile. 'Helpfully, there are no working CCTV cameras on the top level of the Monument, so we can't just look at what happened the moment before she went over the edge. However, witnesses say that one minute she was there, and the next the screaming began as she hit the ground. Whatever happened, it was sudden. If she was pushed, it happened so quickly she didn't even have time to struggle, scream or cause a scene. At this point, we think it's suicide.'

Then, almost to herself, she added: 'Which may be a blessing.'

'How so?' Doug asked, not taking his eyes from the page he was rapidly filling with shorthand notes.

'Because we caught a break with identifying the body.' Susie paused for a moment, closing her eyes and shuddering slightly at the memory of what she had just seen at the lock-up. 'How so?' Doug asked again, trying not to sound like he was pushing and failing miserably. 'Surely there was some identification: driver's licence, credit card, wallet, something on the body?'

Susie sat upright, forcing back images of gore-streaked blonde hair. 'None that we found. Which is why we're not ruling out a robbery gone wrong, despite what the circumstances point to. All we found on the body was some change and a set of keys.'

'So, how did you get a break?'

'Although there were no working cameras at the top of the Monument, there was one on the entrance,' Susie said. 'It records the face of everyone going in to the Monument through the turnstile, so the wardens can track down any possible vandals or people who throw things off the Monument.'

'Including themselves?'

Susie snorted a dry laugh in spite of herself.

'Hold on a minute, though,' Doug continued. 'Even if you could tie a face from the video footage to the body, then how does that help you? I mean, she's still just a face unless...'

'Exactly,' Susie nodded as she watched Doug arrive at the answer himself. 'Given the mess the body was in, we couldn't get a visual ID. There wasn't much left of her face, and Dr Williams found most of the teeth had also been shattered on impact. All we had was a record of who had gone up the Monument that day, the clothes and rough build of the deceased. We knew her hair colour too, but that didn't help as the CCTV footage was black and white. So we went over the footage for someone whose clothes and build matched and...'

'And you saw someone you recognised, a familiar face that matched what you had,' Doug interrupted. She had his full attention now. He was like a child being told a bedtime story. 'Who?'

Susie finished her drink in a gulp. Took her time replacing the glass on the table as she looked around the bar, making sure no one else was listening.

'Katherine Buchan,' she said.

Doug tried the name out, ran it through his mind. It didn't ring a bell.

'Sorry, who?' he said. 'Someone with previous? Drug dealer, shoplifter, prossie, what?'

'Try daughter of Richard Buchan,' Susie replied.

'Richard Buc...' The sentence trailed off as Doug's jaw fell open. Susie had never seen it happen outside of cartoons before. The effect was almost surreal.

Doug cleared his throat, buying time as he tried to put his thoughts in some vague semblance of order. 'You don't mean *the* Richard Buchan?' he whispered, leaning closer to Susie over the table. 'Not Far Right Marmite?'

'If you mean Richard Buchan, Tory list MSP for the Lothians who just happens to be proposing a Bill that advocates full-term sentence serving for all convicted criminals and the basic abolition of time served or appeal, then yes, I mean Far Right Marmite,' Susie replied. 'A uniform recognised Katherine from a family photograph used by one of the papers in a profile of her dad around the time of the last election.'

'Jesus,' Doug whispered. 'Are you sure?'

'Well, we're still waiting for the DNA testing to be one hundred per cent certain, and the family is being brought in to identify the clothing and jewellery, but yeah, the newspaper shot matches the CCTV footage.'

Doug whistled between his teeth. The daughter of a high-profile MSP dead, apparently by throwing herself off one of Edinburgh's most famous landmarks. The McGinty story suddenly didn't look so important. This was big. National big.

Buchan had risen to prominence after the last elections to the Scottish Parliament, partly because he was one of the few Tories to survive the SNP onslaught, partly because he was defiantly proud of being an old-school Conservative in a country that had never forgiven the party for the legacy of Thatcher. He wasted no time in making his mark in parliament, going out of his way to comment on every controversial or sensitive policy that arose. Gay marriage? Hated it; it was perversion of an age-old institution. Union strikes over public-sector pension changes? Irresponsible and selfish, and any public-sector worker who supported the strikes should be reprimanded. Scottish independence? The politics of grievance pedalled by disgruntled little subjects who were being disloyal to their Queen and country.

But it was on the issue of justice that Buchan really made his name. A lawyer by trade, he turned his legal expertise to campaigning for full-term sentences for all prisoners, doing away with appeal for all but the most questionable cases. He latched on to the release of the terminally ill Lockerbie bomber on compassionate grounds, saying this was the action of a soft-touch government that lacked the 'moral fibre or conviction' to see justice done.

So far, so Tory. His plan was, naturally, controversial, and the debate raged across the media, from late-night politics shows to newspaper columns and colourful online blogs.

Somewhere along the way, Buchan earned a nickname: Far Right Marmite. He was loathed by liberals and the Cameron-era Tories, who were trying to rally around a smear of paint that looked vaguely like a tree with the cry of 'we're all in this together', but he was loved by the Presbyterian right-wing torchbearers of the party; the twinset, pearls-and-perm brigade who applauded his hard line on everything that threatened 'traditional morals and standards'.

So he was already big news – and now his daughter was a bloody smear across Princes Street Gardens. Love him or loathe him, Marmite was now flavour of the month.

'Well,' Doug said, trying to stop his mind from racing ahead. 'What can I use?'

'Like I said, this is anonymous for the moment, Doug. In the meantime, this gives you lead-time on everyone else. Understandably, the bosses are keen to be seen to be taking action on this, given the media shitstorm that's about to hit, so make sure you talk up the "investigation is ongoing" angle and the fact we need to track down anyone who was up the Monument or in the Gardens at the time who hasn't come forward yet. There was a lot of screaming and hysterics after she landed, so a few people could have just bolted.'

Doug ignored the flash of anger he felt at being told how to write his copy. 'And when will my "source" confirm that the body is that of Katherine Buchan?'

'As soon as the family confirms the clothes and effects are Katherine's and we get her medical records from her GP.' Susie glanced at her watch. 'Buchan's going to be at the morgue about four. We've sent a uniform to pick up Katherine's records, so it won't take long for Dr Williams to match things up. The DNA tests will take a day or two, but they're really just a formality.'

'So, if I called you at about seven tonight…?'

Susie smiled briefly. 'I might have something interesting to tell you.'

'And then what happens?'

'Buchan will probably clear us to make a statement tomorrow, after he's made arrangements for the family to visit the body if they want to, by which time you can have a full background piece ready to go. As Buchan's got pull, we won't have an official release ready to go until the line has been agreed by him and his family, so the story will be too late for the morning papers, but the *Tribune* will have it, and quotes from an unnamed source, all to itself.'

'Except for the TV and radio,' Doug muttered.

Susie shrugged. 'Them's the breaks. Katherine's body won't be released to the family until our investigations are complete and the report's been sent to the fiscal, so you can bet Buchan is going to be bending the ear of his brethren in high places to push for an early result.

'The important thing is you're getting the story, and we're seen to be acting. The last thing we need is some crime and punishment nut with friends in high places taking aim at us because we're not doing a thorough or quick enough job on his daughter's death.'

'Understood,' Doug said. 'I'll let you see my quotes from "a police source" before we run anything.'

Susie nodded agreement.

'One more question,' Doug asked. 'The guy she scared the shit out of when she jumped, any chance of…'

Susie she shook her head, ponytail flicking lazily against her shoulder. 'Don't even think about it. The poor bastard's been through enough. He's in the Royal Infirmary at the moment, doped up to the eyeballs pending psychological evaluation.'

'He got a name?'

Susie sighed. Thought it through. The poor sod's name was bound to come out sooner or later, there was no real harm in Doug having it, but still…

Still….

'No, Doug,' she said. 'Give the guy a little privacy. And please, for me, don't go looking for him, okay? Trust me, if you'd seen what he did, you wouldn't be too bright just now, either.'

Doug nodded. Same old Susie. Still trying to balance the hard-nosed cop routine with the caring person she was underneath. He hoped she never stopped trying.

'You want another drink?' he asked, noticing the way she was playing with her empty glass and eyeing it nervously.

'Yes,' she sighed. 'But I better not. I've got work to do.' She glanced at his near-empty pint glass. 'And I think you do too, Doug.'

'Understood,' he replied, folding away his notepad. 'Thanks, Susie, that's one I owe you.'

'Yeah, yeah. Just make me sound good without sounding like me, okay?'

'No problem,' he said as he drained his pint and made to leave. He didn't quite run out of the pub for the car and the phone call that would make Walter's day.

But he didn't quite walk calmly, either.

7

The city was always at its best in the rain. Charlie Morris sat calmly, watching the rain spattering on the window and smear the night into a palette of warm orange streetlights and flashes of red from brake lights as he listened to the phone ring. Normally, the delay in answering would have annoyed him but, after everything that had happened already today, he would make allowances.

Only small ones, though. Only small ones.

'Hello?' The voice on the other end of the line was tired, wrung tight by stress. Charlie wasn't surprised.

'It's me.'

'*I thought I told you never to call me here!*' the voice hissed. 'We agreed...'

'No,' he interrupted; voice little more than a whisper. 'You dictated. I never agreed. Now shut up and listen. He's on the move.'

A pause on the other end of the line, silence interspersed with soft scrapings and shuffling as the phone was lifted and carried to a more private position.

'You... you've found him?'

'Not yet, but I know where he's going to be.' It wasn't hard – a phone call, a promise, a threat; the information came quickly enough. 'I take it you want me to proceed as agreed?'

Another pause on the line. The sound of a lighter being sparked, a cigarette being lit. A sharp, greedy intake of breath – a smoker desperate for a fix. He'd heard the same sounds from junkies when he'd handed them bags of smack or speed or E. The substance changed, but the language of addiction stayed the same.

Charlie looked at his watch. It was getting late, and he was a busy man. So many deliveries to make, so many addictions to satisfy, so many accounts to settle.

'Well?'

'Yes,' the voice replied in a whispered monotone. 'As agreed. I trust I can count on you to be discreet, as usual?'

Charlie grunted harsh laughter down the line. He couldn't help it. After everything that had happened, this bastard was still more concerned about reputation than anything else. Wanker.

'You don't need to worry. I'll take care of it. But there's a lot of heat around this, I've heard that bastard McGregor is poking around for a start. I'll be wanting a little bit extra for this one.'

'Don't worry,' the voice said, colder and more remote than ever now. 'You'll be well paid for your services. Just get it done, and make sure the bastard suffers.'

Charlie felt a smile cross his lips in spite of himself. 'Oh, don't worry,' he replied. 'He will. I guarantee it.'

8

Doug knocked gently on the door of the editor's office, wincing slightly as the noise echoed through the open-plan newsroom, drawing a few curious glances from the subs and reporters busy working on the next day's paper.

'Come!' came the call from the other side of the door. Taking a steadying breath, Doug stepped inside.

Jonathan Greig was sitting barricaded behind his huge oak desk, a hard copy of what Doug had written so far strewn out in front of him. With his dark, swept-back hair, angular features and immaculate suit, he looked more like a lawyer than an editor. Or an undertaker.

Walter sat at the opposite side of the desk, the pen he was playing with looking like a twig in his hands. It was a standing joke at the *Tribune* that Walter 'Bulldog' McKay was Greig's enforcer. If the boss didn't like a story, he would send Walter – who was 5ft 6ins with a weightlifter's physique – to sort you out. Standing there, both of them glaring at him expectantly, Doug didn't find that joke quite so funny anymore.

'Well?' Greig asked, his voice as stiff and exact as the suit he wore. 'What's the news?'

'I've just been on the phone to my police contact,' Doug said, glancing down at his notepad as he spoke in an attempt to get away from Greig's stare. 'She's confirmed it. Richard Buchan and his wife visited the city morgue earlier tonight, where they identified jewellery and personal effects recovered from the Scott Monument jumper earlier today as belonging to their daughter, Katherine Patricia Buchan. Final DNA tests are pending, but the blood tests match the medical records Katherine's GP supplied. They also matched the scar from where Katherine had an appendectomy two years ago and a tattoo she had on her left shoulder. There's no doubt, boss, it's her.'

Greig rocked back in his chair, nodding slowly. Doug was fairly sure he could see a smile twitching at the corners of his mouth. 'So, now that we know, is there anyone you can get to comment on this while keeping it semi-quiet until the official statement is made?'

Doug chewed on the end of his pen. 'Well, the Tory press office will be in full swing to get the release agreed with the police, so I could start there. They'll be desperate to get as much early coverage as possible. I know a couple of people who work down at the morgue, too, so they could give me "sources said" reaction pieces; how the Buchans took the news, that sort of stuff. Other than that…'

Greig raised a thin hand, gold cufflink winking in the light. 'That's enough to be going on with, don't you think, Walter?'

Walter clicked the top of his pen a couple of times, then pocketed it. 'Yeah, that should do it for starters. We want to get the story in for first edition, break it before anyone else. We can get all the big quotes after the official press conference tomorrow. What time's that going to be at, anyway?'

'About noon in police HQ at Fettes,' Doug replied.

Walter nodded. 'Perfect,' he muttered. 'We can cover it for second edition.'

Greig grunted in agreement. 'Right, Doug,' he said as he sat up straight in his chair, smoothing his tie as he did. 'You going to be okay with all this, or do we need to get you some help while you're still trying to track down Derek McGinty?'

Doug shook his head. No way. These were his stories. In a way, newspapers operated by playground rules; this is mine, and I'm no' sharin'.

'No, it's fine. To be honest, McGinty's not likely to show up in Prestonview, but if he does, I'll be told. In the meantime', he waved his notepad in front of him, 'I've got this to keep me occupied.'

'Get to it, then,' Greig said, returning to his work. 'And forward me your story before you go, I'll want to check it over personally.'

Doug nodded and headed for the door.

He finally stepped out of the *Tribune* offices at just past 11pm. A thirteen-hour day, give or take. Not bad. He'd passed a few poor sods on the way out who had been there since seven that morning. Young wannabes fresh out of college, trying to show how committed they were to a career in journalism by letting management work them into an early grave. He sometimes felt he should say something to them, but what? After all, he had broken into the business the same way.

He had always known he wanted to be a journalist. For Doug, it was the only game in town. He was born a rarity in Scotland, some might say a freak: a boy with no interest in football or sports in general. He flirted with football at school, mostly to try to fit in, belong, but he quickly found that the boredom and frustration of not being able to control the ball or understand the offside rule outweighed the acceptance of his peers. So he retreated into the classroom, to the books in the library and the stories they held. But unlike Susie, Doug had no interest in literature. The great works with their archaic language bored him. Shakespeare was a chore, Dickens a trip to the dentist. He wanted stories, plain and simple.

It was, his mother told him, an impatient streak he inherited from his dad. 'You want it all and you want it now, son,' she said once, after one too many glasses of white wine. 'You want to take the shortcut, get to the end, have the answer. Your dad's just the same, and look where it got him.'

Yeah, Doug thought as he looked at her, half-cut on the sofa – hair the colour of smog, a tidemark of heavy make-up creeping down her neck – just look.

He dabbled with writing fiction, found he had a knack for short horror stories that revolted and scared the shit out of his friends. But he didn't have the patience to sit down and plot out a novel then write it. He wanted to know the stories. Wanted to tell them.

It was that impatient streak which kept Doug out of university, rejecting the thought of four more years studying in favour of an HND college course in Communications. From there he freelanced for a while, then blagged a work experience place at the *Capital Tribune*; never left. Worked his way up from subbing the obits and letters to general reporter. Took his NCTJ exams to get the qualifications he needed to report on crime then stepped into the job when the previous reporter, who encouraged him to go for his exams in the first place, moved to the nationals. The hours were long and the pay was crap, but it was worth it. He had the stories and the chance to tell them, all against the ticking of a clock as deadline loomed.

He stood in the chill air for a moment, rocking his head from side to side as he tried to ease the knot of tension in his neck. The rain had slackened to a soft drizzle, and he enjoyed the feeling of the fine spray on his face. He could hear cars and lorries on the city bypass behind the *Tribune*'s offices, heading west toward the airport and Glasgow. He wished he could join them. Just drive to the airport, jump on a flight somewhere, anywhere warm. No deadlines, no stress.

Ah, who was he kidding? He'd be bored shitless after the first sangria.

Sighing, he headed for the car, massaging his stinging eyes. Got in, slid the key in the ignition and stopped. He knew he should head home to the flat – Musselburgh was only a twenty-minute drive and he had another early start in the morning – but then what? Pace the floors, lie in bed pretending to sleep, lobotomise himself with some pointless late-night TV? Drink? It was a common enough problem when working on a big story; the mind kept on ticking long after the body had called it quits for the day.

He could go for a drive, maybe down the coast towards North Berwick or across the bridge to Fife, but he knew he was too tired to enjoy it. A thought occurred to him as he started the car. He got his wallet out of his pocket and checked for cash. Thirty quid. Not a lot, but enough for a couple of hands at the casino. The Maybury was only a five-minute drive away, hell, he could walk it in ten, it was open all night. He could get a drink, play a couple of hands of poker, relax a little…

As long as he could leave it at £30. No more. No more cashing cheques, no more running up a tab of £500. He'd done that once, about a month ago, and what had scared him more than the amount was how easily he got there in the first place. It hadn't even taken an hour.

£30. Could he leave it at that? Could he? *Would* he?

Doug slipped the car into gear and headed out of the car park. Gambler in the house.

• • •

Even muffled by his jacket, the sound of the window smashing seemed to fill the street. Derek McGinty tensed for a moment, scanning the houses in front of him for a light going on or a door rattling open as someone came to investigate. Surely someone must have heard?

No one had, or they weren't bothering. He couldn't blame them. He'd chosen this car – a battered-looking Polo – because he knew it stood the least chance of being alarmed. With its rusting bodywork, sagging tyres and dirt-smeared windscreen, why bother?

He pulled up the door lock, swept glass from the driver's seat and slid inside. Breaking open the steering column was laughably easy – it crumbled when he gave it a good knock – then he busied himself twisting wires together to jumpstart the car. The engine coughed into life after a moment, like a sixty-a-day smoker trying to get out of bed in the morning.

Nice one, Derek. Nicked a real beauty here, didn't you? Ah well, at least the tank was half-full. The joke was, with the money he had in his pocket, he could have rented a car, bought one even. But he didn't want the attention. And besides, old habits died hard. He drove away slowly, eyes sweeping across the street to make sure no one was about to try and stop him. No, still in the clear.

He headed out of Gilmerton and on to the bypass. Took out a cigarette, then rolled down the remains of the window he had smashed and stuck his elbow out. To the casual observer, or any half-asleep copper, he was just having a smoke while driving.

He drove down the slip road, instinctively putting his foot down as he joined the bypass. The Polo coughed in protest as the speedometer climbed shakily to 50 mph.

It would be good to see home again. He had been away too long, living in self-imposed exile, dragging himself around the country when, by right, he could go anywhere he wanted. He had seen a few articles in the *Tribune* about how Prestonview was 'living in fear' of his return. He even recognised one of the names quoted, an old prune-face fucker called George Amos who used to chase him off the playing fields when he took his airgun down there as a boy. 'We don't want his sort around here,' he told the reporter, some shit-stirrer by the name of McGregor. 'Derek McGinty has been nothing but trouble to this town and his parents since the day he was born. If he had any decency, he would stay as far away from here as he could.'

Decency? That one made Derek laugh.

Fuck 'em. Fuck 'em all. If he wanted to go home, he would. He had served his time, he was a free man. During the trial, and afterward, he had been branded a monster, a pervert and worse. People were quick to judge – his jury took less than two hours to do that – but throughout the whole trial, no one had asked one simple, obvious question: why?

But then, the answer was obvious, wasn't it? Bethany Miller was a beautiful young woman. He had seen her and decided to have her by any means necessary. That's just what monsters do, that's what perverts do. Isn't it?

Maybe. And what he had done was monstrous and perverted; he was old enough and self-aware enough to admit that. He was ashamed of what he had done, more ashamed of what his mum and dad thought about it – and him. But still, the question had never been asked, not even by them.

Why Derek? Why?

He had spent a long time asking himself, though. And, although it wasn't a justification, he kept coming back to one answer. Love.

He swiped at his eyes angrily, mashing away the tears as he stomped down on the accelerator. He forced the Polo up to 60 mph, feeling it shudder slightly as he ground the gearstick into top. He offered a silent prayer. All the car had to do was last him to East Lothian. After that, the fucking rustbucket could fall apart in the street for all he cared.

Not much longer, he told himself. Soon it would be payday. Soon he could say goodbye to shitty little jobs, petty thieving and scrounging from the bottom of the barrel to get by. Just a little business back home, and that would be it.

He would demand what he – what *they* – deserved. And if he didn't get it, he would take it. By force, if he had to. For them. For love.

The thought kept Derek warm as he drove.

9

Hal Damon stepped out of the arrivals lounge at Edinburgh Airport into a near-deserted concourse at just after 11pm, his only company an exhausted-looking man pretending to read a magazine as he glanced nervously up at the arrivals board, and a cleaner making herself busy moving non-existent dust from one moulded plastic seat to another.

So much for the red-carpet welcome.

It had started earlier that day, with a call from Conservative Campaign Headquarters. He'd listened carefully, agreed to take the job, then put the phone down slowly, cursing softly under his breath.

Edinburgh. Fuck.

He had stood in the calm of the kitchen, surveying the wreckage of baby bottles, sterilisers, soiled bibs and abandoned cups of half-drunk coffee in front of him. Absently, he'd wandered around, picking up cups and placing them in the dishwasher, pulling bottles apart with practised ease and loading up the steriliser. From the living room, he could hear Colin cooing and soothing Jennifer. Hal had smiled, made a bet with himself that they were standing in front of the window that looked out onto the back garden.

'It's the way the light catches in her hair,' he told Hal one rare, rare night when they got Jennifer to sleep in the cot next to their bed and managed to steal five minutes together. 'I just can't get enough of looking at her in that light.'

She had arrived three months ago, the product of Colin's sperm and a surrogate's egg. They had been together for eight years by that point, bought the trendy garden-flat conversion in Kensington, built up careers, friends, a life. Had a wedding – or as near to one as closed-minded bigots thought acceptable at the time – then convinced themselves they were ready to be parents.

Then found out how wrong they were when Jennifer arrived. They transformed from a quiet, professional couple into a pair of sleep-deprived zombies who shambled around a home that looked as though Hurricane Mothercare had ripped through it. Luckily, Hal was able to work from home, advise most of his clients by e-mail or phone, while Colin's work as a graphic designer allowed him to choose his own hours.

Slowly, the sleepless days and nights became weeks. A juddering, faltering routine had started to form – Colin would take the days and then work at night, leaving Hal free to deal with his business, which was concentrated on more traditional working hours.

And now, one phone call had screwed it all up.

Hal had run through a mental list of what he would have to do. Phone his mum and Colin's dad, get them to come round and help Colin when they could. Dig up background on the shitstorm he was flying in to – Janey at the office could do that – book flights for Edinburgh. Janey again. Get a hotel. Pack.

Oh, and tell Colin he was abandoning him with their three-month-old daughter so he could go and clean up someone else's crap.

Hal headed for the living room, already readying his excuses and reasons. Colin would understand, grudgingly, he always did. But he wouldn't like it. Hal didn't, either.

Edinburgh.

Fuck.

Now, several hours later, he wandered out of the terminal

building, flicked his phone on and thumbed in a quick text to Colin without really thinking about it. '*Just arrived. Miss you both. Give J a kiss from daddy. Love you both, Hx.*' Hit send, told himself it was better than calling, just in case the phone woke Jennifer. He knew it was shit, he just didn't want another argument about leaving so soon.

He shrugged off the thoughts, suddenly angry that his promised lift wasn't here to meet him. Started thumbing through his phone contacts, looking for a name to call and rant at.

'Ah, Mr Damon?' A timid voice, heavy West Coast accent. A thin-shouldered kid with perfect hair and a suit that looked like it had been ironed on smiled at him nervously. 'Mr Damon, I'm Jonathan. Jonathan Parker. Sorry for the delay in meeting you, the parking here…' he nodded slightly over his shoulder, 'is a nightmare.'

Hal took the kid's hand, shook it. Tried not to wince at the sweaty palm. 'Don't worry about it,' he said.

Jonathan's face cracked into a horrible fixed smile. All teeth and twitching dimples. It didn't hit the eyes. Politician in training, Hal thought.

'Shall we?' Jonathan asked, motioning towards the double doors. 'We've got you booked into The Royal Scot on Princes Street. Shouldn't take too long to get there at this…'

Hal shook his head. 'Forget that. Get on the phone, round everyone up, tell them to meet us at the parliament. Sooner we start getting some lines on this, the better.'

• • •

'So tell me, ladies and gentlemen, how the *fuck* did this get out in the open?'

DI Jason Burns was not a happy man. He was pacing around in front of the assembled officers in Gayfield Place police station's CID suite, trying to give his best pissed-off sneer. His jowly face reminded Susie of raw cookie dough, and it had turned an angry scarlet that eclipsed even the shock of thinning bright ginger hair on top of his head, which, coupled with his blunt, relentless style in the interviewing room, had earned him the unkind nickname of Third Degree Burns around the station.

He was holding up a copy of the morning edition of the *Capital Tribune* – complete with the headline 'MSP'S DAUGHTER IN "SUICIDE" DEATH RIDDLE' and a huge picture of uniformed officers cordoning off the Scott Monument yesterday – as though it were the head of some enemy he had just decapitated.

So much for the hope of a better day. Susie had woken up early, been staring at the ceiling when the alarm screeched at 5.30am. Thought about going out for another run but the dull ache in her legs from the previous night talked her out of it. She had finally got home at 10pm, head swimming with forensic reports, witness statements and the hellish freeze-frame images of Katherine Buchan's shattered body. Before she left last night, she had called the hospital to see if Brian Edwards, the poor sod who had been closest to Katherine when she landed, was in any fit state to talk.

After being bounced from extension to extension at the Edinburgh Royal Infirmary for a good five minutes – her nerves becoming increasingly frayed every time she was subjected to another synthesised version of Madame Butterfly when she was put on hold – Susie had managed to speak to the nurse on Edwards' psychiatric ward.

'There's no real change, DS Drummond,' the nurse, whose name Susie had forgotten, told her. 'We've managed to get him sedated, but he's still in deep shock. When they brought him in, he was manic, clawing at his face, screaming about the blood and brains.' The nurse sighed, his deep voice at the wrong end of a very long day. 'Poor bastard. Seeing something like that...'

Susie murmured agreement. She didn't need reminding. She thanked the nurse for his time, got him to promise he would call her if Edwards improved, then headed for home; a two-bed flat a ten-minute walk from the station on Broughton Road.

She had fought the temptation to just flop down on the couch and flick the TV on, got into her running gear and hit the streets. Ran along Bonnington Road then took a left down to Leith, following the coastal path. She ran for an hour, heavy bass pulsing in her ears, trying to shut out the day. It didn't work. Home, and with mind still racing, she hooked a chin-up bar to her bedroom door frame and put herself through a circuit of pull-ups, press-ups and sit-ups, only stopping when her arms were numb and shaking.

After a shower and a tasteless microwave meal, she flopped into bed and pretended to concentrate on re-reading *The Old Curiosity Shop* before falling into a sleep that was more blackout than restful.

And now, here she was, confronted by an enraged DI. Perfect.

She resisted the urge to slump into her chair and drop her gaze. No one knew it was her who had given the story to Doug, and no one would. But in a room full of detectives, and with Burns glaring around the room, looking for the smallest sign of guilt, any embarrassed shifting in her chair would be the same as hanging a sign reading 'IT WAS ME' around her neck. Doug had been as good as his word, talking up the fact that suicide was the way the police were thinking and witnesses were being sought urgently, but keeping her quotes just bland enough to make sure they couldn't be tied to her.

But still, she wondered, had she done the right thing? She had gone to Doug because she knew she could trust him, knew he was the best way to get the story out and handled – at least, initially – the way she wanted it to be before it was thrown into the bear pit of national coverage. But he was getting more out of it than she was. His editor was no doubt ecstatic that Doug had managed to bag an exclusive, but what did she get in return? Answer: nothing, or a severe bollocking, suspension or worse if she was found out.

No matter how much she owed him, was it worth the risk?

Case in point, the fuming DI Burns now pacing up and down in front of her. His skin was a dusty purple now, nostrils flaring wildly as he spoke. He looked ready to have a stroke.

'If I find out who leaked this, I'll rip their balls off,' he whispered. 'This is a delicate case. Yes, we need witnesses, but we need to go through the right channels. King!'

DC Eddie King jumped in his chair. He'd been half-asleep throughout Burns' rant. 'Yes, boss?'

'Head down to the press conference at Fettes. I've no doubt our friend Mr McGregor will be there. Have a word with him, will you? He's not going to finger his source, but remind him this is a police investigation and we don't need hacks getting in the way. Right?'

'Yes, sir,' King whispered. He sounded like he'd just been handed a life sentence.

Burns stopped pacing and glared out at the officers in front of him. 'No more fuck-ups people. This is a sensitive case. We need to know what Katherine Buchan was doing before she took a dive from the Monument. We need to know who was up there with her, if anyone saw anything suspicious. What type of woman was she? Did she have a reason to top herself, if that's what happened? Any friends, enemies, lovers in the picture? What was her state of mind? Any money problems, debts, drugs or alcohol problems? We've got a lot of questions here, and having a fuckwit MSP who's on first-name terms with the Chief isn't making our lives any easier. They want answers. I want the right answers. So no fucking shortcuts. Understood?'

A general murmur of agreement filled the room as officers got to their feet. Susie headed back to her desk to get ready. She had an appointment with the Buchans in half an hour. It wouldn't do to keep them waiting.

10

Charlie could feel the bass of the music vibrate through the floorboards and up through his spine as he stepped out of the shower. He paused for a moment in front of the mirror, casting an appraising eye over his reflection.

Not bad. His shoulders were wide and heavily muscled, like his arms, the waist tapered and lean. Although he didn't really work at it, he had a fairly reasonable six-pack, which was only spoiled by the long, ugly scar twisting its way across his stomach and down towards his left hip. He smiled slightly at the memory of how he got that scar.

Twenty-one years old, ready to take on the world. He was small-time muscle at the time, little more than a rent-a-thug for bigger fish, so when a debt collection went wrong and a knife was pulled on him, he wasn't overly surprised. He was, however, careless. He let the guy he was collecting from, a ratty-looking smack-head by the name of Stevie Jones, slice his guts open before he got the knife away from him. He had made Stevie pay for that.

Charlie walked away with a scar. Stevie lost an eye and an ear. Lesson learned.

Wrapping a towel around himself, he padded into his bedroom. He opened a drawer beside his bed, pushed his socks and pants aside and pulled out the knife. The very knife that had carved the scar.

He flicked it open, the blade catching the watery morning light shining in through the window blinds. Despite its age, the blade was immaculate, razor sharp. Since his meeting with Stevie, he had found the knife to be an invaluable tool in his work, and only a sloppy workman neglected his tools.

He ran his thumb down the blade, watching as a thin line of blood formed in its wake.

'Make sure the bastard suffers,' his client had said last night.

He glanced at the clock. Still early. Perfect. Plenty of time to plan for this evening.

Gently, he sucked the blood from his thumb, relishing the hot, coppery tang in his mouth.

Anything to keep the customer happy.

11

Despite an enthusiasm as disgusting as his choice of tie, Jonathan proved to be a very useful little go-fer. He had arranged a meet and greet with the party chiefs while driving Hal into the city last night, had them all assembled in a pine-panelled meeting room by the time they pulled up in front of the parliament, which was, Hal thought, the ugliest building he had ever seen. It was all concrete and what looked like bamboo, glowing in the dull orange of streetlights that only served to make the incongruous angles and shapes stand out all the more.

Hal was greeted with muted politeness by the politicians, party workers and officials Jonathan had assembled. He shook hands and exchanged warm words, could almost smell the suspicion of him as the 'big gun' sent in by CCHQ in London to make sure the situation didn't blow up in the party's face.

Hal had made the move into freelance PR about five years ago, taking most of his client list with him when he bailed out on the marketing agency he had worked with since leaving school. He had made his name as a PR fixer fairly quickly, lucky that some of his clients – ranging from a major high street retailer to B-list celebrities –found themselves in trouble more often than not.

But this one had caught him by surprise. One call from Tory headquarters looking for some PR advice on a 'delicate situation north of the border', the promise of a mid-five-figure payday and the hint of future work, and here he was. Although, given the move to get him on board, Hal wasn't sure the Tories really needed another spin doctor on the case: they seemed to be masters at the game themselves. After all, who better to defend a man known for his objections to gay marriage and threats to 'traditional values' than a gay man with a husband and baby at home? The party could bleat on all it wanted about 'getting the best man for the job', but Hal knew he was the message as much as the messenger. And the message was clear: 'We're supporting Buchan in his time of need, but any views he has that could alienate voters are his alone. Just look at who we've got to work with him.'

After assuring everyone in the room that he wasn't there to impose the CCHQ line, Hal had got to work crafting a response to the Buchan situation. The reactive stuff was easy; go heavy on the family grief line, release a prepared statement (that he would write) and get them off the stage as quickly as possible.

The trickier part of the problem was the bigger picture. Public sympathy for Buchan could galvanise support for his 'full-term sentencing plan', and that was what had the London Tories' blue blood running cold. With the independence referendum looming, they didn't need or want anything that cast them in the light of the bad old days – crime and punishment nuts who didn't give a fuck for a non-existent society. And Buchan's plan was too hardline for them to stomach. But the harsh truth was that there was also mileage in his daughter's death; public sympathy to capitalise on. And if he could be softened, if Far Right Marmite (Hal hated the nickname) could be shown to be a vulnerable, grieving father, it was a vote winner.

They had worked late, crafting a line that was respectful yet emphatic. Agreed a statement from the family for the press conference the next day, made sure Jonathan got it to the family for sign-off. Hal then made the MSPs brief him on the wider picture – the support for Buchan across the parliament, who might decide to back him, who could carry a Bill forward in his name.

That done, and satisfied that everyone was on message, Hal

had got Jonathan to drive him to his hotel. He checked in, ordered a drink from room service then, restless, walked out into the rain. Wandered along Princes Street, which, from what Hal could see, was nothing more than a cheap outdoor shopping arcade stuffed with discount stores and burger joints with a castle looming over it. He stopped a block from the hotel at the police tape that was fluttering in the wind. Looked up at the ornate stone monument that Katherine Buchan had thrown herself from. He stared at it for a moment, touched the phone in his pocket, willed it to ring. For Colin to phone him, tell him it was okay, he understood.

When it didn't happen, Hal had headed back to the hotel. Read for an hour, press clippings, mostly, from reporters likely to be at the press conference.

He had woken up late, was just pouring his first cup of coffee when Jonathan knocked on his door. The horrible fake smile was even more grotesque in the daylight.

'It's all ready,' he told Hal. 'Police have a room set up at their HQ, they'll take the lead and we… ah, you, of course, can present the family statement. We'll e-mail it out when the presser starts. I've also got hard copies here', he waved a thick sheaf of papers in front of Hal's nose, 'in case anyone needs them. Oh, and I got you the morning papers like you asked for as well. They're in the car.'

Hal nodded, murmured thanks between sips of coffee. Useful little go-fer.

'Right, then,' he said. 'Let's get going, shall we? After all, we don't want to keep the press waiting.'

• • •

Home for the Buchans was a Georgian townhouse down a tree-lined, cobbled street in Stockbridge, a fairly well-heeled area of Edinburgh only a couple of miles from Fettes and the Botanic Gardens.

The drawing room that Susie had been ushered into by Linda Buchan, the small, matronly looking woman who had answered the front door, was immense, there was no other word for it. The far wall was dominated by a large window, which looked out onto the street below and flooded the room with natural light. A few tasteful – and no doubt expensive – watercolours hung from the cream walls, while a display cabinet of what looked like antique crystal shimmered lazily in the sunlight. With its high, corniced ceilings, ornate wooden fireplace and stripped wood floors, the room couldn't have been more different from the two-bedroom, Ikea-furnished flat in Broughton that Susie called home.

The drawing room door swung open and Susie was startled from her thoughts by the echoing report of shoes on the polished floor. She turned to see Richard Buchan striding towards her, hand already reaching out to shake hers.

If Susie had been asked to draw a photo fit of a stereotypical Tory, Buchan would have been roughly the opposite. Growing up with a father who worked through the miners' strike, forced to face friends at the picket lines, called 'scab' and attacked, she had been raised to believe that all Conservatives were either starch-haired, severe-looking women with a penchant for power suits and vampiric overbites, or tired-looking old men in pinstripes who peered out at the world from behind thick-framed glasses.

Buchan, though, was something different. He was about the same height as Susie; 5ft 9ins, with the thick-set, stocky body of a rugby player gone to seed. His neatly styled back hair was peppered here and there with the first tinges of grey – either that or the grey was staging a defiant fightback through Grecian 2000. His glasses, which slightly magnified his watery blue eyes, were wire-framed and unobtrusive.

She noticed dark rings under his eyes and the sparkling, slightly wild-eyed look of a man deprived of sleep but, other than that, he was hiding his sorrow well. It must, she thought, have something to do with his legal background. As a QC, Buchan would have projected an air of unflappable confidence. In grief, he seemed little different.

‘Richard Buchan,’ he said, giving Susie’s hand a brief squeeze as he shook it. ‘My apologies for keeping you waiting, but, as you can understand, there is a lot to organise at the moment.’

‘Not at all,’ Susie replied, giving Buchan what she hoped was understanding smile. ‘I’m Detective Sergeant Susie Drummond. I’m sorry to intrude on you and your wife at such a difficult time, but, if you could perhaps answer a few questions...’

Buchan nodded his head slightly. ‘Of course,’ he said, gesturing towards two large, black leather couches that faced each other over a coffee table. ‘Shall we sit down?’

Susie took a seat, Buchan adjusted his suit as he sat on the other couch. She reached into her bag and produced a notepad and pen.

‘Is Mrs Buchan joining us?’ she asked.

Buchan sighed slightly. ‘I’d rather she didn’t if you don’t mind,’ he said. ‘This has almost been too much to take for Linda. I think she’s still in shock. Going over it all again, talking about Katherine...’

Susie nodded, remembering the blank gaze and small, disconnected voice that had greeted her when Linda Buchan opened the door. ‘No, that’s fine, Mr Buchan. As I said, I’ve only got a few questions, and they’re merely routine.’

Buchan nodded but said nothing, happy to sit in silence until Susie made the first move. She took a deep breath, ran through the questions she wanted to ask in her mind, and then got started.

‘When was the last time you saw Katherine?’

‘About a week ago,’ he replied, eyes drifting towards the window as he spoke. ‘Last Monday, it would have been. She had a little time off and was in town for the day – shopping, or something – so we met up and had lunch.’

‘And where was that?’

‘The Grain Store restaurant on Victoria Street. It’s only about fifteen minutes’ walk from the parliament at Holyrood, so it was ideal.’

‘And how was Katherine when you saw her?’

'Fine,' Buchan replied. 'Her usual self; better, in fact. She had just started planning a new exhibition, and she was quite excited. Something about landing a famous photographer for the show.'

'Show?' Susie asked.

'Why, yes,' Buchan replied, the sofa creaking slightly as he shifted his position. 'Actually, I'm surprised you didn't know. Katherine works...' He paused, lowered his head and took a ragged breath. 'Sorry, worked, as the manager of an art gallery in the Old Town. Modern art, glasswork, photography, that kind of thing.'

Of course, Susie already knew that. But sometimes, playing dumb in an interview yielded results. Like now. She could have sworn there was something else in Buchan's voice. Disapproval? The proud father disappointed by the path his little girl had chosen? Maybe. Or maybe she was just hearing an echo of her own dad in Buchan's words.

'And she said nothing to indicate that she was depressed or worried about something?'

'No, nothing at all. I wish she had, though, wished I'd paid more attention when I saw her. If she'd just told me what was troubling her, or if I'd noticed something, I would have been able to help her, avoid all...' he gestured aimlessly with his hands, '...this.'

Susie shook her head slightly. She'd seen enough suicides and those affected by them to know that, more often than people liked to admit, there were no telltale signs. The decision to take your life was a secret you kept locked away.

You would live your life as normal, meeting family and friends, talking, laughing; your thoughts of bottles of pills or slitting wrists safely locked away. Until the moment you were alone, the door bolted, the safety rail on the bridge climbed, the knife resting against your wrist. And by then, it was too late. It was your decision, yours alone. Live or die?

She studied her notes, searching for a way to phrase her next question as delicately as possible. She couldn't find one.

'Mr Buchan... did your daughter have any enemies that you

know of? Anyone who might have wanted to hurt her?'

Buchan gave a harsh, humourless laugh. 'If you had known Katherine, you'd know how ridiculous that question was,' he said. 'She would never hurt a fly. Why? Surely you don't think someone did this to her?'

'No,' Susie said as apologetically as possible. 'As I've said, these questions are purely routine. We're just covering all the possibilities.'

'Ah,' Buchan said slowly. 'Like that reporter from the *Tribune*, you mean?'

Susie felt heat flash through her cheeks. Shit, she thought she had got away with it, that he wasn't going to mention it.

'Yes, sir,' she said quietly, raising her eyes to meet the intense stare challenging her. 'We can only apologise for that and assure you…'

He raised a dismissive hand. 'Forgive me, that was a cheap shot. Besides, I've already spoken to the Chief Superintendent, who's given me a full apology and assurance it won't happen again. No need for you to worry.'

Chief Superintendent? Oh fuck.

Susie cleared her throat, forced herself to concentrate. 'Did Katherine have a boyfriend, Mr Buchan? Or a close friend she may have confided in?'

'Not that I can think of, no,' Buchan replied, just a fraction of a second too quickly for Susie's liking. 'Oh, she was friendly enough with Lizzie.' He noticed Susie's quizzical glance. 'Elizabeth Renwick from the gallery, but you must understand, Detective Sergeant, Katherine was an intensely shy, private person. She loved her art and her work, but she always found being with people… tiring.'

'Including you and Mrs Buchan?'

'Of course not,' he snapped back, impatience bubbling below the veneer of civility. 'We were her parents. She knew she could come to us at any time, with any problem, no matter what it was.'

Ah, but she hadn't though, had she? Whatever had happened

at the top of the Scott Monument had either happened on the spur of the moment, or Katherine had kept whatever was bothering her from her father when they met for lunch. Susie was trained not to jump to conclusions, to follow the chain of evidence one link at a time, but her gut told her this was a suicide case. There were hundreds of more discreet ways to kill someone than pushing them off a tourist attraction. And if it had been a robbery, surely Katherine would have screamed or lashed out – something, anything, that would have attracted more attention.

No, it was a suicide. Susie was sure of it. And, if that was true, and Katherine had decided to end it all, then she had been keeping a secret, whatever it was that spurred her on, from her parents.

What? And, more important, why?

In the hall, the phone began to ring. Buchan glanced at Susie. 'Will that be all, Detective, or is there something else I can help you with?'

Susie shook her head as she stood up to leave. 'No, Mr Buchan, I think that's it for just now. We'll be in touch if there's anything else.'

Buchan nodded, offering his hand to Susie again as he escorted her to the door. In the hallway, Linda Buchan was standing with the phone cradled to her ear. When she saw her husband, she held out the phone to him and mumbled, 'It's for you.' Her eyes were still blank.

'Thank you, dear,' Buchan said, taking the phone and giving his wife a supportive squeeze on the shoulder. He put a hand over the receiver and turned to Susie with an apologetic glance.

'No problem,' she said. 'I'll see myself out. Thanks again for your time.'

Linda Buchan watched Susie leave as her husband turned his attention to the phone. It was like being watched by a statue.

12

It was 2pm by the time Doug got back from the press conference at the Fettes police centre, feeling for all the world like he had wasted his time. Most of what the police had given him merely confirmed what Susie had told him last night. The only new lines were the official statement from Katherine's family telling of their 'shock and heartbreak' at their daughter's death. The statement was read out by a guy so well-manicured Doug knew he had to be a hired mouthpiece, along with a direct appeal for anyone who had seen anything or was up the Monument at the time, to get in touch 'so we can ascertain our beloved daughter's final moments and find some peace.' The suit also released a family picture of Katherine in the hope it would jog some memories.

Sitting in his car outside, reporters and TV crews milling around in the street like supporters dispersing after a football match, Doug had written up the story and sent it to Walter at the *Tribune* by e-mail so it could go in the second edition. He was just waiting for Walter to call to tell him whether the story was fine or missing something when there was a soft tapping on his window.

Doug rolled down the window, and a reedy-looking DC stuck his hand through to introduce himself as Eddie King. He had heard Susie mention the name before, not always in the kindest of terms.

'Yes, Eddie, what can I do for you?'

'Well, I've been asked to have a word with you by DI Burns,' Eddie said. He was, Doug guessed, aiming for a tough, official tone. It came out more school prefect than CID officer.

'Ah, and how is the Third Degree?' Doug asked. 'Still brow-beating suspects into submission?'

King bristled noticeably. The friendly, we're-men-of-the-world smile slipped from his face. '*Detective Inspector* Burns has asked me to remind you this is an official police investigation, Mr McGregor. He was none too pleased to read your "exclusive" this morning, especially with this being such a delicate case.'

On the dashboard, Doug's phone began to ring. Saved by the bell. He flicked answer. 'Hold on a minute, Walter, I'm just finishing something up here,' he said as he turned back to Eddie. 'Thanks for the advice, Eddie. I'll bear it in mind. Oh, and remember to tell Third Degree I said hello.'

King was still trying to think up a comeback when Doug turned his attention back to the phone. He spoke to Walter for a couple of minutes, going over the story and press conference, making sure he hadn't missed a line from the story he had filed. When they were both satisfied he hadn't, Walter had told Doug to head back to the office.

Now, sitting back at his desk, the soft cacophony of phones, chattering keyboards and undercurrent of conversation surrounding him, Doug slumped in his chair. He hadn't got home until three in the morning – blame a blazing run on the poker table which saw him climb from £30 to £400 before he came crashing down to earth – and he was back in the office at 7am. His stomach burned from all the coffee he had drunk to try and stay awake, and he could feel the caffeine jangling sourly through his nerves, but still, all he wanted to do was sleep. Just five minutes, that was all, just a little shut-eye…

His phone rang, jarring him from his dazed near-sleep. He fumbled for the handset, almost missing it and knocking over a thankfully empty coffee cup in the process.

'Hello, *Capital Tribune*.'

No answer on the other end of the line.

'Hello?'

A pause. Then a man's voice. Soft-spoken, hesitant. 'Can I speak to Doug McGregor?'

'Speaking.'

'You the one who wrote the story about the girl who died at the Scott Monument?'

Naw, Doug felt like saying, *I just put my name on it for the fun of it*. He sighed internally. So began the nut calls. It was always the same with the big, colourful stories. They attracted nutters like flies. He would have to talk to Emma on reception again, ask her not to put everyone who called for him straight through.

'Yes, that's me,' Doug said. 'Can I help you at all, Mr…?'

'Disnae matter whit ma name is,' the voice said, growing harder. 'What matters is you don't believe what they tell you.'

'What who tells me?'

'The polis,' came the reply, an edge of frustration and anger creeping into the voice. 'They're trying to say she killed herself. She didn't. Believe me.'

Doug sat bolt upright, fumbling for a pen and notepad. Ignored the curious glances from around the room. 'What do you mean, she didn't kill herself?'

The reply was flat, final. 'She was pushed.'

Be calm, Doug told himself as he scribbled notes, this could just be another hoax, another nutcase. But he didn't think so. There was something in the voice, wasn't there?

'You saw her being pushed off the Scott Monument?'

'No, but I know she was pushed. Know it.'

'How do you know?'

'Because I fuckin' *DO*, okay?' the man bellowed, voice raw with fury and something else. It took Doug a moment to catch what it was. Sorrow.

'Look,' Doug said slowly, 'whoever you are, you're not giving me anything to go on. You say you know Katherine Buchan's death wasn't an accident, but you won't tell me anything about yourself, how you know this, or even how you know her. If you think someone pushed her, then who?'

Another pause on the line, the only sound harsh, uneven breathing. And then, just as Doug was beginning to think the caller was about to hang up, he spoke again.

'It was McGinty,' the voice said. 'Derek McGinty pushed her, McGregor. Derek fucking McGinty. You know, the bastard you wrote all those stories about?'

Doug felt as though he had just taken one too many fast turns on a rollercoaster. McGinty? Jesus Christ. It sounded insane, unreal. Why would McGinty, whose face had been splashed over every newspaper and TV station in Scotland, be in the centre of Edinburgh when he was trying to keep a low profile? And, even assuming he did, why the hell would he spontaneously decide to throw a woman he had never met off the top of a busy tourist attraction?

It made no sense. Didn't add up.

Except…

Except McGinty hadn't been seen since being driven out of Cairneyhill. If the thinking that he would head for his parents was true, and he didn't have a car, he'd have to go through Edinburgh to get to Prestonview. He'd need money to get there.

Susie's words now, ringing in Doug's ears: *We're not ruling out a robbery gone wrong.* Something else flashed across his mind's eye, caught, then disappeared again like the afterglow of a camera flash. What…?

Doug closed his eyes, trying to rein in his thoughts.

'What makes you think it was McGinty who murdered Katherine?'

'I don't think, McGregor, I know,' the voice spat. 'You're meant to be the crime reporter, do some fucking reporting. Derek McGinty pushed Katherine Buchan to her death. I know you don't believe me, but don't worry, I'll send you a little reminder of our chat. Something to convince you.'

'Look, if you're worried about being named, don't. I'll keep you anonymous. If we can just meet and...'

'No fuckin' chance,' came the harsh reply. 'But don't worry, like I said, I'll send you something special.'

'Hold on, I...' Too late. Whoever had called, they'd hung up.

Doug cut the connection then dialled 1471, only to hear the 'sorry, the caller withheld their number' message. Predictable.

'Shit,' he whispered. Now what? Derek McGinty? Could it be true? The rational journalist in Doug was telling him it was a hoax – that someone had seen the stories he had written in the *Tribune*, added two and two and come up with five. But, then again...

And what did whoever had just called him mean by 'I'll send you a little reminder of our chat, something special'?

Doug wasn't sure he wanted to find out.

13

Rita McGinty was just settling down to her nightly soap ritual – *Emmerdale, Coronation Street* and *EastEnders* – when Sam shrugged his jacket on. She glanced up at him, worry etching its way across her face.

'You're going out? Again?'

He had nipped to the shops earlier this afternoon, 'just to get a pint of milk,' he had told her. Which was true. What he hadn't told her was he wanted to pick something up for tonight, just in case.

'Yeah,' he said. 'Just for a little while, love. Thought I'd get out, see Mike and the boys down at the House. Give you peace to watch your soaps. I won't be long, promise.'

Rita glanced nervously at the curtains. 'But what if they…?'

Sam went to her, leant over and kissed her gently on the forehead. He could kill Derek for this. Rita didn't deserve any of this. Neither of them did.

'They won't, love,' he said, as soothingly as he could. 'It's dark now and getting cold. There's been no sign of Derek for a month. He's not coming back here, they know that. And besides, they've got that poor girl's family to go and pester now.' He nodded to the copy of the *Tribune* lying on the coffee table in front of the couch.

Rita nodded, curling her feet under her on the couch. He could tell she wasn't convinced, but she wasn't going to stop him, either.

'Right, I'll see you in a bit,' he said, heading for the door.

'Don't be too long, love,' she said, the pleading tone in her voice stabbing at him.

'I won't, love. Love you.'

'Love you, too.'

The night was cold and clear, the stars bright chips of ice. Sam kept his eyes straight ahead, watching his breath as it plumed out in front of him in frosted clouds. At the end of the street he came to the small vennel that would lead out of the estate. If he turned left and kept walking, he would come to the Halfway House. Straight on took him across the fields and towards the old railway line.

Sam paused, undecided. The thought of just turning left and heading for the pub flashed across his mind. It would be so easy. A five-minute walk and he would be there, sharing a joke with Mike and the others, warming himself beside the open fire as Denver farted his way through another evening while the regulars made their usual jokes about it. Just one of the guys. Just an old man living an ordinary life. A man whose wife was at home waiting for him, happily watching her soaps, not glancing nervously at the phone every two seconds, body tensed for the next call, the next knock at the door, the next question. A man whose son wasn't a rapist.

But then, if he abandoned Derek, what would that make him? Just the same as his father, who walked out on his mother after fucking his way through most of the women he met on his all-too-frequent 'boys' nights'? The rest of the world had given up on his son, but Sam hadn't. He could not, would not.

Would he?

He had crossed the road and was heading for the railway line before he knew the decision had been made. As he walked, a growing unrest filled his mind. It wasn't fear exactly – even after everything that had happened he wasn't afraid of Derek – it was more unease at not knowing what was coming next.

He hadn't seen his son in years – he had visited briefly when he was released from prison – and it had been one of the most excruciating experiences of Sam's life. Rita sat in her chair, glaring at Derek with open contempt and hatred. It hadn't surprised Sam. Rita's upbringing had been small-town strict; a steady diet of strict morals, propriety and church on a Sunday. The opposite sex were a temptation, and sex itself outside marriage a sin, she had been taught. So when her son, her *only son*, was convicted for a depraved sex assault on a defenceless, innocent young girl, her reaction was predictable.

Trying to get beyond that, Sam attempted to break the ice, tried to engage his son in small talk about the future and his plans, flailing for something, anything, to rebuild their relationship on. To try to understand what had driven Derek to do what he had done.

He had failed. The oppressive silence in the house proved too much for Derek, who stormed out of the door, telling his parents to go and fuck themselves. And that was it. They hadn't heard from again since. Until yesterday.

Sam climbed over a stile and trudged across a field – frosted mud crunching beneath his boots – then headed down the path that led onto the old railway line. Somewhere in the distance a dog barked, and he could dimly hear traffic on the new stretch of A1 that ran behind Prestonview, linking East Lothian to the main road down to Newcastle, but, other than that, everything was silent.

The tree he had arranged to meet Derek at was an old, gnarled oak about five hundred yards in front of him, its thin, skeletal branches the colour of bone in the moonlight. Sam walked up to it and stopped, heart pounding in his ears. He looked around. Nothing. Typical Derek. Come out of nowhere, upset everything, and then...

'Dad?'

Sam jumped back as a shape emerged from the shadows

that pooled around the tree's trunk. He peered into the darkness. 'Derek? That you?'

'Naw, it's fuckin' Santa,' Derek snapped. Stopped. Sighed. Forced back the anger and churning in his guts. Spoke more softly. 'Yeah, Dad, it's me.'

It took Sam a moment to believe it. The last time he had seen Derek, his son had been overweight and flabby, his face drooping with jowls of fat. The man who stood in front of him now was gaunt, almost overly thin, with defined cheekbones and a square jaw. He was wearing a heavy jacket, but Sam could still tell that underneath it, Derek's beer belly had gone as well.

'It's… it's good to see you, son,' Sam whispered, trying to keep his voice even as he spoke.

Derek laughed sharply. It wasn't a pleasant sound. 'We both know that's a pile of shit, Dad, but thanks anyway.'

'Look, son,' Sam said, 'we haven't got much time, what with all these reporters hanging around. When you called, I thought you might need some cash, so…'

Derek reached forward, taking hold of Sam's arm as he reached inside his pocket for the cash he had withdrawn earlier in the day. His grip was strong.

'No, Dad,' Derek whispered, his voice unusually soft. God, but he sounded tired. 'That's not why I called, just the opposite in fact. Here.'

He handed over a large brown envelope. Sam tore it open, his breath catching in his throat when he saw the contents. Even in the moonlight he could see that the envelope was stuffed with money – £20 and £50 notes, by the look of it.

Sam looked up, straining to read his son's face in the darkness. 'Derek? What's going on? Where did you get this money? Oh God, please don't tell me you…'

'Give me a fucking break,' Derek snapped. 'Christ all-fucking-mighty, Dad, it's always the same, isn't it? What, you think I broke into the offy on the high street, emptied the till on the way here?'

'It wouldn't be the first time, would it, Derek?' Sam snapped, voice trembling with the old anger. What the fuck was he doing here? Trying to buy them off, say sorry for all the stress and pain he had put Sam and Rita through with a wad of cash and a half-arsed poor-me plea? Fuck that.

Derek took a step forward, saw the way his dad's shoulders straightened, felt the prickle in the back of his neck that told him violence was on the horizon. Closed his eyes. Took a deep breath. *I believe in you, Derek, I have faith.*

Bit back his rage. Forced his voice to be calm. 'I didn't do anything, Dad, I just collected some of what was owed to me. Look, I don't have much time. I just came back to give you this and tell you I'm leaving. I've got a couple of things to sort out, and then that's me. Gone.'

'Wh… where?'

'I don't know,' Derek shrugged. 'Anywhere away from here. Where they don't know my face.'

'So that's your answer is it, run away? Buy your mum and I off with some cash that you got from God knows where and then just disappear? Is that it?'

'Fuck off,' Derek sneered. 'What choice do I have here, Dad? It's not like anyone is going to forgive or forget what I've done, not like I can start again.'

'You think you deserve that? After what you did?'

'No, Dad,' Derek sighed, 'I probably don't. But I'm going to try anyway. So take this. Do something for you and Mum. Christ knows, you deserve it.'

Sam was stunned. He couldn't believe Derek was talking like this. What had happened to him?

'Son, I…'

'Don't, Dad, just don't. Just take the cash and go. Please. Tell Mum you won it on the lottery or something, if you have to.'

'Will… will you let us know where you are when you know?'

It was hard to tell in the light, but Sam thought he could see

Derek smile. 'Aye, I'm sure Mum would love a postcard from me an' aw. Now go on. If you hurry, you've got time for a pint before you get back to Mum. Have it on me.'

Sam opened his mouth, closed it. He didn't know what to say. He took a step forward, grasping his son with all his strength. The arthritis in his hands and arms snarled angrily. He barely felt it.

'You take care,' he whispered.

'I will, Dad, I will.' And then he was gone, jogging down the railway path and into the shadows. Sam stood watching him for a moment, fighting back the tears welling in his eyes.

It was a fight he never won.

• • •

Derek had left the Polo in a small car park about half a mile along the track from where he had met his dad. He ran the whole way back, lungs burning by the time he got there, eyes dry from the cold and reddened by tears.

It wasn't much, but the car would do for tonight. He would drive up behind Pencaitland, find a wooded lane or farm road, park up and sleep there. He had the money for a hotel, but this way was easier. Less chance of being recognised, less chance of some night receptionist phoning the police. The last thing he needed right now was the pigs crawling all over him.

As he approached the Polo, he noticed something was wrong. The car was sitting at an odd angle. Getting closer, he saw the driver-side tyres were flat.

'Oh sh...'

He had just enough time to register something glinting in the corner of his eye before his head exploded in agony. Darkness rushed in on him like a wave as he crumpled to the cold ground, blood spurting from his skull and soaking his hair. He cried out, but couldn't be sure if he would be heard over the roaring that seemed to fill the world. He tried to get up, tried to move, but couldn't. It was as if he had been disconnected from his body.

'Hiya, Derek,' a voice said from what seemed to be very far away. He knew that voice. Tried to place it, lost it. Wasn't important, anyway. He was going to pass out soon.

'Long time, no see. How are ya? Me? I'm fuckin' great.'

Derek folded over as a boot was driven viciously into his ribs. He felt one crack, screamed as bone ground against bone. The kick was swiftly followed by another. And another. Then, more talking, that same naggingly familiar voice. Dimly, he could hear the sound of boots crunching on gravel as his attacker circled him, gloating. He shut out the words, focused on staying conscious.

Breathe, Derek, for fuck's sake, breathe!

He shook his head, trying to clear the fog in his mind. If he didn't shape up now, he was in serious trouble. He lay on the ground, gasping for air, willing himself to stay awake. No good, his vision kept on blurring. Desperately, he bit down on his tongue, hard enough for hot, bitter blood to flood his mouth. The pain surged through his body, excruciating, but the world was back in focus.

'You know, when I took this job, I didn't realise it was going to be so much fun,' his attacker said. And in that moment, Derek knew who he was. Saw in his mind's eye a young, brutal man with a taste for violence and knives.

Charlie Morris.

Charlie was pulling him up now, dragging Derek's face close to his, filling his lungs with his sour breath. 'Come on, Derek, open your eyes at least, so you can see what I'm going to…'

Derek drove his head forward with all the strength he had left. Charlie uttered a high, muffled scream as Derek felt a nose snap sharply against his forehead. To his left, there was a heavy clanging sound.

The knife!

Derek rolled away, pushing Charlie back. He groped desperately at the ground in front of him, got the knife in his hand, closed his fingers around it.

Play time.

He stood up, body still feeling shaky and foreign after the blow to the head and kicks to the torso. He wiped blood-soaked hair from his eyes. A hot lance of pain flashed through his side every time he took a breath. One rib broken definitely, maybe two.

Time enough to worry about that later.

About two feet away, Charlie had pulled himself upright. The blood gushing from his nose looked black in the dull orange glow of the car park's meagre lighting.

'Fugging bastard,' he gurgled as he spat out a wad of phlegmy blood. 'Fugging bastard!'

'Who sent you, Charlie?' Derek asked as he began to shuffle forward slowly, willing his legs to keep working. 'You said this was a job, so who sent you?'

'Fuck you!' Charlie barked.

Derek raised the knife to eye level. The blade caught what little light there was, seemed to bathe in it. Charlie always was proud of that knife. 'Look, Charlie, I'm not fucking around here, tell me. Was it...?'

Charlie surged forward, catching Derek off-guard and driving him back onto the bonnet of the Polo. He screamed as his ribs exploded in pain, arms flailing out to the sides, knife squirting from his grip. Charlie grabbed a handful of hair and smashed Derek's head backwards into the bonnet. Derek lashed out wildly, felt his fist connect with jaw. They tumbled from the car and onto the ground in a tangle of flailing arms and legs, punching, kicking, clawing. Somehow, Derek managed to flip himself on top, using his weight to pin Charlie down.

'Tell me, Charlie!' he screamed, spittle and blood flying from his mouth and peppering Charlie's face. 'Who sent you, was it *him*? WAS IT?'

Charlie hawked back and spat in Derek's face. Rage flooded through Derek, drowning out the pain, the exhaustion, the fear. He pulled back, swinging with all his strength. Teeth bit into his knuckles, bone gave a horrible, liquid snap. He swung again and again and again, only stopping when his arms were too heavy to lift and the world gave a sickening, dizzy lurch.

Derek got up, staggered away from the pulped mess of sinew and bone before him. Closed his eyes and wished to die as he vomited. Was it always going to be this way?

He took a moment to pull himself together and make sure he wasn't going to pass out, then lurched back to where Charlie lay. He fully expected to find he had killed him, but Derek could hear soft, gurgling breathing, and felt a steady pulse when he pressed his fingers into Charlie's neck. He didn't know whether to be disappointed or relieved.

He patted Charlie down, finding a wallet, some cash and a set of keys. Stashed them in his pocket and lurched back to the Polo. It was a struggle to keep moving. All he wanted to do was lie down and sleep. It didn't take long to realise the Polo had had its day – Charlie had slashed all the tyres. Always the professional.

Derek fished the keys he had taken from Charlie out of his pocket, held them up to the light and examined them. One of them was an oversized car key with a built-in switch for an alarm. Squinting, Doug made out the BMW logo. Despite himself, he laughed. Same old Charlie, always the show-off.

There were no cars in the car park, but that was to be expected: Charlie wasn't that sloppy. He would have parked the car somewhere close, hidden but near enough to make a quick getaway. His legs feeling like lead pillars, Derek headed for the lane that led from the car park to the main road.

About three hundred yards up, he saw a BMW tucked away off the road in a small bank of bushes. He flicked the switch on Charlie's car key and the car bleeped obediently.

Derek climbed in, careful to cradle his ribs. He sat behind the wheel for a moment, enjoying the soothing comfort of the leather driver's seat. It was the most comfortable seat he'd had in weeks. His eyelids slid down. It would be easy to take a nap, so easy. No one would know, he was safe enough. And it was comfortable here. Quiet…

So easy…

He jerked forward, wrenching himself from sleep and started the engine. Fuck it, he was finding a hotel for the night. An out-of-the-way travel stop on the motorway would be safe enough, surely. It was worth the risk. Derek gunned the engine and drove away as, in the car park, Charlie Morris lay in a widening pool of his own blood.

14

Hal skimmed through the news websites, watching the reruns of the press conference. He hated the way he looked on camera – face pinched and sallow, those high cheekbones, which Colin said were his best feature, appeared blade-like in the glare of TV lighting. His glasses glinted like mirrors, masking his eyes as he turned his head to make sure he was reading to the whole press pack, not singling out one reporter. His voice, which he tried to keep even and sombre, grated like a pop song on his ears. And was he really going that grey already?

He turned from the screen, focused on the newspapers in front of him that had managed to cover the press conference in their later editions. There weren't many surprises; most of them focused in on Hal's statement from the family, backed it up with the police appeal for witnesses and the handout picture of Katherine that he had released. He worked through the papers quickly, taking notes on how the lines he had given played, what might work as a follow-up if needed. Finally, he came to the *Capital Tribune*. As with most of the other papers, the splash image was a picture of Katherine. What was different was that the headline between first and second edition hadn't changed. While other papers had re-nosed their stories once Katherine had been officially named, the *Tribune* hadn't. Because they had already known.

Hal wrote down the reporter's byline. Doug McGregor. Forced himself to slow down and read the copy rather than just skim it, comparing the later version with the morning edition before the press conference had been held. It told him two things: McGregor was a good writer, and he obviously had brilliant contacts in the police. The whole story was there in the first edition; Katherine being identified from CCTV footage, the family going to the morgue to identify the body, the ongoing investigation, the police appeal for witnesses.

McGregor had also been cute, alluding to the suicide line being the favoured police theory, but leaving it open-ended and hinting at an ongoing criminal inquiry. As he already knew Katherine's name and family connections, McGregor had also managed to write some fairly in-depth background pieces on the Buchan family and, in particular, Richard Buchan's work in parliament.

McGregor's job must have been easy after the press conference, all he had to do was take Hal's statement and bolt it onto the copy. But instead of just lumping it in as a three-par addition at the end, Doug had woven it into the story, using the statement to give the family's grief and shock greater resonance. Hal circled McGregor's name and made a note to do a bit of digging on him. He was one to watch.

He was topping up his coffee when his mobile chirped, the ringtone he used only for Colin making his breath shallow and sharp.

'Hey,' he said.

'Hey, yourself,' Colin replied, his voice a flat, almost matter-of-fact tone that gave Hal's guts an oily chill. 'How's it going?'

'Yeah, not bad. Had the first meet and greet with the press today, just getting some lines together at the moment. Should calm down soon. How are you and Jennifer doing?'

'We're fine. She misses her dad though, I think she was looking for you last night.'

Hal shoved his glasses up his nose, rubbed at his eyes hard enough to see dark stars. Guilt. Colin was always good at playing the guilt card.

'I miss her too, Col,' he said. 'I miss both of you. This shouldn't take too much longer. Then I'll be home.'

'You shouldn't be there in the first place,' Col hissed, jagged blades of anger glinting through his indifference. 'What the fuck were you thinking, Hal? Taking this job? I mean, you do know who you're representing, don't you? Or did you think I'd be too busy looking after Jennifer to catch the news?'

Hal sighed. He had known this was coming. 'Col, please, I told you. We need this job, and it's not Buchan I'm representing, it's the…'

'Oh, don't lie to me, or yourself, Hal. If he's not who you're representing, why were you reading out a statement on his behalf today? I wonder what he'll say when he finds out that the man hired to media-manage his daughter's death is one of those nasty queers he doesn't want tarnishing the institution of marriage?'

'Hopefully, he'll say that his party had the common sense to see through petty prejudice and hire the best man for the job,' Hal snapped back, his own anger rising. 'Look, Col, I don't like this prick much either, but he's a means to an end. There's a big payday at the end of this, and I'm doing this for us – you, me and Jennifer. For fuck's sake, it's not like every design brief you work on is for a cure for fucking cancer, is it?'

Silence on the other end of the phone. In his mind, Hal could see Colin standing in the kitchen, his tall, lithe frame leaning against the breakfast bar. He would be chewing his lip, running his free hand through his blonde hair. If he stayed on the line, he would start wandering through the kitchen soon, absently pulling open cupboards and staring inside as he spoke. It was his routine.

'Look, Hal, I'm sorry,' he said. 'But I'm pissed that you upped and left us, especially to go and help a bigoted little fuck like this guy Buchan.'

'I know, Col, and I'm sorry. But it shouldn't take too much longer, I'll be home soon.'

'I hope so,' Col said, his voice softening. 'We miss you, Hal. Your mum's great, but she can't make a cup of tea for shit, and if she keeps trying to reload the dishwasher after I've done it, I might have to kill her.'

Hal laughed, mostly out of relief. 'I'll be home as soon as I can, promise. But now I've got to…'

'I know,' Col said. 'Get back to work. Love you, Hal.'

'Love you, too,' Hal said. 'Give Jennifer a kiss from me. I'll call later tonight, let you know how it's going.'

'Bye.'

Hal cut the line, sat back in his chair, relief flooding through him. He may be a selfish prick for taking this job, but at least Colin had forgiven him for it. Again.

And, Hal thought, he had raised an interesting point. Why had Buchan's party decided to hire him for the job? His answer to Colin had been spur of the moment, but surely there were PR firms closer who could have done the job?

Colin's words now: *You do know who you're representing?*

No, Hal thought, thumbing through his contacts list. I don't, not really. Not yet. But I intend to find out.

15

'So?' Doug asked. He took a long drink from the soda and lime in front of him, grimaced. He wanted a pint, but he was driving. 'What do you think?'

'To be honest, not a lot,' Susie replied. 'It sounds like a crank, Doug. I mean, both Katherine Buchan's death and Derek McGinty on the loose have been big stories, you said so yourself. Like you said, some lunatic's probably just decided to put the two together to try and get some attention.'

They were in the Freehope, a small pub that lay on the boundary between Leith and the more industrial Newhaven further along the coast. It wasn't the most luxurious of pubs, but it had the virtue of being out of the way. Susie had told him about Richard Buchan's little chat with the Chief Superintendent concerning Doug's story, so he figured the less they were seen together at the moment, the better.

It probably wasn't wise for them to be meeting at all, but Doug was curious to see if Susie had turned up anything new. He also wanted to get her opinion on his little phone call earlier on. And, as he was the only one with whom she could share her fears about what the Chief Superintendent could and would do, it was a meeting of convenience as much as need.

The more he thought about it, the more he agreed with Susie. It had been a crank. Nothing more. But still, something about the call nagged at him, something that just refused to show itself. And then there was what the man had said before he hung up: *I'll send you a little reminder of our chat. Something special.*

Doug shrugged, forcing the thought away. A crank. Nothing more. Leave it there.

'So, what did you think of Richard Buchan?'

Susie took a moment, turning her glass slowly in her hand, remembering the way Buchan had answered her questions. That one, almost too-quick response that had put her on edge.

'I'm not sure,' she said. 'He's not what I expected. Very controlled, disciplined. Oh, don't get me wrong, you could see he was cut up about what's happened, but he's refusing to give in to it. I suppose he's got to be that way, especially now.'

'How so?'

'His wife,' Susie replied, remembering Linda Buchan's slack, empty gaze. 'She's completely lost it, Doug. I mean, totally. The poor woman was walking around like a zombie. I think he's the only thing holding her together just now.'

Doug nodded. It would be bad enough to lose a child, but to lose one the way the Buchans had? Jesus.

How would it have felt, he thought, to hit the ground from the height? Did you die instantly, or would you linger for a moment, just long enough to feel the agony surge through your ruined body and hear your last breath rattle from your ruptured lungs? He shuddered. Not a way he would want to go.

Doug shook his head, took another swig of his drink. Maybe he just needed to get used to the taste. 'So, any witnesses come forward yet?'

'Well, we've had a few...' Susie was cut off by the sound of her mobile ringing. She smiled apologetically then flipped it open and held it to her ear.

'Drummond. Oh, hi, Eddie.' She flashed Doug a sharp but not unamused glance. 'What's up?' Pause. 'Uh, yeah.' She took out a notepad, started scribbling. Doug hoped the fact he was trying to read what she was writing wasn't too obvious. 'Okay, fine, 10am tomorrow. Great. Thanks, Eddie. Night.'

'So, what was all that about?'

'Nothing interesting,' Susie replied, reaching for her drink again. 'Buchan mentioned that Katherine was quite close to a friend at the gallery, Elizabeth Renwick. I tried calling her earlier on today to arrange a meeting, left a message. Your friend Eddie was just telling me that she's phoned back, wants to see me at the gallery tomorrow.'

'That the Altered Perspective gallery on Candlemaker's Row?' Doug asked, smiling as Susie's eyes widened slightly. 'I did a little checking on Katherine myself. Bit of an artist, apparently. Modern art, photography, stuff like that.'

Susie nodded. If there was something to be found, Doug had to find it first. She often wondered what type of detective he would make.

She knew the place Doug was talking about, had walked passed it a few times on nights out. From what she remembered, it didn't seem big enough to be a gallery, with only one small window and a single wooden door. Then again, she wasn't an expert. And with what passed for art these days, who knew?

Doug drained his glass, felt his stomach gurgle. 'Right, I've had it. Let's get out of here. Fancy something to eat?'

'No, thanks,' Susie said, draining her glass and then stretching theatrically. Her legs ached from the run, arms still sore from the pull-ups. 'I'm beat, I need to get to bed.'

'No probs,' Doug said as he pulled on his jacket and checked for his car keys. 'I should probably do the same myself.'

Doug walked Susie to her car, hands buried in his pockets against the cold. They stood for a moment, staring up at the night sky. The air was heavy with the smell of salt from the Forth – and less savoury smells from the industrial units and sewage plant further down the coast.

'Well, thanks for listening,' he said as she unlocked the car and got in. 'And thanks again for your heads-up on the Buchan story.'

Susie busied herself getting her key into the ignition. Was she blushing slightly? 'No problem,' she said. 'Just remember, you didn't hear any of it from me.'

'What's that? I can't hear you.'

'Very bloody funny,' she snorted, slamming her door and starting the car. She waved as she drove out of the car park, mind already turning to thoughts of a quick run before bed.

Doug waved back, watching her go. He headed for his own car, mentally sorting through the menu of his local Chinese takeaway, trying to decide what to order when he got there.

He never saw the figure standing in the shadowed alley down the side of the pub. The figure that watched as Doug drove away, memorising his car's number plate. The figure that smiled slightly, thinking he would be well paid for a job well done.

16

Every step was agony.

Charlie shuffled from the bed, where the sheets and pillow were stiff with his blood, and made his way to the kitchen. He fumbled through a cupboard, found a bottle of whisky, opened it with a shaking hand, took a mouthful. His jaw screamed in protest as he opened his mouth, pain like cold steel needles lancing through the bone and down the side of his neck. He tried to force back the pain as the whisky hit his stomach and spread bitter heat through his body. But it was difficult to stay calm when you were trying to breathe through a broken nose.

He lurched from the kitchen to the bathroom, bottle of whisky still in hand, to survey the damage again.

He had become a monster. His entire face was a bruise, a shifting kaleidoscope of dusty purples, angry reds, blacks and greens. His eyes glittered from hollow pits surrounded by swollen tissue and split skin. His nose was worse. It sat at a horribly crooked angle, bent flat at the end and plastered against his cheek like a wad of plasticine. Blood was caked around both nostrils, making it hard to breathe.

Slowly, he opened his mouth and leered at the mirror. His front teeth were little more than ragged stumps. He looked across to where his toothbrush and toothpaste sat. Somehow, he didn't think Sensodyne was going to help this time.

The joke of it was that this was the face of a lucky man. He didn't know how long he was out after McGinty had finished with him, but, when he came to, he could feel frost forming on his face. Maybe that was what had saved him, forced him to wake up, he didn't know.

It didn't take long to realise that McGinty had robbed him, taking both his car keys and wallet.

With no cash or means of transport, he had been forced to be creative. He had staggered up into the town, careful to stay out of the light and away from people, found a quiet estate and walked around for a while. If Charlie had been told that Derek had used more or less the same techniques when he stole a car from Gilmerton the night before last, he wouldn't have been surprised. After all, he had taught the little shit how to steal in the first place.

He only remembered the drive home in snatches. A blurred roadway here, a street sign there. Somehow, he managed to get back to his flat without attracting any attention, using the spare key he kept hidden on the sill above the front door to get in. He parked a few blocks away – the last thing he needed was pigs at his door, enticed by the stolen motor that was sitting outside it. If he wasn't so badly hurt, he would have dumped it further away, but it would do where it was. In this part of town, stolen cars weren't exactly a rare occurrence. If he was lucky, it would be torched before he had to deal with it.

He headed back to bed, whisky bottle still clutched tightly in his hand. McGinty would pay for what he had done. Oh yes.

He had been sloppy, underestimated the bastard and paid the price. But he knew what he was up against now. His fee would be higher, but he would get the job done. Next time he saw Derek McGinty, he would walk up to him and gut him like a...

Charlie's eyes flew open. The aching wound that was his head roared in protest as he sat bolt upright.

His knife! He had it last in the fight with McGinty. Did the bastard have it now, along with his car and keys, or...?

Or was it still lying in that car park, waiting to be found by anyone who happened to come along?

He slumped back in the bed. What could he do? The answer was nothing. One way or another, the knife was gone. Either McGinty had it, or someone else would find it. He was in no condition to go and get it.

Something else to make McGinty pay for. When he found the bastard – and he *would* find him – he would make him pay. If he had the knife, and he gave it back then maybe, just maybe, he would earn an easier death.

But not much easier. Oh no. Charlie owed Derek much more than that. He rolled over and reached for the phone. Noticed he had a message and pressed play. Mark Kirk's whining, Leith-stained tones filled the room, amplifying Charlie's headache. 'I did whit ye asked likesay, Charlie,' Mark said on the answerphone. If a rat could talk, Charlie imagined this was what it would sound like. 'Gote the car nummer here, it's...'

Charlie listened, eyes closed. Thankful when Mark hung up and the message ended. An annoying little cunt, but useful. Especially when he was offered an extra half-gram in his next hit for doing a little legwork.

He sighed and picked up the phone. No more putting it off. Dialled the number and waited. He could imagine what the response would be to him breaking the golden rule and phoning not once but twice in two days.

Fuck it. From now on, they were doing this his way.

17

After getting through first edition, Doug managed to slip out of the office and head back to Prestonview. The Buchan story was more or less dying away to aftermath now, anyway. A few more politicians had come forward to offer their sympathy to Richard Buchan and his family, and the DNA tests confirming it was Katherine had come back, but other than that, nothing.

All that was left now was for her family to bury her and then try to find an answer, a justification, for what had happened.

He had heard talk in the office of the *Tribune* running a feature on suicides; the psychology, the warning signs, what family and friends could do and what groups like the Samaritans were doing to help prevent things like this happening, but Doug didn't want any part of that. He'd done his job. Reported a crime, got the story ahead of everyone else. The rest was clean-up duty.

Mike started pulling a pint of Guinness almost as soon as Doug walked in the door. After all the Chinese last night, he didn't particularly feel like it, but he smiled and paid for it anyway. It wasn't worth upsetting the landlord for.

'So, Mike, how's it going?'

Mike gave Doug a world-weary smile. 'Ack, you know, same old same old. Nothing much happening, really. Still no sign of Derek, although his old man, Sam, was in here for a wee while last night.'

'Oh aye,' Doug said. 'S'been a while since he's been around, what with all the cameras up at his place. What was the occasion?'

'None from what I could tell,' Mike said. 'He just said he wanted to get out of the house for a bit. All this is getting to the guy, though, poor bastard was as white as a sheet.'

'I'm not surprised,' Doug murmured. It couldn't be easy living in a small town where your son was regarded as the devil.

'So, I see you got the story on the girl who jumped off the Scott Monument,' Mike said, attempting to change the subject.

Doug just nodded. Again, he wondered if stating the blatantly obvious was a required skill for being a pub landlord.

'Terrible way to go,' Mike said, shaking his head slowly.

'Yeah,' Doug said flatly.

'So, do the police know what happened?'

'Not completely, not yet, although they're leaning towards the suicide angle. If someone killed her, they would have had to be Houdini to get away from there without being noticed.'

Mike grunted agreement, then disappeared behind the bar. He was just starting to clean glasses when the door opened and a tall, thin man with a wisp of pure white hair walked in, dragging an ancient-looking Golden Labrador with him.

'Morning, Mike,' he said, ignoring Doug completely.

'Morning, Jimmy,' Mike replied. 'That you and Jess just heading home from your walk?'

'Yeah, and an interesting walk it was, too,' Jimmy said as he patted what was left of his hair back into place.

'Oh, how so?'

'Well,' Jimmy said, his tone showing he had been aching for someone to ask him that very question, 'we were out on our usual walk down the pathway, and you'll never guess what we found. An abandoned car, which had been vandalised.'

Ooh, Doug thought, hold the front page.

'Badly damaged?' Mike asked.

'Not too badly,' Jimmy replied, annoyed to be interrupted

mid-story. 'Tyres slashed and a window smashed. But that's not the interesting thing. What is, is what else we found.'

'And what was that?' Mike asked. Doug could tell he was quickly growing bored with the conversation.

'This,' said Jimmy, theatrically pulling his prize from his pocket. It was a wicked-looking lock-knife, blade about ten inches long with a heavy, brass-and-wood handle.

Mike put aside the glass he was worrying at with a tea towel and leaned forward, eyes fixed on the blade. He seemed to go pale. Doug suddenly lost the little interest he had in his pint. 'That's some knife,' he said. 'You said it was next to the car?'

Jimmy looked at Doug as though he were seeing him for the first time. 'Yeah. Down by the side of the car.' His voice rose with excitement as he delivered his knockout blow. 'There was blood there, too. A lot of it. It wouldn't surprise me if someone was mugged down there. Or worse.'

He rambled on, explaining his theories about what might have happened, but Doug wasn't listening. He was too busy trying to fit scenarios together. A wrecked car. A pool of blood. A knife that looked like it would be more at home hacking its way through jungle than in Prestonview. Prestonview. Home of Derek McGinty's parents. Had their boy made it home? Jumped someone and tried to steal their car? Or had he forced that person to drive him here and then decided to get rid of the witness? Where was he now? With his parents?

'So,' Doug asked, interrupting Jimmy mid-sentence. 'You taking that knife to the police, Jimmy?'

Jimmy gave Doug a look of open disgust. 'What else can I do?' he sneered. 'Keep it? What do you think I am, a ghoul or something? I'm goin' straight up to the polis station with this,' he waved the knife in an alarming arc in front of the bar, 'just as soon as Mike gets me something to steady my nerves.'

18

Ronnie Selkirk slurped noisily at his coffee as he surveyed the dining room of the Royal Scot Hotel, his face twitching with disgust at the tables of dead-eyed executives, business travellers and affluent tourists who thought Scotland began at 'Lock' Ness and finished at 'Edinbro Castle'. At the table next to them, a bored-looking teenager toyed with the shredded remains of a sandwich; a watch worth more than a mortgage payment glinting on his wrist. Ronnie felt a surge of contempt for the little shit, swallowed it down with another mouthful of coffee.

'You've done okay for yourself, Hal,' he said. 'Nice digs they've got you in here.'

Hal smiled and nodded slightly, knowing a place that reeked of money like this would be driving Ronnie nuts. He had no objection to wealth – Hal's conservative guess was Ronnie had made a few million in his time – he just hated people who flashed the cash. It was a very Edinburgh attitude.

They had met years ago, when Hal was working on a product launch for an insurance firm getting into banking. Hal had organised the media and the press work with Ronnie, who led the firm's legal department and insisted on seeing every line of copy before it went out.

'I'm gieing those bastards not one line they can use against us if this goes wrong,' he had told Hal in his office, which was at the other end of Princes Street in the West End – at the time, known as the heart of Edinburgh's thriving financial industry.

They had worked together closely, Hal briefing executives and staff who they offered up for interview to the press on the lines that Ronnie insisted on. With Ronnie also handling the work that made the bank a legal entity, he ultimately set the timetable of when the bank was ready to go and Hal could launch.

As they worked together, a grudging respect and then friendship grew between them. While Ronnie would drive Hal nuts with his unwillingness to embellish a line for a press release or an interview, he also had a dry wit and easy charm that made him a popular boss, and Hal quickly learned that his nickname in the office – though never repeated to his face – was Uncle Ronnie. It wasn't long before Hal was being invited to dinner with Ronnie, his wife, Angie, and their three-year-old girl, Amy, at the family home just outside Edinburgh. Even now, years later, they kept in touch, swapped Christmas cards and baby pictures, kept each other up to date with the latest relevant gossip that could lead to business for either of them.

'So,' Ronnie said, leaning away from the table and running a smoothing hand over his goatee, 'you didn't ask me here for morning coffee. Whassup, Hal?'

Hal smiled again. All business. Typical Ronnie. 'Well, you know I'm up here working on the Buchan story,' he said, dropping his voice slightly and leaning across the table a little. 'The party wanted a sympathetic media line, especially with all the noise Buchan is making with his sentencing ideas. I just wanted to check with you, see if there was anything you thought I needed to know?'

Ronnie grunted slightly, took a moment to study his friend closely. He genuinely liked Hal, Angie and Amy did too, and it was good to see him again. Though not under these circumstances, and not when he was about to fall into such a deep pit of shit.

'What's the background you've been given by the party?' he asked.

'Not a lot,' Hal replied. 'I got a briefing from the guy who hired me, Edward Hobbes, who's one of the party chiefs at CCHQ in London. He got my name from a client I did some damage control work for about eighteen months ago.' Hal shrugged. 'Anyway, Buchan's seen as a bit of a loose cannon, not the most popular in some circles when they're trying to make Scotland love the Tories again. Seems to have been a bit estranged from the daughter; nothing major, I'm told, just didn't like her choice of career. Married for twenty-seven years, happily enough, apparently. But...'

'But what?' Ronnie asked. Stupid question, he already knew.

'So far, so boring. I dunno,' Hal shrugged, stirred his coffee, 'I just get the feeling I'm missing something, you know? And I thought maybe the name rang a bell with you, maybe you knew him when he was a full-time lawyer and just starting out? After all, the ages tally.'

Ronnie smiled. Typical Hal. He always was creepily intuitive. Like when he caught a whiff of what was going on with Ronnie and Megan at the bank.

He never said a word though, never threw it in Ronnie's face. Even when he took him home to meet Angie and the family. It was, Hal told him one night after too any brandies, his business. Do what you need to do, Ronnie, just keep it away from home and your family.

Do what you have to do. Good advice.

'Come on,' Ronnie said, finishing his coffee in a gulp and standing up. 'Let's go for a walk. There's a few things you need to know and', he cast a scornful gaze around the dining room, 'we don't want to upset folks at their breakfast.'

19

Lizzie Renwick had the most violently coloured hair Susie had ever seen. It was dyed a bright, almost gaudy shade of purple and braided with green, orange, and yellow beads. It must, Susie thought, be hell to live with when she had a hangover.

They were sitting in a small workroom behind the main display area of the gallery on Candlemaker's Row. Despite her reservations about the size of the place, once inside, Susie found herself standing in a huge, open-plan space filled with sculptures, murals and paintings. Photographs – both landscapes and portrait shots – lined the walls, vying for attention with elaborate glass sculptures, friezes and prints.

The shop, Lizzie had explained, would remain closed for the immediate future, but she had thought Susie would like to meet her there in case she wanted a look at Katherine's desk.

Lizzie was a tall, angular woman with a flat chest and incongruously wide hips. She moved with neat, birdlike motions, worrying at a nail as she smoked a cigarette and perched opposite Susie on a high stool. It reminded Susie of the type of seats she had been forced to sit on in high school art classes – her least favourite form of torture.

'So, how did you and Katherine meet?'

'At an exhibition opening at the Fruitmarket gallery.' Lizzie's voice was coloured with the faint lilt of an Irish accent. 'We got talking, found we had similar tastes in art, wanted the same things, and stayed in touch.'

'So how did all this...' Susie nodded out towards the main area of the gallery, 'come about?'

'Oh, it was Katherine's idea. She'd seen some of my work, said she would like to try and get one of the galleries in the town interested.

'When she couldn't, she decided to open a place where she could display the works that she – we – like, and promote them.'

Susie could see tears form in Lizzie's eyes. When she spoke again, her voice was wistful. 'That was Katherine, once she decided to do something, there was no stopping her.'

Thinking how she had died, Susie could believe it. The strength of will it must have taken to throw herself from the top of the Scott Monument, knowing it meant death.

'And how is the business doing?'

'Oh,' Lizzie said, shaking herself slightly, 'very well. We were just getting ready to start drawing up plans for a new exhibition by Eric Mullard, the photographer.'

'I'm sorry, I don't know...'

Lizzie flashed uneven, yellowing teeth in a small smile. 'No reason for you to,' she said. 'He's not well known. Nude poses and abstracts, that sort of thing.'

'Ah,' Susie nodded, none the wiser. 'Lizzie, Katherine's father said that you and her were close. Did you notice anything in the last few weeks that was out of the ordinary? Did she seem distracted or worried about something? Did she say anything to you?'

'No... she seemed her normal self. I mean, she was excited about the new show and everything, but nothing out of the ordinary. Although...'

Susie looked up. 'What?' she asked gently. 'It could be important.'

'Well, there was one thing, about a week ago. I came back after lunch, and she was on the phone. I don't think she saw me, and I didn't want to interrupt, but I heard what she was saying.' Lizzie looked away. Susie could tell she felt guilty about eavesdropping on her friend.

'Who was she on the phone to?'

'I don't know, but whoever it was, she wasn't happy with them. She kept on saying "It's the price we agreed. It's the price you pay."'

'Can you remember anything else?'

'No, not really. Except that she slammed the phone down and swore. Katherine never swore. That's why I remember it. I thought it was just a customer who was getting pissy about paying, but it really upset her.'

'Could you check the books for me just in case, see if there are any accounts outstanding?'

'That's the thing,' Lizzie replied, worrying at her nail more ferociously than ever. 'I already have. You see, Katherine was never the most... forceful... person in the world. She found it difficult talking to people. The poor girl was painfully shy. I think that's why she wanted me to work with her here, to help her with the business side of things.

'Anyway, I checked the accounts – I was going to phone the customer back and try to sort it out myself – but I couldn't find anything.'

'You mean there were no outstanding accounts?'

'No, none at all. So, whoever it was Katherine was on the phone to, it wasn't a customer. Or at least, not a customer I knew about.'

Susie nodded. Could mean anything. Worth looking at, anyway. She pushed the thought aside, wanting to get on with the interview and ask the question she had been wanting to ask since her encounter with Richard Buchan yesterday.

'One other thing, Lizzie,' she said. 'Did Katherine have a boyfriend or anyone else that she saw regularly? Someone else, who may have known her as well as you, that we might be able to talk to?'

'Eh, no, not that I know of,' Lizzie said, her eyes darting away. She was lying – or covering for someone. Susie could feel it.

'You sure about that?'

'Absolutely,' Lizzie replied brightly, grinding out her cigarette and meeting Susie's gaze as she did so. Good recovery, Susie thought to herself. Almost too good, practised. 'I'm a little thirsty. Would you like a cup of coffee?'

'Oh yes, please,' Susie replied, making sure Lizzie knew she would leave when she was good and ready and not before. 'I've only got a few more questions. Shouldn't take long, but a coffee would be great.'

Lizzie hid her disappointment well. 'Coming up,' she said, hopping from the stool. 'How do you take it?'

'Black,' Susie replied. 'Just black.'

20

Derek shifted slightly in the driver's seat, trying to find a comfortable position as he drove. No use, no matter what he did, his ribs moaned in protest. Fuck it, he would just have to live with it.

After his run-in with Charlie, last night had worked out better than Derek could have hoped. He managed to drive to a small Travelodge just outside North Berwick, where the kid at the desk was too busy trying to hide the porn magazine he had been looking at to bother about the fact his latest guest looked like roadkill. He had handed over a key with no hesitation, not even looking twice at the room card Derek had filled in using Charlie's name and address.

In his room, Derek tried to tend his wounds the best he could. He tore up a towel to make bandages for his ribs, tying them tight to hold them in place, then checked the wound on his head. He had been lucky. It was a deep cut, about three inches long, and the pain was incredible, but at least he could still feel it. If Charlie had decided to use the blade instead of the handle to hit him, he'd be dead now.

He didn't think he'd be able to sleep, too wired from the fight, but the moment he lay down, he passed out. After the last few weeks, it was luxury. A warm, soft bed. He woke up at about eight that morning, his entire body bruised and aching. He comforted himself with the thought that he felt better than Charlie, if he had even survived.

He had no sympathy for Charlie, or what became of him. He had taken his chance, and Derek was in no doubt that Charlie had been intent on killing him, and failed. The consequences were his own fault. He was playing with the big boys now.

Driving back into Edinburgh, Derek went over last night in his mind. It was pitifully obvious who had sent Charlie, and why, but the question was, how? How had *he* – or Charlie – known that he had gone back to Prestonview?

It was possible they would know he was back in the Lothians, but in Prestonview, on that night? Nah, someone had told them. But who?

Derek considered his dad, then dismissed that idea, ashamed. His dad may have loathed him for what he had done and the trouble he had brought down upon him and his mum, but there was no way he would have sold Derek out. His mum might have for the right price, Derek was pretty sure of that, but not his dad. Never.

So how? Derek had told no one and, as far as he was aware, neither had his dad. So how had he – how had they – known?

He pushed down harder on the accelerator and pulled out into the fast lane, eager to be in Edinburgh. Eager to see *him* and ask that very question.

• • •

Back at his desk, Doug went over the notes he had taken during his talk with Tom Allan, a sergeant at Prestonview police station. Although Allan was one of those cagey police officers who thought every question a journalist asked was a trap waiting to be sprung, he had revealed that the car park where Jimmy had found the knife and blood was being sealed off pending forensic analysis.

Luckily, he said, it hadn't been raining the night before, so there was a chance that there were still some clues – other than the obvious – about what had happened there. He had been reluctant, but finally relented and agreed that Doug could call him later on in the day to see if anything had turned up.

It wasn't strictly by the book – officially, all press enquiries were meant to go through the press office – but Allan was enough of a realist to understand that just meant more paperwork and bureaucracy for him to deal with.

Doug was itching to phone him, but forced himself to wait. Patience, he told himself. Forensic tests take time. Hours. Sometimes even days. But he needed to know if they had found anything. Anything that might show McGinty had made it back home. A blood-stained car park and a knife were right up his street. But was Doug reaching, was it just something unrelated that he was trying to shoehorn into fitting somewhere else because he wanted it to?

He had phoned the McGinty home, no answer, and when he had gone round, the other reporters and TV crews camped outside said there had been no movement all morning. Was Derek there? Doug didn't think so. He had rung the door anyway and Sam McGinty had answered. His response to Doug was terse and gruff – no change there – but Doug had seen nothing in his tone or manner to indicate Sam was hiding his son indoors. And, without anything else to go on, what could he do? Nothing.

He needed Allan to give him some proof. Needed something concrete. Walter had mentioned that Greig was getting tired with the whole Derek McGinty story – or lack of it – and was ready to pull the plug. Doug couldn't argue, but he wasn't quite ready to give up on it yet, and at least this gave him a link to the town.

He was just trying to write up a story on the latest crime-fighting initiative in Edinburgh city centre – the controversial and ground-breaking 'put more officers on the street' strategy – when his phone rang.

'Hey, Doug, it's me.'

'Hey, Susie,' Doug replied, slightly surprised she was calling.

'What's up?'

'Not much,' she said. 'But I was wondering if you could do me a favour?'

Doug felt his eyebrows rise slightly. Unusual. 'Sure, what?'

'Can you check in your library, see if the *Tribune*'s ever done anything on the Altered Perspective art gallery or a photographer called Eric Mullard?'

'That spelled like it sounds?'

Susie spelled the name out for him.

'So,' he asked, 'I take it this has got something to do with your chat with Lizzie Renwick this morning. How'd that go?'

'Interesting,' Susie said after just enough of a pause to let him know she wasn't going to give him any details. 'But I'm not too sure how much of what she said is of any use.'

'That why you want this info, try and fill in the blanks yourself?'

'Yeah, but it's more for my own curiosity than anything else.'

Doug doubted it, but he didn't say anything.

'I'll get back to you if I find anything,' he said, ready to hang up the phone.

'Thanks for that, Doug. Oh, one more thing. Have you heard anything about the knife from Prestonview you were asking about earlier?'

'Now how the hell did you know about…?'

'You're not the only one with contacts, Doug. Let me know if you hear anything interesting. See ya.'

Doug hung up, a smile on his face. Typical Susie.

He called up the online library on his computer, punched in 'Altered Perspective gallery' and sat back to see what it gave him. The answer was nothing. As usual, the damn thing refused to work, giving him a standard 'too many users logged on' message.

'Brilliant,' he muttered. So much for that idea. There was always the actual library in the basement of the building, where all the back issues of the *Tribune* stretching back over its eighty years were kept. All he would have to do was phone down, give some rough dates and ask a librarian to dig the stuff out for him. He looked at the clock on his screen. Later.

Doug turned his attention back to the story on screen. It was terminally dull, but at least it was something to do, something to keep him from phoning Allan and quizzing him.

Twenty minutes and a few phone calls to the relevant police officers, shop owners and councillors later, it was done. He read it through one last time, used the spell-checker, then sent it across to the newsdesk.

Thank God. Done. What now? He smiled. Dumb question.

He dialled Tom Allan at Prestonview.

'Hi, Tom,' he said as the sergeant answered the phone. 'It's Doug McGregor. I was just wondering if you'd found out anything on that car and knife yet?'

'Ah, Doug... good to hear from you,' Allan stuttered, sounding like a man who had just got a bad call from the clap clinic. 'Eh, no... no. Not yet. Listen, why don't you give me your number and I'll call you back when I do?'

Doug reeled off his work and mobile numbers, wondering what the hell had gotten into Allan. Probably nothing, he realised, more likely was the fact he just didn't like being phoned by a quote-hungry, impatient hack at work.

He was just hanging up when Penny, one of the other reporters who Doug occasionally wished he had the looks and courage to ask out for a drink sometime, wandered up to his desk. He swallowed back the sudden dryness in his throat, had a sudden pang of paranoia about having a bit of breakfast stuck between his teeth.

'Hiya, Doug. Sorry to interrupt, but this was delivered for you when you were out earlier on.' She handed him a letter-sized envelope.

'Thanks,' he murmured, forcing his gaze to remain on her face. She smiled and wandered off, leaving him to watch her go.

What a useless wanker, he thought. Patter like that, no wonder no woman will come within ten feet of you. He tore open the envelope. Inside was a folded piece of paper, with a note beside it:

I told you I'd send you something to prove it. Here you go. McGregor pushed her.

Doug felt a cold knot twist in his stomach. Quickly, his fingers numb, he unfolded the piece of paper, which felt laminated and smooth like a…

…photograph. It was an old and battered photo of a group of people standing in the sun, smiling for the camera. There were about six of them, standing in a rough group in what looked like a park. Behind them there was a building, the sign on which Doug couldn't quite read.

He scanned the faces, looking for detail. Then stopped. Heard breath wheeze out of him as though he was a tyre with a puncture… felt his pulse roar in his temples.

No. No, it can't be.

He flailed for a second edition of yesterday's paper and flicked through the pages. When he found what he was looking for, he held the photograph up to it. No mistake. It was. Oh Jesus, it *was.*

Two pictures of Katherine Buchan stared up at Doug from his desk. One was from the *Tribune*, the photograph her parents had released as part of their appeal for information. The other was battered, old, tatty. In it, she was smiling at the camera, just another young woman with a group of friends.

But standing behind her, one of those friends was Derek McGinty.

21

Hal shook Ronnie's hand at the main entrance to his offices – a huge castle-like building with a two-storey glass frontage that dominated a corner of Lothian Road.

'Just remember, that's all off-the-record gossip,' Ronnie told him, 'I'm not sure what use any of it'll do you. But I hope it helps.'

'"Help" isn't really the word I'd go for,' Hal said with a smile. 'But thanks, anyway.'

Ronnie gave a theatrical half-bow. 'Happy to help any time. You take care, Hal. Give Jennifer a kiss for me, tell Colin I said hi.'

'I will. Give my love to Angie and Amy.'

Ronnie nodded, then waddled up the steps to the double doors. Turned to wave one last time, then disappeared inside.

Hal crossed the road, then walked down a narrow lane beside a multi-storey car park and towards the Grassmarket and the main run of pubs in the city. It had been an after-work favourite area when he had been working with Ronnie, and it was also popular with tourists and students. From here, he could follow the road all the way down to the Scottish Parliament at Holyrood.

He made a quick call, got Jonathan to make sure everyone was gathered for a meeting in an hour, then gave him a couple of phone numbers to chase down and text back to him. As always, Jonathan was his sickeningly enthusiastic self. Hal wondered how long that enthusiasm would last when he told them Buchan was going to be taking a leave of absence from his parliamentary seat to look after his wife at this 'traumatic and painful time'. Wondered how much of what Ronnie had told him he would have to share to make them see it was the only thing to do.

Buchan had first dipped his toe into politics as a local councillor for Stockbridge back in the late Nineties. Given his legal background, it wasn't a surprise that he ended up on the city council's board for the then Lothian and Borders Police, making a name for himself by challenging the Labour administration of the day on every decision they made that was seen to erode the ability of the police to do the job.

'A lot of folk at the time thought the Chief Constable, who's now Chief Superintendent after the shift to Police Scotland, was helping him with his lines,' Ronnie had said. 'Buchan was the mouthpiece and got the headlines, the Chief got his points across about budgets and staffing levels. Win-win all round.'

Win-win, indeed. Until Buchan did his best to fuck it all up.

It happened, according to Ronnie, at the time of Buchan's campaign for a Scottish Parliament seat. The official version of events was that Buchan was out late and driving home after tirelessly campaigning for the people. His head full of great and noble thoughts, he missed a corner, tried to overcorrect and ploughed his car into a lamppost.

Hal paused in the street, used his iPhone to find the news articles from the time and read them. It wasn't a big story. 'Would-be politician in car crash shock' was about the size of it, although one of the papers had a bit of fun and headlined it '*Tory has an illuminating moment and veers to the left*.' Buchan was quoted being suitably embarrassed, promising to pay for the damaged lamppost and gravely warning that he had learned the lessons of driving while overly tired.

No harm. No foul. Except not one of the reports mentioned the young woman who had been standing between the lamppost and Buchan's car when he ran off the road.

According to Ronnie – who had heard the story from a colleague who worked for the police and had a tongue that was easily loosened with just the right blend of whisky and flattery – Buchan's first call after hitting the girl had been to the Chief Constable. Forget an ambulance to help the poor kid, who had been thrown across the pavement by the force of the impact, breaking her arm and a couple of ribs and leaving her face looking as though she had tried to exfoliate with a cheese grater. No, Buchan was more concerned about how he would get by with a little help from his friends.

The Chief got personally involved, spoke to the police officers and ambulance crew who were called to the scene, and made sure the girl was effectively deleted from history. According to Ronnie's contact, she was never mentioned in the police reports and, when taken to hospital, the ambulance crew reported her as being found about two miles west of where the 'accident' took place.

'Don't worry about the kid,' Ronnie had told Hal, 'she was well taken care of. Got a wee visit from her friendly polis, along with a nice payday to make sure she wasn't too inconvenienced by the whole ordeal. Made a full recovery, I heard, living up in Dundee now.'

Hal stopped at a coffee shop, ordered a strong black to take away. Cursed slightly as the first mouthful scalded his tongue.

Whatever way he looked at it, it was a PR disaster. He wrote the headlines in his head, didn't like what they were telling him. '*Crusading MSP in hit-and-run cover-up shocker*', '*Justice Bill Tory covered up crime with Police Chief*'; the bad news just kept on coming. It didn't matter if it was true or not, with all the coverage that was being generated by his daughter's death, the mere hint of scandal would mean Buchan would be plastered over the media 24/7. And it was only a matter of time before a reporter somewhere stumbled on the story, made the connections. A reporter with police contacts, say. A reporter like Doug McGregor.

So much for my mate Marmite, Hal thought bitterly.

He briefly toyed with the idea of leaking the whole thing to the press himself – McGregor was the obvious choice – and just gutting Buchan there and then. But if he did that, the party would be guilty by association, giving the press a free hand to look at other leading Tories who had broken the law. The names tripped off the tongue: Archer, Hamilton, Aitken. No, better to keep quiet, quell press interest in the daughter suicide story as quickly as possible, and get Buchan off the stage by announcing a leave of absence. It was an easy enough sell after his daughter's death: it would only be natural that the grieving father would want to take some time off to be with his wife.

Hal was getting ready to phone Edward in London, fill him in on the latest. He was halfway through keying the number in when a text flashed up from Jonathan. The message was simple: '*Chief Superintendent Adam Paulson's number as requested, boss. Will ping you McGregor's in a mo. See you at the meeting. J.*'

Hal sent back a quick thanks, then dialled the number. Mr Paulson liked to help his friend out, and the best way he could do that now was to finish up the investigation into Katherine Buchan's death ASAP. As he listened to the ringtone, his phone beeped; Jonathan, no doubt, sending him McGregor's number. While he wasn't ready to sacrifice Buchan yet, it wouldn't hurt to build a few bridges.

Just in case.

22

Susie shifted uncomfortably in the small, moulded plastic chair she was perched on in DI Burns' office. Across a table cluttered with paperwork, a computer and half-drunk cups of coffee, Third Degree sat reading her report on the interview with Lizzie Renwick. His lips moved silently as he read.

Burns' office was a small, sparse box of a room, which had been partitioned off from the rest of the open-plan CID suite with plywood walls that shook whenever the door was opened or shut. Despite a strict non-smoking policy in the building, the smell of stale cigarettes hung in the air and, glancing up, Susie could see the telltale muddy-brown stains creeping up the walls in the corners of the room.

Rank, and an office with a window, had their privileges.

Apart from the stains and the institutional dull green paint, the walls in Burns' office were bare, except for a single large photograph that hung behind him. In it, Burns and his family on some foreign beach, squinting into the camera for the classic family pose. His wife, a full-figured woman who was a good three or four inches taller than Burns, cradled a small baby to her more-than-ample bosom as two other small children – Susie guessed they were both seven or eight years old, at most – clung to her, beaming with gap-toothed grins.

The boys looked like shrunken versions of their father: heavy brows, thick-set bodies that were obviously no stranger to the Scottish staples of grease and fat, flame-red hair. Susie could only imagine the torments they endured at school.

'So,' Burns said, jogging her from her thoughts as he leaned back, his chair squealing a soft, resigned protest as he shifted his considerable bulk, 'what do you think?'

'I'm not sure, sir. There's something she's not telling us, though. The way she reacted when I asked if Katherine had a boyfriend, or someone she would talk to if she had a problem, was a little too sharp for my liking.'

Burns nodded agreement. 'Hmm, and what about this phone call she mentioned,' he flicked through the pages of the report again, 'when Renwick says Katherine was upset and shouting, "it's the price you agreed"?'

Susie shrugged her shoulders. 'She says she doesn't know what it was about, sir. I've checked the gallery's books, and she was telling the truth about one thing, at least: there are no outstanding invoices to be paid.'

'But you think there's more to it than that?'

Susie thought back to the way Lizzie had recovered from her questioning. Too practised. Too professional. She would expect that from someone used to being interviewed by the police, not a gallery assistant. 'Just an impression, sir, but yes, I think there's something there worth our attention.'

'Well,' Burns sighed, reaching forward for one of the cups of coffee in front of him. He took a noisy slurp, grimaced. Cold. 'Keep digging. But I'm already getting heat from the powers-that-be to wrap this up. They're keen to keep Mr Buchan happy, and a protracted investigation into his daughter's tragic suicide isn't seen as the best way to do that.'

'So, we're definite on the suicide angle?' Susie asked. It was the way she was thinking herself; the fact that they had found Katherine's purse and credit cards in her flat earlier in the day only ed to the theory that it was a suicide rather than a robbery gone wrong. But still, there was that phone call Doug had received. It wasn't unusual for reporters to get crank calls or letters when there was a high-profile death in the news – she remembered Doug telling her he had once received a letter from a man claiming to have killed Michael Jackson by psychically ordering his doctor to give him an overdose of sleeping pills and Pepsi – but, there were loose ends to be tied up here, and she was damned if she would let them be swept under the carpet in the name of political convenience.

'It's looking that way,' Burns nodded, not sounding entirely convinced. 'And the Chief's not keen on making Buchan unhappy by dragging this out. But,' he sighed, adjusting himself in his chair again, 'I meant what I said, Susie, no shortcuts. If you find anything interesting in the background checks on Renwick, then let me know.'

Susie nodded and got up, glad to be out of the ass-numbing chair. She got the feeling Burns wouldn't be quite so eager to let her keep digging around if he knew some of the sources she was using. She didn't think Doug McGregor was on Burns' Christmas card list.

She had just settled back at her desk when her phone began to ring. By the time she reached for it, it had gone dead. She was about to pick it up and dial 1471 when she noticed a manila envelope had been put on her desk. Glancing at the front, she saw it was internal mail from the records department. Susie fished out the papers and began reading. After about three lines she forgot all about finding out who had just called her. What she had in front of her was far more interesting than any wrong number.

• • •

Doug dropped the phone back into its receiver, closed his eyes and took a deep breath. After the initial shock of seeing McGinty and Katherine Buchan together in the photograph had worn off, his first impulse had been to phone Susie. A story was a story, but this… this changed everything. It meant there was a very good chance that whoever had called him the other day wasn't just another crank, that McGinty had indeed pushed Katherine from the top of the Scott Monument. If the bloodbath in Prestonview was McGinty's handiwork, then the times and locations fit. It meant that the police should be looking at a murder rather than a suicide. It meant that McGinty was in the area.

It meant Doug had a chance of finding him.

He had snatched up the phone and got as far as dialling Susie's number before the journalist in him spoke up. What did he have? An old photograph with a handwritten note tying the daughter of a well-known politician to a convicted rapist.

An envelope with a postage mark too smudged to be read. It could have been posted from anywhere, from Edinburgh to Essex. And if he called in the police now – even Susie – he would lose an exclusive on the biggest story of the year, and all because he played by the rulebook.

Nah. Playground rules. Mine. He would share with Susie soon. First, he wanted to see what he could find out.

He took the photo over to the picture desk where Terry Hewson, the *Tribune*'s picture editor, was hunched over a screen, pouring over images that were being sent to the newspaper via an international wire service.

'Got a minute, Terry?'

'For you, Douglas, anything,' Terry replied as he swung round in his chair. He was a small, compact man with neat dark hair carefully combed to hide a growing bald spot. A pair of half-moon glasses perched precariously on the end of his nose, meaning he was always tilting his head up when he spoke. To Doug, he looked like one of those lecturers he'd seen on Open University programmes.

'Could you have a look at this photo, tell me a bit more about it?'

'Hmm.' Terry held the picture close to his face to study it, adjusting his glasses as he did. 'What do you want to know?'

'Anything you can tell me,' Doug said, trying to keep the pleading tone out of his voice.

'Well, there's nothing much I can tell you about the photo itself,' Terry said. 'Seems to be a fairly standard Polaroid, but…' He paused for a moment.

'Jesus, have you seen this?' He pointed to the note that was in the envelope, which Doug had clipped to the picture.

Doug bit back the thousand sarcastic responses that flitted through his mind. 'Why do you think I'm so interested in it?' he said, careful to keep his tone neutral.

Terry said nothing, merely nodded. 'You think there's any truth to it?'

Doug felt a scream tickle the back of his throat. 'I don't know, I really don't. But I want to find out. So is there anything you can do to help…?'

'Well, we could scan the photo in, see if we can sharpen up the background, try to give you a better idea of where they are?'

'Great,' Doug replied. He felt like grabbing Terry by the scruff of the neck and screaming at him to get on with it. He resisted the urge, but only just. In frustration, he wheeled away and strode down the newsroom. He barely stopped to knock as he burst into the editor's office.

'Doug, what…?'

'Sorry, Jonathan, but I think you should come up to Terry's desk for a minute. I've got something I think you're going to want to see.'

23

It was one of those pubs where everyone turned round the moment the door squealed open. But when they saw Charlie's ruined and bruised face, the curious suddenly found their pints fascinating. In a place like this, it didn't do to ask any questions.

Charlie walked into the pub, pausing briefly to order a double Grouse at the bar. The barman, a twitchy-looking kid whose left forearm was dominated by a maroon heart-shaped tattoo around which the legend '*HMFC Forever*' was tightly curled, made sure not to catch Charlie's eye as he served him. Charlie was something of a regular in the bar. His face spelled trouble on a good day. But today...

Taking his drink, Charlie headed for the back of the pub, where two old and tatty-looking pool tables sat surrounded by three booth-style seating areas. It didn't matter what condition the tables were in, they were never used anyway. This was not a place for games, it was a place for business. Very serious business.

Charlie slid into the booth nearest to him, nodded a greeting to Henry, the mass of muscle prowling like a bulldog in the shadows at the back of the pub – the criminal equivalent of visible deterrent. Henry's arms were even more ornately decorated with Hearts FC tattoos than the barman's.

A cadaverous-looking man with cheekbones so sharp they threatened to poke through his jaundiced skin looked up from a racing paper as Charlie settled into the seat opposite him.

'Charlie, Charlie,' he drawled, small beady eyes darting across Charlie's injuries, 'you have been in the wars, haven't you?'

Dessie Banks may have looked liked a frail old man with a liver problem, but he was one of the most feared and respected men in Edinburgh. From his 'office' in this Gorgie pub, Dessie organised protection, extortion, and contract deals for more than half the city. Someone owe you some cash and unwilling to repay? No problem, see Dessie. For a small fee, he would see you got the money back, plus a few of the debtor's teeth as a souvenir. Someone else shagging your wife? No problem, one meeting with Dessie and the guy was landfill. The wife, too, if you had the cash. And so on. Charlie had worked for Dessie a few times himself, collecting debts and occasionally dealing for him in some clubs around town and, during that time, the golden lesson he had learned was simple and absolute. Do not fuck with Dessie Banks.

'You could say that, Dessie,' he sighed, taking a gulp of his whisky, grimacing at the bright flash of pain as he opened his mouth. 'Do you have it?'

Dessie smiled slightly, revealing a row of rotting teeth. 'I wasn't sure why you wanted this when you first called,' he said, reaching into a small bag that sat beside him. 'After all, I always thought you were a knife man. But now that I see this,' he waved a bony, claw-like hand in front of Charlie's face, 'I understand. You after a bit of payback, are you, Charlie?'

Charlie's eyes burned from the swollen mass of bruising surrounding them. 'Oh yes,' he whispered, his voice a lisping rasp thanks to his shattered teeth. 'That's exactly what I'm after.'

'Hmm.' Dessie nodded, placing the bag on the table between them and resting his hand on it. 'Payback costs, Charlie, you of all people should know that. Do you have the money?'

Charlie fished into his pocket and threw a fat wad of cash onto the table. His employer hadn't been happy at having to pay for this, or the fact that Charlie had insisted this was the only way to get the job done, but what did he know? He wasn't the one getting beaten half to death and then robbed in a shit-stained car park. He wasn't the one feeling like someone was gouging the marrow out of his teeth with blunt needles as a steel band was tightened around his head.

Fuck him. They had tried it his way, and Charlie was paying the price. Now they did things his way.

Dessie fingered the cash greedily then slid the bag across the table. Charlie dropped it into his lap and unwrapped the greasy towel the bag held. What was there was surprisingly heavy for something so small, so lethal.

'Think that'll get the job done?' Dessie asked.

'Oh yes,' Charlie replied, eyes not moving from the pistol. Pain flared across his face as he smiled. He didn't care. 'Thanks, Dessie, I think this'll do very nicely.'

24

Doug was just passing the 'Welcome to Prestonview' sign when his phone rang. He glanced down at the screen, winced, then hit answer.

'Susie,' he said, trying to keep his voice as casual as possible. 'What's up?'

'Hey, Doug. Where are you, I thought you were going to be in the office this afternoon?'

'Ah… yeah, I was, I was. But something came up. I'm just heading to an interview.'

'Hmm,' Susie replied. She sounded impatient. 'Anyway, I was just phoning to see if you had found anything on Altered Perspective yet?'

Doug glanced at the clock on his dashboard. 3.30pm, just over an hour since she had last called. Susie never hassled him about stuff unless it was important. She was onto something, he was sure of it. Question was, what?

'Eh, not yet, I kind of got caught up and haven't heard back from the library yet.' It was half-true; he hadn't called the *Tribune*'s library at all, but he had got caught up once the picture of McGinty and Katherine together had arrived.

After he had barged in on Greig and filled him in on the situation, a hasty conference had been called. Walter – whose only comment on the photograph had been a whispered 'not exactly a good quality pic for the front, is it?' – had been called into Greig's office, along with Terry and, at Doug's request, the *Tribune*'s political editor, Andy Wilkes.

Walter's first thought, to run a late second edition with a new front page and a story about the picture, had been grudgingly dismissed by Greig, but Doug could tell he wasn't totally happy with the decision. He couldn't blame him. On the one hand he had every editor's dream: an exclusive angle on the biggest story of the day linking the tragic daughter of a well-known politician with a notorious criminal. But on the other hand, he had nothing.

Sure, he had the picture, but what else? An anonymous note saying McGinty had killed Katherine. Not exactly a trustworthy source. And while the picture itself raised more than a few interesting questions, it wasn't proof. It didn't show McGinty was connected to Katherine's death. No, the story was theirs, an exclusive. Better to wait, do a bit of digging and see what they could find.

Terry reported that the picture had been scanned into the computer, and he was going to see what he could do about sharpening up the image and getting more details. Part of the problem, he said, was that the picture was faded and crumpled, with heavy creases across the main frame, but he would do what he could. Again, Doug bit back the urge to grab Terry and frogmarch him back to his machine. He wanted answers. He wanted the story. Now.

'Oh well,' Susie sighed, shaking him from his thoughts. 'Guess it's not that important, anyway. Can you let me know if you find anything, though?'

Find anything; that was a laugh. He'd found something alright. And he was going to have to tell her about it sooner or later. But not yet. He had a few questions he wanted to ask uninterrupted first. And to do that he would need the photograph, a copy of which was tucked in his jacket pocket.

'Sure,' he replied. 'Listen, Susie, you going to be free in about an hour?'

'Maybe,' she said, a note of caution her voice. She was still worried about them being seen together while the Chief Superintendent was inquiring about how the *Tribune* had got the inside track on the suicide of his friend's daughter. 'I've got an interview myself. What's up?'

Doug took a deep breath. Why did lying to her feel so wrong? 'I've found something I think you're going to want to see.'

'But I thought you said you hadn't had time to look into the gallery for me?'

'I didn't. It's not that, it's something else.' He turned off Prestonview Main Street and into the small estate where Sam and Rita McGinty lived. He noticed that a couple of the reporters' cars had disappeared and couldn't help but smile. 'Listen, I've got to go. I'll phone you when we get done and we can maybe meet up, okay?'

'Yeah, okay.' Susie let the silence hang on the line for a moment, giving Doug time to volunteer some details. It made her nervous when he got mysterious, but it was clear that was the way he was going to play it. 'Speak to you soon, Doug.'

'Yeah, I'll give you a call,' he said and cut the line.

He parked his car, picked up his notepad and got out. Nodded a few hellos to the reporters and TV crews he knew as he walked up the pathway. He knocked on the door of the McGintys' home and waited. After a moment, Sam McGinty opened the door slightly. He left the door chain on.

'You again,' he hissed. 'Look, I thought I told you this morning, I don't know anything. I haven't seen Derek and even if I had…'

Doug held up the copy of the photo, making sure it was facing straight towards Sam McGinty, mindful of how many bored journalists with telephoto lenses were sitting in the street behind him. He watched as Sam's eyes went wide with shock and recognition as he realised what he was looking at.

Bingo.

'I think you do know something, Mr McGinty,' Doug said slowly, trying to sound as friendly as possible. 'I think you have seen your son, or at least spoken with him on the phone. Look, my paper is going to run this picture, one way or another. Now, do you want us to go with what we usually do – Derek McGinty, the infamous rapist – or do you want us to tell our readers about the man in this picture, the man who looks like he doesn't have a care in the world?'

Sam McGinty opened his mouth, but it was a woman's voice that spoke. She sounded exhausted. 'Let him in, Sam,' Rita McGinty said, her hand appearing on her husband's shoulder. 'They're just going to keep coming until we speak to one of them, might as well be him.'

The door swung shut while the chain was rattled free and then it opened again. It seemed to take forever.

'You'd better come in, then,' Sam McGinty sighed as he turned round and headed back down the hall.

Doug didn't need to be asked twice. He followed them into the house.

The living room reminded Doug of his grandparents'. The McGintys had the same style of crocheted headrests thrown across the back of their chairs that he had seen his gran make when he was a child. Like his grandparents' home, the McGintys' living room was compact and neat, dominated by an open fireplace, which had once been for coal and now contained a gas fire. And, like his grandparents, the McGintys had a small television stashed in the corner of the room, almost an afterthought, while a radio took pride of place in a display cabinet on one wall.

But, where Doug's grandparents' home had been light and airy, with a huge bay window from which a set of flimsy sheer blinds hung, the McGintys' was dark and gloomy, the light blocked out by heavy curtains drawn tight across the windows. Seeing those curtains, and the gloom of the room, Doug felt a sudden pang of guilt.

Rita McGinty motioned to the couch. 'Take a seat, Mr…'

'McGregor, Doug McGregor.'

Rita nodded slightly, committing the name to memory.

'Well then, can I get you a drink, Mr McGregor?'

'It's Doug, please. And a coffee would be great if it's no bother. Black, no sugar.'

Rita's lips twisted into a humourless smile. She was a tall, thin woman with a tight, pinched face and eyes that seemed to be everywhere at once. It may have just been the light, but her skin had a greyish, washed out look to it. Again, Doug was reminded of his grandparents. Rita McGinty looked like his gran had after her first stroke.

'Sam, do you want anything?' she asked.

'No, love, I'm fine,' Sam said, his tone implying he was anything but. He waited for his wife to disappear into the kitchen, and then leant forward so violently Doug thought he was trying to headbutt him.

'Why are you here?' he hissed. 'Can't you see what this is doing to her? Why can't you just leave us alone?'

'Look, I'm sorry,' Doug said. He hated this part of the job, going where he wasn't welcome, asking the questions no one wanted to be asked. 'I'll be out of your hair as quickly as I can. But I need to know if you can tell me anything about that picture, Mr McGinty, anything you know about your son. You saw him last night, didn't you?'

'How did you know…?'

'Good guess,' Doug said. 'There was a bit of bother down at the car park leading to the cycle track last night, and I heard you were in the Halfway House looking a little shaken up. Doesn't take much of a jump to guess that Derek is the common thread in those two events.'

Sam McGinty blinked rapidly. 'What bother? Is he in more trouble?' There was a noise from the kitchen and his eyes darted to the door. 'She doesn't know,' he whispered desperately. 'Please, don't say anything. It would kill her if she knew I'd seen Derek last night, it would...'

'Right,' Rita said, carrying in a tray laden with biscuits and mugs and placing it on a small table between Doug and Sam. 'Now, what do you want to ask, Mr McGregor?'

Doug cleared his throat. 'Is there anything you can tell me about this photograph?' He passed it to Rita, who perched herself on the arm of her husband's chair. They studied it together for a moment, then Rita nodded slightly and said, almost to herself, 'Yes, it's her. It must be.'

Doug's breath caught in his throat. 'Who?'

She looked up at Doug. When she spoke, her voice wasn't quite steady. 'We never met her, Mr McGregor, and I've never seen a picture of her before. But, given the way Derek looks here, this photograph must have been taken when he was about eighteen years old.'

Derek had been eighteen when he attacked Bethany Miller. Interesting. Doug nodded his head. 'That would mean that picture was taken in '91 or '92,' he said.

'Quite. He was working in Edinburgh then, Mr McGregor,' Rita continued. Doug wondered what it would take for her to use his first name. The second coming, probably. 'We didn't see much of him then, but he did phone home from time to time. And, of course, he visited when he needed a hot meal or was running short of money.'

'Now, Rita...' Sam began before being silenced by a withering glance.

'Anyway, on one of those visits, he seemed different.'

'Different? How?'

'Happy, Mr McGregor, he was happy. Derek was hardly ever happy. He seemed to think that being surly was the only way to get ahead in life; that he was owed something because he had been born in a small town with not much to do and few jobs going.'

Doug tried to ignore the pained look on Sam McGinty's face

and the anger in his wife's words. 'And did you find out what made him happy?'

'She did, Mr McGregor. As I said, we never met her – he must have thought we were an embarrassment or something – but he said it was serious and the way he described her matches that picture.' Her eyes strayed back to the picture, studying her son. When she spoke again, Doug couldn't tell what he was hearing in her voice. Regret, maybe. Or sorrow. 'He said he wanted to make a go of it, find himself a proper job and settle down with her. It could have just been puppy love, a teenage crush, but...'

'But?' Doug prompted.

'But I believed him,' Rita snapped. 'Whether he loved that girl or not, I didn't care. He *thought* he loved her, and that was enough.'

Doug rocked back in his seat. Derek McGinty and Katherine Buchan, together. Jesus. Is that why he killed her? Spurned lover seeking revenge? Or worse, had he tried something on top of the Monument and she had fought him off, losing her balance and toppling over the edge as a result? Again the whispered voice on the phone: *Derek McGinty pushed Katherine Buchan to her death.* Doug fought to focus on the questions he wanted to ask. He could figure out what it all meant later.

He heard Rita gasp sharply, saw Sam take his wife's hands in his. 'What is it, love?'

Rita shook her head from side to side, tears welling in her eyes. Doug felt his stomach give a sickening lurch as he saw her eyes stray to the coffee table in the middle of the room. The coffee table with yesterday's *Tribune* on it, complete with his story on the Scott Monument 'suicide death riddle'. And a photograph of Katherine Buchan.

Rita lunged for the paper, knocking over the plate of biscuits she had brought from the kitchen with Doug's coffee. The sound of the plate shattering was deafening. She rifled through the pages manically and then dropped the paper, fell to her knees and wailed. To Doug, the sound was barely human.

Sam shot Doug a poisonous look as he leapt out of the chair and put his hands around his wife's shuddering shoulders. 'What is it, love?' he whispered, rubbing her back, trying to rock her gently back and forth to comfort her. 'What's wrong?'

'It's her!' she screamed viciously through choked sobs. Sam flinched away. 'Don't you see, it's her! The picture in the paper, the girl who died yesterday, it's HER!' She whirled around to face Doug, glaring at him with bloodshot eyes as tears streamed down her cheeks. 'You think he did it, don't you?' she cried, voice rising to a near scream. 'You think he killed her, don't you? DON'T YOU?'

Sam wrestled the photo from Rita's grip, eyes darting between it and the paper. 'Oh Jesus,' he whispered. 'Oh Jesus Christ.'

Doug got to his feet. His legs felt numb. What had he done? They were an old couple, for God's sake. Their only crime was to have a son who turned out to be a monster. They didn't deserve any of this.

'Mr McGinty,' he whispered. 'I… I'm so…'

'GET OUT!' Sam McGinty roared, drowning out his wife's hysterical sobs. For an old man he moved quickly, grabbing Doug by his shirt and pushing him towards the door. Doug could feel McGinty's arms tremble with rage, could smell peppermint on his breath. His face was twisted into a hateful sneer. For Doug, it was like looking at Derek.

Here I am, motherfucker. Come and get me.

He let McGinty manhandle him to the door, had the breath knocked out of him when the old man pinned him against the front door as he tried to fumble the chain and open it.

'Look, Mr McGinty, I'm sorry, really I am. I didn't think…'

Sam hauled him forward to swing the door open. Their noses were almost touching. 'I never want to see you again,' he spat. So that was where Derek got his temper from. 'If I do, it won't be Derek you'll have to worry about, it'll be me. I swear to God, I'll fucking kill you.'

'Mr McGinty, Sam, I...'

No good. McGinty shoved Doug backwards out the door. He stumbled and fell back down the doorstep. 'And take this shit with you,' McGinty hissed as he crumpled up the photo and threw it at Doug. The front door slammed shut, the bang echoing down the street. Doug scrambled to stuff the photograph into his pocket as he heard footsteps run up the path towards him.

'Jesus, Doug,' he heard Julie McCabe, a reporter he knew from the *Record*, say as she helped him to his feet. 'What the hell was all that about? The old guy looked like he was ready to kill you.'

Doug got to his feet and made a fuss of straightening his jacket and tie, giving himself time to collect his thoughts. 'Just asked a question he didn't like,' he said.

He could see Julie wasn't convinced. 'What was that he threw at you, then?' she asked.

'My business card. I asked him to call me if he heard anything about Derek. Must have been the wrong thing to say. Listen, you get shots of all that?'

Julie jerked a thumb back over her shoulder to her car and the pony-tailed giant sitting in the front seat with a camera pointing out of the window.

'Gary did,' she said. 'He's been looking for something to do all day.'

Doug nodded slowly. 'Good. Terry will probably be in touch for one of the snaps later.'

'Mmm-hmm.' Julie crossed her arms across her chest in the classic you're-fooling-no-one-pal stance. 'Doug, what the hell is going on?'

'Good question,' he said as he headed for his car. 'Soon as I know, I'll let you know.'

He unlocked the car and got in, rocking his head back against the headrest as he closed the door.

Just what the fuck *was* going on? So Derek and Katherine knew each other; were, according to Derek's mother, a serious item in her son's mind. Had Katherine felt the same way? And why, Doug wondered, had none of this come up when reporters and police had been combing over McGinty's life during his original trial?

Doug straightened in his seat, started the engine. Driving would help clear his mind, it always did. It was like a meditation to him. Some people listened to music when they wanted to think, some went for a walk, others had a pint. Doug sat behind a wheel and drove.

He turned the car and headed back down the road. Yes, a drive was just what he needed. But first, he had another stop to make in Prestonview.

• • •

The desk sergeant at Prestonview police station wouldn't have won any prizes for most welcoming host, Doug thought as he stood in the main reception area. When he had asked to speak to Sergeant Allan, the response had been a gruff 'He's no' here, pal.' No 'Can I take a message?' or 'Give me your number and I'll get him to call you when he gets back in.' Nothing, just stonewalling. Which, after his earlier conversation with Sam McGinty, made Doug think that Allan *was* in the station, did have some very interesting news about his little blood-stained crime scene at the car park, and had then told the desk sergeant he didn't want to be disturbed – especially if an overly nosey journalist turned up and asked for him.

'Hokay,' Doug said, turning to go. 'Thanks, anyway. But, when you see him, could you tell him it's okay, I know they found Derek McGinty's fingerprints all over the knife that was handed in earlier on. If he wants to know any more, tell him he can read it in tomorrow's *Tribune*.'

He had got as far as the door when Mr Congeniality called him back. 'Haw, hold on a wee minute there,' he said, a phone clamped to his ear. He mumbled into it, nodded and grunted a response, then sat the phone down and fixed Doug with his best you're-shit-pal stare.

'Sergeant Allan will be down to see you in a moment,' he snarled.

Doug gave him his best smile and took a seat. Sometimes, it was amazing how winging it could achieve results. Five minutes later, he was sitting in a small canteen with a tar-black cup of coffee and a very agitated Tom Allan opposite.

'How did you find out?' he asked.

Doug took a sip of the coffee, tried not to shudder. 'Digging,' he said, not willing to share his reasons for visiting the McGintys or why that had made him think Derek was in the area. Susie deserved to know about the photograph first. And he would tell her, as soon as he got what he wanted from Allan.

'So, if you already know, what do you want?'

'Confirmation,' Doug replied. 'And don't worry, I won't name you. As far as my readers are concerned, you're "a police source who asked not to be named", okay?'

'And what happens if I don't want to say anything?'

'Then I go to the press office, they come to you, I still get what I'm after and you get the headache of dealing with enquires you could have dealt with in two minutes. So, what do you say?'

Allan shook his head slowly. He knew when to admit defeat.

'So, what did you find?' Doug asked.

'Fingerprints,' Allan replied. 'Specifically, McGinty's fingerprints, and lots of them. On the knife your friend brought into the pub and all over a wrecked car we found at the scene.'

The Polo, Doug thought. 'It was stolen, right?'

'Yeah,' Allan replied, a surprised tone in his voice. He opened his mouth to ask how Doug knew, then thought better of it and pre-empted the next question instead. 'We ran the number plate. The car was reported stolen from the Gilmerton area a couple of nights ago. Although why anyone would be bothered if someone had stolen that piece of crap...'

Doug laughed. So Allan had a sense of humour, after all. 'So, is there anything else you can tell me? Jimmy said there was a lot of blood on the scene. Has a victim come forward, or is it McGinty's?'

Internally, Allan sighed. Thank Christ. He didn't know everything, then. 'No,' he said, 'the blood wasn't McGinty's and no victims have come forward.'

'So, where did it come from?'

'We don't know,' Allan said, hoping his tone or expression didn't give away the lie.

'Hmm,' Doug said, chewing on the end of his pen. 'So, what happens now? I take it you've got officers out looking for McGinty? Are you drafting in extra manpower for the search?'

'McGinty would have to be a fucking moron to stay around here after that. And we don't usually draft in extra officers to look for a car thief, Mr McGregor.'

Not yet, you don't, Doug thought. But wait until you hear about this photograph. Then wait and see what happens. You'll have cops from all over crawling up your arse.

'Is there anything else?'

'Nope,' Doug said. 'That about does it, Tom, thanks for your help.'

'And you won't name me, right?'

'Right,' Doug replied, winking. 'As far as I'm concerned, you're the man with no name.' He saw Allan's shoulders sag with relief, and couldn't resist adding: 'Just make sure that desk sergeant of yours knows the same. After all, he saw me coming in here, knows you spoke to me.'

Doug left Allan to his panic.

25

The deep leather sofa creaked slightly as Susie shifted her weight, trying not to get sucked down into it. Sitting opposite, immaculate as ever in a dark suit with black tie, Richard Buchan adjusted his glasses on his face, waiting for her to get comfortable.

'I'm sorry to intrude on you and your wife again so soon after my last visit,' Susie said as she finally got into a comfortable position. They were back in the drawing room of the Buchans' Stockbridge home. Late afternoon light was spilling in through the window, stretching long shadows across the floors. The silence in the room reminded Susie of a library. Or a museum.

'Not at all, DS Drummond, although I must admit, I was rather surprised by your call. You say you've found something odd?'

Susie nodded and produced a manila envelope from her briefcase. 'Yes,' she said as she handed it over to Buchan. 'As I said on the phone, we've been trying to build up a picture of Katherine's movements shortly before her… ah, death. As such, we been looking at her phone records, bank statements and the like, which is what you have there.'

Buchan studied the pages in front of him, smooth brow darkening as it was creased by a frown. He ran a finger along the page, then looked up. '£5,000?' he said.

'Yes, sir. As you can see, it was withdrawn from Katherine's account the day before yesterday.'

'The day she died,' Buchan mumbled.

'Exactly. The bank has provided us with details of the time and location of the withdrawal. It appears she went in to the Royal Bank of Scotland on St Andrew Square and made the withdrawal at about 11am that day.'

Buchan nodded. Susie noticed a muscle in his cheek flutter. 'Which would have been just before she went to the Monument. Do you have any idea why?'

'No, sir, none. That's what we were hoping you could tell us. We've checked her other accounts, her mortgage, credit cards and the like, and there are no records of £5,000 being either deposited into another account or being used to pay for something else.'

Susie would have been surprised if there had been. In her experience, you didn't get your hands on a large chunk of cash just to pay a bill or open another account on the day you planned to kill yourself. No, there was something else to it.

'And you have no idea where the money went?' Buchan asked, his eyes falling back to the papers in front of him, as if studying them hard enough would yield an answer.

'We were hoping you could help us with that, sir,' Susie replied. 'There was no trace of the money on…' – she caught herself before she said 'the body' – '…Katherine when she was found, and there's no record of the money being deposited anywhere else.' All of which put the robbery theory back in the frame. Or gave the suicide theory a nasty new spin.

'Can you think of any reason why she would need that amount of cash, Mr Buchan?'

Buchan took of his glasses and rubbed his eyes. In that one moment, he looked his age. 'No,' he muttered, 'I cannot. I assume you've checked with Lizzie that Katherine didn't need the money for something at the gallery?'

'Yes, we have. As far as Ms Renwick knows, there were no outstanding bills for the gallery to pay, other than the usual gas and electric bills, which are taken directly from the business account.'

Buchan nodded slightly. Susie took a deep breath and then asked the question she had wanted to ask since he had let her in.

'Mr Buchan, can you think of anyone who may have been blackmailing your daughter?'

Buchan's head snapped round suddenly, his eyes settling on hers. 'Of course not,' he said, his tone as cold as his stare. 'As I said, Detective, Katherine was a very shy, introverted girl. I can hardly think of any reason for her to be… Wait, wait a minute, you think someone pushed her from the Monument, don't you? That she gave someone that money and then they shoved her over the edge?'

Susie raised a hand. 'We're not ruling anything out, sir,' she said. 'We're just examining the facts. And that', she nodded towards the papers in Buchan's hand, 'is one of the facts that we need to look at, and find an answer for.'

Buchan opened his mouth to say something, closed it again.

'Sir, when we last spoke, you said Katherine didn't have a boyfriend or anyone else other than Lizzie Renwick that she would talk to if she had a problem. Are you sure there's no one else we could talk to about this, sir? Someone she felt might have needed that kind of money?'

'Of course there isn't,' Buchan snapped again, a moment too quickly for Susie's liking. He was hiding something, she could feel it. But what? And, if he wanted to get to the truth of his daughter's death and lay her to rest as he had said, then why?

Good questions. Susie wished she had some answers.

'Sir, I…' Susie was cut off by the shrill ringing of the phone from the hall.

'Excuse me, Detective,' Buchan said as he got up and strode or the door. 'But my wife is resting, and I don't want the phone to disturb her.'

Susie nodded and watched him go. She looked down at her notes. This case, like her handwriting, was a mess. So many questions, so few answers. Burns hadn't been too happy when Susie had told him about the £5,000 missing for Katherine's account. The missing money put the whole suicide angle in doubt, which would drag out the investigation. And the longer the investigation ran, the longer Katherine's body lay in the morgue, the longer the Buchans would have to wait to bury her.

Susie knew as well as Burns that that wouldn't sit well with Richard Buchan, who would make his displeasure known to his friends in high places. Fuck 'em. Let the heidyins grumble as much as they wanted. A woman had died in a horrible, brutal way, either driven to it or murdered. Susie didn't know which it was yet, but she was determined to find out.

She could hear Buchan speaking from the hall. He didn't sound happy.

'Ah, Andy. Yes, thank you, thank you. Linda? She's coping, as you can imagine, this isn't easy for any of us. What can I do for you?'

A pause as Buchan listened to his caller. When he spoke again, his voice was a shout that made Susie jump in her seat.

'What? What photograph? What are you talking about? What do you mean, Katherine's in it?' Another pause. 'WHO?'

Susie was on her feet now. What the hell was going on?

'No,' Buchan snapped, his voice rising with anger. 'I know nothing about this, nothing at all. How did you get this, anyway?' Another pause. Then Buchan, voice heavy with disgust. 'Oh, and you're going to publish it, I take it? I expected better from you, Andy, I thought you had morals. Don't you think we've been through enough?'

Pause.

'That's shit, Andy, and you know it. No, I have no official comment to make, thank you very much, other than that my lawyers and I will be studying your *work* very closely and will no doubt be in touch with your editor.'

The sound of the phone being slammed down was like a gunshot. A moment later, Buchan strode back into the room, door banging against the wall as he threw it open.

'Mr Buchan, what…?'

He glared at her, then remembered himself and the mask of civility slipped back down. He took a deep breath, straightened up and ran a hand down his chest to smooth his already perfect tie.

'I suggest you have a word with your superiors,' he said, the anger still present in his voice. 'That was Andy Wilkes, the *Tribune*'s' – he said the name as if it were an obscenity – 'political editor. It would appear they have received a photograph of Katherine with a less than savoury character.'

Susie blinked, why hadn't she heard anything about this? Then, Doug's words: *I'm heading for an interview*. The way he was being mysterious when she had called him. What the hell was going on?

'Who did they say is in the photograph with her?' Susie asked.

Buchan's shoulders slumped slightly. 'That rapist who's been in the papers recently.'

'McGinty?' Susie offered. 'Derek McGinty?'

Buchan nodded. He wouldn't look Susie in the eye.

Susie felt a headache snarl behind her eyes. Derek McGinty. Doug's pet subject. Derek McGinty, who had been chased out of his Fife home a month ago and hadn't been seen or heard from since. Derek McGinty, just the sort of man to whom five grand would come in very handy.

'Could there be any truth to what they're saying?'

Buchan ignored her, heading for a drinks tray in the corner of the room. He poured himself a large whisky, downed it. 'Please, just leave,' he whispered.

'Of course,' Susie said as she headed for the door, trying to keep her pace casual. 'But I'm afraid this means I will have to...'

Buchan waved a dismissive hand as he pushed his glasses aside and massaged his eyes. His skin was the colour of rotten paper. 'Yes, yes. You will have more questions, no doubt. But please, just not now. Not now.'

Susie nodded and kept walking. Paused on the doorstep after she stepped outside. A photograph of McGinty and Katherine together. Jesus. Why hadn't the paper, why hadn't Doug, told her?

The answer was depressingly obvious; Doug had to know what the story was. And to do that, he needed to poke around without the police getting in his way. Wherever he had been heading when she called him, it was connected to the picture, she knew it.

Back at her car, she punched in Burns' number and listened to it ring, trying to keep her anger in check. She had to remain calm, let Third Degree know what was going on. She could only imagine what his response would be.

Everywhere she turned, there were questions. Most of them, she couldn't answer yet. But Doug, it seemed, had more answers than she did. And, as soon as she had finished with Burns, he was going to share them.

26

The conference room where Jonathan had assembled the MSPs and party officials for the briefing was in chaos by the time Hal walked in. Even Jonathan had lost some of his enthusiasm, and was standing in the corner busily running a pen over a document as his lips moved silently.

About four different arguments were going on at once, all of them focused on how fucked they were and what the hell could be done. Hal felt a moment of panic so strong it was like vertigo as the thought flitted across his mind that they had found out about his chat with Ronnie and his follow-up call to the Chief Superintendent. Knew that wasn't the case when he felt the weight of the room's gaze fall upon him, eyes looking for answers, not his head.

'So,' he said quietly, keeping his voice low so the others in the room would have to shut up to hear him. 'What's happened?'

Three people – two balding MSPs and a party official who looked like she had been freeze-dried in the early 1970s – tried to tell him at once.

'The papers have got a hold of this picture...'

'Rapist everyone's looking for...'

'Buchan's daughter with...'

Hal held up a hand, waited for them to stop talking. 'Please,' he said softly, 'one at a time. Jonathan?' The kid jumped in the corner as though he'd been electrified. 'Why don't you tell me what's going on?'

'Me? Ah...' Red crept up from his collar, as though bleeding from his lurid tie. 'Well, ah, ah...'

'Oh, for God's sake,' snapped The Creature The Seventies Forgot. 'What's the point of getting...?'

'Because,' Hal said sharply, voice hardening, 'I want to know what the hell is going on, without the hysteria and politics. Jonathan can tell me that, then we can figure out what we're going to do. Go ahead, Jonathan.'

'Well, ah, Mr Buchan just took a call from a reporter at the *Tribune*.'

'McGregor?' Hal asked.

'No, ah, Wilkes. Andy Wilkes. Something about a picture of his daughter with that rapist that has been all over the TV recently. Asking for a statement; reaction.'

'Hmm.' Hal sat back in his seat, tension in his chest easing. Nothing to do with Ronnie's chat, then. Thank God. 'How old is the picture?'

'Ah, not sure.' Jonathan said. 'Can't be that recent though, there's no way it would have stayed quiet until now if McGinty had been spotted since he disappeared from Fife.'

Hal raised an eyebrow. Smart kid.

'Good. Simple response for us, then. Jonathan, type this up, will you? Get it out on the wires for the later editions: "This is a personal matter for Mr Buchan and his family, and we are not going to add to their distress at this time with lurid speculation about who his daughter may or may not have known."'

He paused for a moment, smiled. This actually worked out quite well. '"Mr Buchan has today indicated that he will be taking a leave of absence from his seat as the MSP for Lothians as he and his wife attempt to come to terms with the tragic loss of their daughter."' Paused. Looked around the room for disagreement. Didn't get any. Good. He didn't have time for it.

'We'll follow that up with a few calls to the newsdesks. Go heavy on the line asking for them to respect the family's privacy at this time.'

'And what the hell are we meant to do now?' a florid-faced suit asked.

'Support your colleague,' Hal replied. 'Don't deviate from the line I've just given you, don't go looking for interviews. You need to keep this low key, let it die out on its own.'

Murmurs of agreement around the room. Hal took this as his cue, got up and headed for the door. 'Now, if you'll excuse me, I've got to tell Mr Buchan about his decision. Jonathan has my number if you need me.'

27

By the time Doug got back to the *Tribune*, Susie was already waiting for him in Greig's office. She had called him just as he was driving into Cockenzie, a small town on the East Lothian coast memorable only for the large, glass and concrete-faced power station that dominated it. He had hit the road hoping for a chance to think, find some answers. For all he good it had done, he may as well have saved the petrol.

'You little bastard,' she had hissed when he answered the phone. 'What the hell do you think you're playing at?'

Doug swallowed, flailing for a response. 'I don't know, I…'

'You know Burns is spitting bullets about this, don't you?' Susie snarled. Doug didn't think he'd ever heard her so angry. It wasn't a pleasant experience. 'He's talking about charging you with obstructing justice and wasting police time, and, you know what, I'm not too sure I disagree with him.'

'Look, Susie, I just wanted to get a few facts before I told you what was going on.' It was a half-hearted excuse, Doug knew.

'Bullshit, Doug. You wanted to get the scoop. You always do. Jesus Christ, after all this time, didn't you think you could trust me or something?'

'Well, I… I…'

'Save it. Listen, I'm heading to the *Tribune* to pick up the photograph now. Let's just hope you've left some trace evidence intact, for your sake and mine.'

'Susie, I'm not a complete idiot. The photo was scanned in and then sealed in a plastic bag, along with the envelope it came in, ready for you to pick up.'

'Oh, and just when was that going to be, Doug? When were you planning to tell me, if I hadn't been there to hear Buchan's conversation with your friend Wilkes?'

'Now, Susie, I…' Too late, she had hung up.

Susie took a deep breath. Forced herself to calm down. Tried not to feel the sting of anger – and, oh, admit it, hurt – at Doug's actions.

'You should know him better by now,' she muttered.

She had first met Doug about three years ago, not long after she transferred to Edinburgh to take the Detective Sergeant job and, on her part at least, it was hate at first sight.

The trouble had started just after Christmas, and the big story of the day was that an Assistant Chief Superintendent, Paul Redmonds, had been caught with his pants down with a female colleague at an office party. The story leaked out after a reporter got wind of the fact Redmond had moved out of his family home – after admitting all to his wife and then being kicked out. The tabloids had a field day: a senior, married officer having a drunken fumble at an office party where those charged with protecting the streets were pissed as farts and acting like horny students? Thank you, Santa, we have been good little journalists this year.

Susie kept her head down, but every briefing she went to, every call she took, she felt the snide, sideways glances, the snickers and sneers, the pointing and elbowing.

'Look, there's the tart that banged Redmonds.'

'Isn't she the new girl from Stirling?'

'Yeah, must be desperate to get up the ladder if she'd fuck that greasy little shit.'

'What a slapper. Bit of a looker, though. Think I'd have a chance?

What the fuck had she been thinking? She'd gone to the party to try and get her face known, try to make a few friends after the move. But when everyone started to divide up into their little cliques, she'd been left on her own, swapping awkward, embarrassed smiles with faces she knew and fending off the drunken dicks who seemed intent on talking to her breasts rather than her face. So she'd floated to the bar, where she bumped into Redmonds. It was a bad combination. Alcohol plus loneliness plus semi-attractive older man, who was more than a little worse for wear on Christmas cheer himself, equalled trouble.

Before she had known it they were back in her room, pawing at each other on the bed as some bimbo blonde with plastic tits and a frozen smile bounced up and down on the screen in front of them. Redmonds had ordered the movie 'for a laugh', but the real laugh had been when he dropped his boxers.

Merry fucking Christmas, Susie. Maybe the disappointment had been why she had clawed at his back so hard – leaving the marks that forced his guilty admission to his wife. It sure as hell wasn't the sex.

Word got round quickly, and she fell victim to typical police humour. The punning asides, from just-loud-enough comments when she walked into the canteen about 'copping a feel' and 'feeling the full force of the law', to a dose of the morning-after pill left on her desk. There were the not-so-subtle digs too, mostly from those who knew Redmonds' wife, Alicia. Hard stares in the bathrooms, the haughty sniff when she walked into a room, as if she was carrying a bag full of warm shit with her.

It felt like being back at school, the bullies singling her out again. Not for being different this time. Just for being a marriage wrecker. Not that she felt much guilt over that – the way she saw it, she had saved Redmonds' wife from a life of quick, blunt sex with a lying prick who thought he was God's gift. The thought of him touching her, that mewling sound as he came, the jerks of his cock inside her as weak as his technique, made her shudder with disgust. Maybe they were all right. If her personal judgement was this bad, what fucking use would she be as a police officer?

She was ready to hand her notice in, just get it over with, when Redmonds called her. Apologised for the position he had put her in – *Missionary and doggie,* she thought, *and you were shit* – and told her to tough it out. He had read her file, she was a good officer, had the makings of a fine copper.

He couldn't help her, of course; after all, how would that look? But the focus of the story was on him, not her. Just keep your head down and it'll pass. After all, the press had nothing to go on to identify her, did they? None of those at the Christmas party (held at a hotel in Glasgow to make sure nobody made a mess at home) had actual evidence who it was he had been a naughty boy with. There were rumours, yes, but unity in the ranks against outside prying made sure no names were leaving the station, especially for a reporter.

Unfortunately, Doug proved a little more creative than anyone gave him credit for. After a few fruitless calls to sources in the police, he had headed for Glasgow and the Hilton Hotel, where the party had been held. After making one more phone call.

By the time he arrived at the Hilton, the staff had printed off a full list of room numbers, guest names and charges for him. Why shouldn't they? After all, as far as they were concerned, Lothian and Borders Police, as it had been at the time, had simply sent one of their accountants to double-check the figures to see what cash they could reclaim from officers and what was a legitimate expense claim. Good idea, really.

He had phoned Susie about an hour later, and they had agreed to meet in a small, anonymous café near the bottom of Broughton Road.

She sat there, staring out the window, coffee forgotten in front of her. Felt angry tears for being so fucking stupid trembling behind her eyes, and rage at this little shite who had found out and summoned her for a meeting.

'Look, I really think it would be a good idea if we had a chat,' he had said on the phone. 'I know I can't force you, I could run the story as it is, but just listen to me first, okay?'

Bastard. Fucking bastard hack.

'Eh, Susie, is it? Hi, I'm Doug.'

He wasn't what she was expecting. With fashionably tousled light brown hair, a face Susie would have called handsome if not for the slightly hawkish nose, and inquisitive green-brown eyes that seemed to be studying and recording everyone around him, Doug McGregor looked more like a student than a reporter. And she'd never seen a man look more uncomfortable in a suit in her life.

She reluctantly took his outstretched hand, eager not to make a scene. He was thin and wiry, but she sensed strength in that handshake.

He smiled at her, revealing a row of white, if slightly crooked, teeth. 'Thanks for coming,' he said as he slid into the chair opposite her, his accent pure Edinburgh. 'I know it mustn't have been the nicest phone call you've had.'

'Look,' she hissed, leaning over the table so she was almost nose to nose with him. 'Let's just cut the shit, okay? So you know about me and Paul. Great, good for you, go write your fucking story. I don't know why you wanted to see me, but if you think I…'

Doug held up his hand. 'I'm not going to write the story.'

'Wh… what?' Susie leaned back, not quite believing what she had heard. 'Then why… what?'

'Look,' he said, leaning forward himself now as he pushed her cup of coffee aside. 'Bottom line? This is a shit story. So you got pissed and went back to your room to enjoy some room service, porn and whatever else you got up to with a senior officer, so what? It's not exactly world-shattering, is it?'

Susie felt her mouth drop open. 'How did you know about th…?'

'Expense records,' Doug replied, pushing a ream of papers

across the table to her. 'I got them from the Hilton. After that, all I had to do was look for anything unusual when the party was in full swing. And look what I found.' He ran a finger down to a highlighted line on the page. 'At 11:24pm on the evening of the party when, according to the hotel staff, the party was in full swing, a bottle of champagne, two glasses and a "movie event" were charged to your room. By the way, "movie event" is hotel code for porn, so business travellers aren't embarrassed about their jack-off entertainment showing up on their expenses.'

Susie felt her face redden as images of that night flashed through her mind. Pushed down a shudder of regret, collected her thoughts. Self-pity could come later. She had a more immediate problem. 'How the fuck did you get these? How? Why…?'

'Brilliant interview technique,' Doug said, smiling slightly. 'Straight to the point. Must be why you're in CID.'

He offered a smile she almost mistook for shyness. 'I did a little checking. You've not long transferred into Lothian and Borders, and I've just landed this crime reporter's job. I figure we could help each other out from time to time.'

Susie snorted and rocked back in her chair. 'Ah, so that's it. You think this gives you something over me, pal? That this makes me a "source"?'

'No,' Doug said softly, his eyes fixed on hers. 'I think this shows you I've got my priorities right. Man and woman shag while pissed. Great story. Sure, it'll sell a few papers, but it's not worth anything, is it? At best, it'll fuck up your career. That what you want? I don't.'

He shoved the ream of papers across the table towards her. 'I don't want to write this up, it's red-top shite at best. So keep all this. You want to cause trouble for me as I got this under false pretences, go ahead. I'm going to tell my boss I couldn't find out who it was. Oh, and don't worry, none of the other papers will find out, I've already told the Hilton staff to be aware reporters might try to get access to their records to get a story. Not that anyone else will probably be as brilliant as me.' Again that smile, almost shy, but the eyes said he meant it. Problem was, the arrogant wee shite was right. It was brilliant.

He stood up to leave. Susie was more confused than ever.

'So why did you want to meet me?' she asked.

'To introduce myself,' he replied simply. 'And to hopefully let you know that all journalists aren't shit-digging scumbags. Look,' he dropped a business card on the sheaf of expense records he had given her, 'here's my number. If you hear something worthwhile that you think warrants attention, or if I can help you get coverage for something, call me. Who knows, I may call you sometime. See ya.'

And that was how it had begun. Since that first meeting, Susie had come to understand Doug was something of an idealist. A story-hungry, ruthless idealist, but an idealist nonetheless. He wasn't interested in gutter press or scandal stories, he wanted to report on the big stories and issues. To start with, he had been good to his word – only calling her when he needed to, never hanging the Hilton episode over her head to get more details. If she didn't tell him, she didn't tell him. He could be useful in getting answers to questions and titbits of information from people who wouldn't talk to the police. And, she almost hated to admit, she loved the thrill of it; throwing him a line that she wanted an answer for, seeing who would get there first. It was almost like a race between them; Doug was smart, resourceful, intuitive, all the traits of a good detective – and Susie thrived on the competition.

But, no matter how productive their relationship had become, and how they were increasingly blurring the boundary between contacts and friends, there were still downsides. Susie took another deep breath, played with the phone in her hand. Toyed with the idea of phoning him back and giving him another bollocking there and then. Just the two of them. Off the record.

But no. No. She could wait. And so could he. Wait and sweat.

• • •

Doug had spent the rest of the drive trying to think what he could say to her. The truth was, he didn't know what to say. He didn't have an excuse for what he had done, other than the story. Susie was right, he had wanted the scoop, wanted to get to the truth, which had blinded him to the fact that what he was doing was wrong. He could, of course, blame Greig and Walter for not ordering him to hand the photograph over as soon as they heard about it, but that would be a cop-out. The decision was his. True, they had backed it, as eager as he was to get the full story, but at the end of the day…

And just what had he got by keeping Susie in the dark? Let's see. He had managed to break an old woman's heart, push an old man to the brink of a nervous breakdown and harass a small-town sergeant who had only been doing his job. And all to prove what he already knew, what the photo already told him. Great day's work, Doug.

Susie shot Doug a cold stare as he took a seat at the conference table in Greig's office. They had been joined by Walter, Andy and a woman in a severe business suit that Doug could only assume was one of the *Tribune*'s lawyers.

'As I was saying to DS Drummond,' Greig said, 'the *Tribune* has already apologised to the Chief Superintendent for this regrettable mix-up. I've spoken to him personally, and he agrees that, although what you did was wrong and irresponsible, it is in no one's best interests to pursue the matter further at this time.'

Internally, Doug breathed a sigh of relief. He wondered how many police-are-great stories Greig had had to promise the Chief to stop him from pressing charges, and how many he would be writing himself.

As if reading his thoughts, Greig turned to glare at Doug. He looked more like an undertaker than ever. 'Do you have anything to add, Douglas?'

'Yeah.' Deep breath, try not to meet Susie's gaze. 'As I've already said to DS Drummond, I apologise. However, I think I may have some information that may be useful to her and her investigation.'

'Oh, and what might that be?' Susie asked, her voice as cold as her eyes.

'Well, according to Derek McGinty's parents, he and Katherine were an item back in the early Nineties, not long before he attacked Bethany Miller.'

'Oh? Anything else?' Despite her tone, Doug could tell he had caught Susie's interest.

He cleared his throat. He didn't like talking to Susie with so many other people around, didn't like sharing leads with other reporters in the room. He had asked Andy to contact Buchan as, with his experience, he might be seen as the friendly face of reporting after Doug had splashed his daughter's death all over the front page. From what Susie had said Andy hadn't got anywhere, and now Doug had a rival on the story.

'Well, according to a source of mine, fingerprints matching Derek McGinty's put him at a crime scene discovered near here this morning. That being the case, there's a good chance he was in Edinburgh recently, meaning…'

'Meaning he could have killed Katherine,' Susie muttered. She was onto something, Doug was sure of it. He could tell by the tense way she sat, the gentle chewing on her bottom lip. But what…?

'Mr Greig,' she said in her most businesslike tone, 'now that we've got all this sorted out, I wonder if I might have a moment alone with Mr McGregor? I need to go over any details he can remember of the phone call he received and the envelope's arrival. Unless, of course,' she fixed Doug with a withering glance, 'you'd prefer to give me a statement at the station?'

'Oh no,' Doug said, rocking back in his seat. 'Here's fine, if that's okay with you, Jonathan?'

'That's fine, Doug. Gentlemen, Ms Ackers…?' They rose to

leave and were heading for the door when the woman in the business suit turned back. 'Would you like me to stay for this, Mr McGregor?' Lawyer, definitely.

'Nope, I'll be fine,' Doug said with more confidence than he felt. 'On you go.'

She nodded and closed the door behind her, leaving Doug and Susie alone.

'Look,' Doug said after a silence just long enough to make it clear Susie was going to make him speak first. 'I'm sorry, okay, I just thought…'

'No, Doug, you didn't think,' she said. 'Do you realise what an idiot you made me look? Not only did I have to deal with Burns screaming down the phone at me, but I also had to listen like a complete idiot while Richard fucking Buchan told me there had been a major development in the case, which he had just heard about from a bloody reporter!'

'Buchan? What were you with Buchan for?'

'Don't push it, Doug,' Susie said, raising a warning finger. 'Just don't. It doesn't matter why I was there.'

'Oh, but it does. You've found something, haven't you? Something you think ties McGinty to being at the Scott Monument when Katherine fell. Come on, Susie, talk to me. After all, who knows McGinty better than I do?'

Susie's face hardened. Damn it, he was right. He had studied the McGinty file in fine detail – almost obsessively – and some of his guesses about the guy had been spookily accurate. Part of her wanted to tell him, to get his opinion, but there was another part of her that was still furious with him for what he had done. And hurt.

She shook her head. No. 'Look, from what you've said, there's a good chance that McGinty was at the Monument. More than that I'm not prepared to say, okay?'

Doug nodded, held out his hand and slapped his wrist. 'Hokay,' he said, flashing his best aw-shucks smile. 'I deserve that,

I've been a bad boy. Seriously, Susie, I am sorry. I won't do it again, okay? I just got caught up in the moment. But I promise, the next time I get an anonymous note, you'll be the first person I call. And I'll get you that info on Altered Perspective tonight.'

Susie held up her hand. 'All right, all right,' she sighed, suddenly tired. 'Come on, I've got to go and face Burns, try to cool him down. He'll be raging now that the Chief Superintendent has saved your arse.'

'So, what am I going to do about that?'

'Nothing,' Susie said. 'But the least you can do is walk me to my car.'

• • •

Doug made a show of opening the car's door for her when she released the central locking.

'Stop it,' she said. Doug hoped he wasn't imagining the smile he heard in her voice. 'I hate it when men get pathetic.'

He smiled sheepishly. He felt pretty pathetic. 'So, how do you feel when men offer to buy you a drink to say sorry?'

Susie laughed. 'Well,' she said, 'I feel kind of...'

Her phone rang, cutting her off mid-sentence. 'Hello, DS Drummond speaking.'

She listened for a moment, clamping the phone tighter to her ear. Her mouth drew in, turning into a thin, bloodless line across her face. 'Hmm, yes,' she said. 'Uh, uhh... Jesus.' She reached up and massaged the bridge of her nose. 'Yes, sir, I understand. I'm on my way.' Then she cut the line.

Doug gave her a quizzical glance. 'Not good news, I take it?'

Susie shook her head and looked at him, torn. Tell him or not? He would find out soon enough, the press office would have to put a release out ASAP, but still...

Still...

'C'mon, Susie, no more secrets. Promise. Whassup?'

Ah, the hell with it.

'That was Burns,' she said. 'There was a report of an alarm going off at a gallery in the Old Town about an hour ago. Uniformed officers went to take a look, found the back door of the premises had been smashed. When they went inside they found a pool of blood and a woman, badly mutilated in the gallery.'

'Wait a minute. Old Town gallery? Woman…' Doug's voice trailed off as his eyes widened.

'Yeah, Doug,' Susie said as she started the car. 'Lizzie Renwick's been murdered. 'Looks like she was stabbed.'

Doug couldn't believe what he was hearing. 'How do you know…?'

'Because Burns just told me the murder weapon is still sticking out of her. Whoever did this, they left a little calling card. Doug, that research you promised me…?'

Doug nodded. It felt as though someone had stuffed his head with cotton wool. 'I'll get right on it,' he mumbled.

Susie nodded, slammed her door and drove away, leaving Doug standing in the car park.

28

The whisky was acid in his throat, poison in his stomach. His eyes, already raw from the lack of sleep, stung as though he were peering through smoke. Above, the floorboards creaked gently as Linda shuffled endlessly between her room and the room that had been Katherine's so many years ago. He strained his ears, waiting for the next inevitable choked sob. Felt empty when he heard it.

Richard Buchan threw back the last of his drink, felt some of it dribble down his cheek. Wiped at his face with a hand that wasn't quite steady, stood up and headed for the decanter in the cabinet. Tore off the stopper, barely fought back the urge to throw the fucking thing against the wall.

He sloshed another whisky into his glass, raised it to his lips. Stopped.

'Control, Richard,' he whispered, his voice sounding dead in the quiet of the lounge. 'Control.'

Ah, but it was tempting though. And who would blame him? After all, he had reason. His dead daughter now linked to a rapist, his wife a basket case, his career brought to a shuddering halt by a fucking poof who thought he could tell him – *him* – what he was going to do next.

Buchan had got the gossip from his few loyal friends in the parliamentary party, and word was that Hal Damon had been brought in from London by the main party. He was, they said, very sharp, very professional. Knew what he wanted and how to get it. And had Jonathan slobbering after him like a lovesick puppy, by all accounts.

It hadn't been a surprise when Damon had demanded a meeting, especially after the call from the *Tribune* linking Katherine to that rapist, McGinty.

What was a surprise was how much he had managed to find out. And how easily.

Buchan had ushered him into the room he now stood in, took a moment to study Damon as he settled back into his seat and waved off the platitudes of sympathy.

A tall man, the broad shoulders and flared back of someone who was a regular at the gym. A face that was too angular to be handsome, smooth pale skin pulled tight over high cheekbones. Close-cropped hair just starting to go grey at the temples, trendy heavy-framed glasses perched on top of a nose that looked as though it had been broken at least once.

He wore his expensive suit with an ease that made Buchan's teeth ache, stood at the window and looked out at the view as though he owned the fucking place.

And worse than all that, he made Buchan speak first.

'Well?' he snapped. 'You asked to see me. I take it this is about that crap the *Tribune* is peddling about Katherine's links to Derek McGinty?'

Damon turned away from the window, a small smile twitching at the corners of his mouth.

'Partially, yes,' he said with an accent that reminded Buchan of the Lake District. 'However, I'd like to focus on what happens next.'

'What do you mean? These rumours are exactly that, tabloid bullshit whipped up to get headlines. Oh, I could sue the papers, but what's the point? I know that...'

'That's not what I meant,' Damon cut in. 'What I meant is, what happens for you.'

'What? I...'

'Let me be blunt, Mr Buchan. Whether or not your daughter knew this man isn't an issue. But the fact the press are looking into it so closely, is. And if they found this out, what else are they going to find?'

Buchan felt a stab of panic, forced his face to remain impassive. *Control, Richard. Control.*

'I'm sure I don't know what...'

Damon held up a hand. 'Please, Mr Buchan. It took me a couple of hours to find out about the favour you pulled in from the then Chief Constable after your little car problem. You've done a good job keeping it quiet so far, but if the press keep looking at you, how long will it take them to find out what I have?'

Buchan felt as though the air was being sucked out of the room. *How had he...?*

'With your sentencing Bill in parliament, the party cannot afford a scandal like this, especially after the cash-for-cooking affair. Can you imagine the headlines? "*Justice crusade MSP in hit-and-run cover-up*"?' He shook his head. 'No. I've discussed it with the parliamentary party and the Whip's office and we agree that the best thing would be for you to take a leave of absence.'

Damon held out a sheet of paper. 'I've drafted a statement. We can release it today.'

Buchan snatched the paper from Damon. Skimmed over it, cold rage scalding the pit of his stomach as the terror receded and the air seeped back into the room.

'And just who the hell are you,' he whispered slowly as he tossed the paper aside, 'to tell me to stand aside?'

'I'm the man hired by your party to make sure this doesn't turn into a clusterfuck in the press, Mr Buchan. You have my sympathies for the loss of your daughter, you sincerely do, but my job is with your party, not you. So I am telling you, you will take a leave of absence while this blows over. I've already spoken to your friend the Chief, and he agrees that a swift end to the investigation into your daughter's suicide would be best to spare you and your wife further pain.'

'Pain?' Buchan sneered. 'What do you think you know about that?'

'Nothing, Mr Buchan,' Hal replied, adjusting his glasses. 'My husband and I just became parents for the first time. A daughter. And I can't imagine what you must be going through. But I *can* imagine the field day the press will have if they find out about your hit-and-run. Do you really want to put your wife – yourself – through that as well?'

Buchan shook his head. He couldn't think straight. He needed this man out of here. Now.

So he played the role, slumped his shoulders, murmured what the prick wanted to hear about it being a relief, really. *After all, Linda hasn't been bearing up well and, to be honest, Mr Damon, neither have I.*

He finally managed to get him to leave after promising to review the statement and get back to him.

Buchan shook himself from his thoughts. Walked back from the cabinet, poured the whisky into the bin beside the sofa – and onto the shredded remnants of Damon's statement.

'"My husband and I,"' he murmured with a shake of the head. 'Jesus Christ.'

He walked to the window, stared out at the night.

Damon had been right about one thing, the press would be looking closely.

But Buchan prided himself on being a cautious man.

And a prepared one.

29

She had never seen the aftermath of an earthquake for herself before, but if asked to describe it, Susie would have said it looked like the scene before her at the Altered Perspective gallery that night.

The sculptures and glasswork, so delicately arranged only hours before, were strewn across the floor, shattered like chunks of rubble from a demolished building. The coloured shards of glass glinted, reflecting the streetlights outside – pathetic remnants of the beautiful objects they had once been. Susie felt heat rise between her eyes at the thought. She wasn't sure why. Photographs and prints had been ripped from the walls – some canvases now lay at odd angles on the floor, frames splintered and broken, while others had been angrily slashed and reduced to streamers.

And then there was the blood. It glistened in the middle of the gallery floor in a dark, oily pool. Susie tried to tell herself that's all it was, oil. Tried to ignore the cloying, bitter smell. She felt the urge to vomit, clenched her jaw against it. She could deal with that later. Right now, she had a job to do.

A trail led off from the puddle, twisting a staggered, smeared path towards the back of the gallery. Scene of crime officers flitted around, taking photographs or bending to take a sample of this or that as Burns led Susie through the gallery to the back office.

Lizzie Renwick lay slumped at the foot of her desk at the end of the blood trail, arms and legs spread out as though she were a doll thrown away by a careless child. Susie had seen bodies before, of course, but just hours ago she'd had coffee with this woman, bullied and intimidated her to get the answers she wanted. Now she was just another victim of violent crime. Just another statistic to be filed away and forgotten.

From near Lizzie's left shoulder a pair of scissors protruded at an obscene angle, framed by a stain of dark blood. Susie felt her gorge rise as she realised the blood was almost the same colour as Lizzie's hair. She overcame a physical urge to touch her. To help. But the police officer in her told her to get a grip. What was wrong with her? Lizzie was quite clearly beyond help.

The office itself was a disaster area. Papers were scattered across the floor, drawers had been pulled from tables and smashed, the two desks upturned. Susie noticed the high stools she and Lizzie had been sitting on earlier in the day lying in the corner, overturned like wounded animals.

'Whatever happened, it looks like she was trying to get to the phone and call for help,' Burns said, jutting his chins towards the trail of blood. He turned towards Dr Williams, the tall, almost gangling coroner who was crouched over Lizzie's body.

'Any idea of a time of death, Stephen?'

Williams sighed as he got up. He was in his late fifties and had been dealing with police officers for a long time. They never learned. 'You know better than to ask that, Jason,' he replied. 'I can't be exact until I can run more tests.'

'I'm not looking for exact,' Burns said, trying and failing to keep the note of impatience out of his voice. 'Your best guess will do for now.'

Williams sighed, pulled off the rubber gloves he was wearing with a theatrical flourish before running a hand through his iron-grey beard. 'Well, this is only a guess…' He fixed Burns with a hard stare to made sure he understood. Burns nodded slightly.

'However, it appears you got lucky. You say that officers found her about an hour ago?"

Burns grunted something that could have been mistaken for a yes.

'Hmm. Well, she hasn't been dead for much longer than a couple of hours at most,' Williams said, turning back to the body.

Susie's throat went dry. If she had only come to the gallery to see Lizzie later in the day…

'Jesus,' Burns whispered. If those bloody uniforms had just got to the alarm sooner. Williams seemed to read his thought, held up a hand, shook his head slowly. 'She was dead the moment she was stabbed,' he said.

'Why's that?' Susie asked, dragging her eyes away from the wound. Her lips felt numb.

Williams pointed to the ceiling, where there was a dark splatter of blood. 'You see that, that's arterial blood,' he said. 'Same as what's around her chest and the wound itself. That's why it's so dark. When she was stabbed,' he brought his arm down in a stabbing motion to illustrate, 'I'm guessing the scissors' blades hit her subclavian artery.'

He was pointing to an area just below his collarbone now. 'It's the artery that supplies blood from the heart to the arm. It would have been like puncturing a high-pressure hose, the blood would have sprayed everywhere, including the ceiling. She bled to death. Unless you had a surgical team on the spot, she was as good as dead the moment the artery was compromised.'

Susie thought for a moment, wished she could sit down. A picture she didn't want to see was forming in her head. 'Hold on, you're saying she died here, at the desk?'

Williams nodded.

'Then what about all the blood in the gallery? What about the trail leading…?' Her voice trailed off as the picture developed fully. The urge to vomit was back now, stronger than ever, a bitter taste rising to the back of her throat. She didn't think she could hold it for much longer.

'You're telling me that someone beat the shit out of her through there, let her crawl all the way here, then stabbed her again?'

'I'm not guessing anything about what happened her,' Williams said. 'That's your job. But, for what it's worth, the facts – and the other wounds on the body – seem to support that theory.'

'Other wounds?' Burns asked.

'Yes. It's hard to tell until I can get her cleaned up and have a proper look, but it seems there are extensive cuts and stab wounds around the body. The hands, legs, torso and so on.'

'Any of them life-threatening?' Susie asked. She didn't like how her voice sounded.

'Again, I can't say with any certainty, but I wouldn't think so. They look like fairly minor injuries on their own. I'd guess some of them are defence wounds. Of course,' he cast an eye over the ruined gallery, 'any injury, no matter how minor, can be potentially fatal, depending on the victim.'

'No,' Susie said looking around the office. The ruined desks, the papers lying across the floor, the smashed drawers, the Edinburgh University mug broken on its side. Her jaw was so tight it ached. She felt her legs begin to tingle, jerk with the need to move. To run. 'They weren't meant to kill.'

Saw Burns give her a questioning glance, ignored it.

'Look around,' she said, hoping she sounded more professional than she felt. 'Whoever did this, they were looking for something. Beat Lizzie up to persuade her to give them answers, tell them where to find what they were looking for.'

'And when she didn't…' Burns nodded slowly. He could see where she was going.

'Doesn't matter,' Susie said. 'Whether Lizzie gave him or her what they wanted is immaterial. Maybe she did, maybe she didn't. But either way, she was left to crawl through here, try to get help and then whoever it was came back to finish her off.'

'So, she was…?'

Susie nodded. The world was beginning to swim. She had to get out of here. Away from the smell of the blood, away from the ruined body that lay in front of her.

'Yes, sir. Lizzie was tortured before she was murdered.'

30

Doug hit the log-off icon on his computer and leaned back in his chair, trying to stretch the stiffness out of his back. Enough. He wondered what Susie had found at the gallery, fought the urge to call her and see. He could say he was only calling to let her know what he had found out about the gallery, but knew she would see that for the lie it was. In the car park, it had felt as though her anger was starting to fade. If he called now, they would both know it was to check if she had thawed any more.

Instead, he settled for printing out his research on the gallery and stuffing it into an envelope. He would drop it into Gayfield station on the way home so she could have it in the morning, for what it was worth.

Doug wasn't sure how much help what he had found would be. After an hour or so digging around the *Tribune*'s library, all he had to show for his troubles were three pieces connected to Altered Perspective.

The first piece, the oldest, was a picture story from the opening of the gallery. It was taken back in 1993 for a columnist's diary piece that was supposed to be a round-up of what was happening in Edinburgh's society circles. Back then, Richard Buchan had only been a QC – although, from what Andy had said, he was already making his voice heard in Tory circles and was said to be a key supporter of the MP Edmund Harrison. The piece ran under the headline '*Straight from the art.*' Doug wondered if the sub who had written it had been taken out and shot for crimes against cliché. They deserved to be.

Under the headline was a picture of Richard Buchan smiling for the camera, a protective arm thrown around Katherine. She looked so different from the way she had in the photograph with McGinty. Her hair was scraped back in a painful-looking bun, her smile nervous and self-conscious. What was it Susie had told him Buchan had said about his daughter? Katherine found people 'tiring', that was it. In the picture, she looked exhausted.

The copy itself was only three paragraphs long:

> *Great day for a show. Pop down to the Old Town and you may find something that will alter you perspective as Katherine Buchan, daughter of QC and Tory VIP has opened her new gallery.*
>
> *Katherine, seen here with her dad at the official opening, says: 'I've always loved modern art, and when the chance of the shop came up, I knew I had to do it. It's a great investment for the future, and, hopefully, I can help people see things the way I do.'*
>
> *Dad Richard, who despite his political shortcomings remains a loyal Hibee, adds: 'I'm just happy to help Katherine do something she loves.'*

Short and sweet, Doug thought, but hardly enlightening. From what he could read between the lines, daddy dearest had bankrolled the project. Interesting, considering Susie had said she got the impression he didn't approve of his daughter's artistic leanings. He mustn't have been that opposed, though. Katherine would have been about twenty in 1992, very young to be set up in business unless her dad had faith in her.

The other two pieces Doug had found in the library were even sketchier than the diary piece. They detailed an exhibition held to commemorate the opening of the Scottish Parliament – there was a picture of the building draped in Saltires with a huge replica of the Stone of Scone taking pride of place in the centre of the gallery, surrounded by artworks and photographs representing key events in Scotland's history. The last piece was a review from the Edinburgh Festival a couple of years ago; the gallery was only mentioned in passing as it was being used as a venue for art works and poetry readings that year.

Doug's research on Mullard hadn't been any more productive. As Lizzie had said, Eric Mullard was a photographer, known for his nude and abstract work. A show he put on in London a few years ago had caused a bit of a stir, being branded pornographic and exploitative by some of the more prudish and conservative commentators of the day. Apart from that one piece of information, nothing. He was a respected photographer known to support small, independent galleries by using them to showcase his work.

Doug packed everything he had found into an envelope, sealed it and wrote Susie's name on the front.

The drive to Gayfield Square only took fifteen minutes. On a whim, he asked the desk sergeant if Susie was around, wondering if she had finished at the gallery yet, but was told that she wasn't available. Doug shrugged, handed over the envelope and left.

Home was a small two-bedroomed flat in an old-style tenement block behind Musselburgh's main street. When he arrived, Doug went through his nightly ritual; drove up and down the car-clogged street looking for a space, found one and managed to squeeze the car into it. He really would have to see about getting a lock-up somewhere, or at least a permit parking space. Another job for another day. He sighed as he killed the engine, closing his eyes. The flat was on the top floor. It was only three flights up, but it felt like it was going to be a long climb tonight.

He got out of the car, walked away, then remembered he hadn't locked it, started to turn to use the remote... and was driven forward as he was body-charged and slammed back into the car.

'Ah, FUCK!' Doug cried as he thrashed against whoever it was pinning him against the car. No good. Whoever had him was strong. He was held tight.

'Shut it,' a voice growled. Pain exploded as a hard jab was driven into Doug's side. He felt knuckle-dusters bite into his kidneys. The breath was knocked out of him as his knees gave way. He was saved from collapsing when a handful of his hair was grabbed and he was yanked back to his feet. Doug yelped and tried to get away, vision blurring with tears as the pain in his side and head competed for attention.

'Now listen, you little cunt.' The voice was closer now, sour breath tickling Doug's ear. 'You've been asking some awkward questions about Derek McGinty. Some people aren't too happy about that. It's going to stop, now. Understood?'

Doug lashed out as best he could, trying to push away from the car and get some leverage. He was rewarded with another punch to the kidneys. He stopped struggling. It felt as though someone was stubbing out matches on his side. He wanted to be sick.

'Don't be a fucking hero, son,' the voice snarled. 'This is your only warning. Next time, I fucking gut you, understood?' Doug jumped as a knife was driven into the roof of his car as though it were a tin can. 'The questions stop, now. Right?'

Doug was too terrified to speak. He nodded feebly, the fight in him gone. He couldn't take his eyes off the blade.

'Good boy,' the voice whispered. The grip on Doug's hair tightened suddenly then his head was pulled back and smashed down on to the roof of the car. He slid backwards, blood gushing from his nose, and crumpled to the ground. Dimly, he heard soft footsteps running back up the street. He tried to roll over, get a look at his attacker, but it was no good, he couldn't make his eyes focus through the tears and pain.

Shaking, sobbing, gulping in huge, panicked breaths, he got to his feet and staggered for the door to his tenement. Halfway up the stairs he doubled over and vomited, agony stabbing into his side where he had been punched as his body was wracked with retching. He felt the world start to spin around him, closed his eyes and leant against the wall until the feeling passed.

Finally he made it to the flat, fumbled his keys into the locks and got the door open. Staggered inside and took his time relocking the door, making sure it was shut tight. He didn't want another visit.

In the bathroom, he bundled wads of toilet paper into his hand and pressed them to his nose. Blood had soaked down his chin and shirt. He stripped off the shirt and turned; angry red welts were on his side where he had been punched. He thought of the knife, the sound it made as it was driven into the roof of the car. He closed his eyes. Jesus. What if that had been him instead of the car?

He staggered into the living room and collapsed on the couch, throwing an arm over his face as he fought fresh tears. Whether he was crying from fear, anger or relief just to be alive, he couldn't tell. He knew he should phone Susie, the police, someone, to tell them what had happened.

But no. No. Cops would mean statements, would mean questions.

You've been asking some awkward questions about Derek McGinty. Some people aren't too happy about that. It's going to stop, now. Understood?

Doug understood alright. But he wasn't going to let it stop him.

• • •

Charlie snatched up the phone on its third ring. It was raining again, but he wasn't enjoying the view as much as he had the other night.

'Yeah?'

'Well, did you get it?' The voice was sharp, impatient. There was a tone there Charlie didn't like.

'Don't worry,' he sighed, trying to move his jaw as little as possible as he spoke. 'I got it, your money has been well spent.'

'Good, good. Have you found him yet?'

'What the fuck do you think I am, magic? He's got my fucking car, he could be anywhere by now.'

'That's not good enough!' the voice snapped. To Charlie, it sounded like an eight-year-old having a tantrum. 'You told me you could find him and deal with him.'

'Calm it,' Charlie whispered, head beginning to throb. He wished he could fire a bullet down the phone line. It would make life a lot simpler. 'I said I haven't found him, and I don't know where he is. But I do know where he'll be.'

Brittle hope in the voice now. 'Oh, and where's that?'

'Wherever you are, of course.'

'Wh… what?' the voice spluttered, spiking with panic. Charlie smiled. 'Wh… what do you mean?'

'Think about it,' Charlie replied as mildly as he could, straining to keep calm. He needed a drink. No, fuck that, he needed a dentist. 'After everything that's happened, you think he doesn't know it was you that put me onto him? He's got scores to settle, and I guarantee you he won't forget.'

'Then you must… you can't…'

'Don't worry,' Charlie interrupted. 'I know what to do. If he's following you, he's not concentrating on me, right?'

'Bu… but what if he sees you?'

'Don't worry,' Charlie said, eyes straying to the gun on the table in front of him. 'He won't see a thing.'

31

By 6.30am the next morning, Doug was back at his desk. After he had managed to stop his nosebleed and the sobbing, he had spent most of the night lying awake, staring at the ceiling, ears straining for the slightest noise indicating that his visitor outside had decided to skip the warning and go straight for the gutting after all.

Five minutes after getting into bed, he had padded through to the kitchen, pulled the largest knife he could find from the drawer and slipped it under the bed, within hand's reach. Having it there helped him settle. But not much.

As he lay there, chewing on paracetamol to dull the throbbing in his side, he tried to make sense of everything that had happened. He thought about Sam McGinty as he forced him out of the door, face a sneer of hate. Remembered his warning: *I see you again, I'll kill you.* Could it have been Sam who attacked him last night? Doug didn't think so. Oh, Sam had the rage for such an attack, but after his warning yesterday, Doug knew he wouldn't have been satisfied with just leaving a couple of bruises.

His mind jumped from question to question like an old record butchered by a dull stylus. What the hell was going on?

He tried to add up everything he knew, testing out different variations to see what he was missing. There was still something nagging at the back of his mind – the way the name of an album or film star leaps into the shadows the moment someone asks you for it – but he couldn't place it. He tried to forget about it, concentrate instead on what he knew. Giving up on the pretence of sleep, he padded through to the living room, knife in hand, and sat down with a notepad, writing down what he knew as a timeline.

Katherine Buchan had fallen to her death from the Scott Monument. Shortly afterward, he got a call telling him it was no accident, that McGinty had killed her. Then came the photo proving that the two knew each other. Who had made that call, sent that photograph? Doug circled the question, moved on.

And then there were the fingerprints found on the stolen car in Prestonview that proved McGinty was still in the area. Doug was also sure Susie knew something else, something she wasn't telling him, some thread she seemed to think tied McGinty to seeing Katherine the day she died. What was it? Another question, another angry circle. And now Lizzie Renwick was dead. Who would kill her – and why?

He stared at the pad, eyes flitting from note to note, trying to make his random jottings coalesce into a picture that made sense. After half an hour he gave up, went back to bed, checking the door again on the way.

Doug slept fitfully, waking suddenly with the terrifying certainty that someone was in the room with him every time he teetered on the edge of deep sleep. Finally, after starting awake for what felt like the hundredth time at 5am, he got up.

He didn't look as bad in the mirror as he thought he would. Dried blood was caked around his nostrils and his nose was swollen with an angry bruise that stretched under his eyes. Running a finger up the bridge of his nose hurt, but it didn't feel broken.

His side was worse. The bruises where he had been punched had spread overnight like malignant stains, while twisting his torso caused a gnawing pain to crawl up his side and across his back. When he went to the toilet, he was sure he was going to see blood in his urine but there was none, just a dull ache as though he had had too much to drink the night before.

He took a long shower, had three cups of strong coffee and left, dumping a plastic bag containing his blood-soaked shirt and tie into the communal bin as he went.

If his injuries weren't as bad as he thought, the car's were worse. He shuddered as he ran a finger along the gash the knife had gouged into the roof. It was only about an inch long, but it had gone clean through, leaving a ragged hole where the knife had been rocked left to right to free it again. Dimly, he wondered how he was going to explain that one to the insurance. He took a rag from the boot and plugged the hole as best he could before heading for the office.

He got to his desk without too many curious glances, keeping his head down as much as possible so, he hoped, the bruises were merely shadows. When he logged in he checked his e-mails, unsurprised to find a release from the police press office about Lizzie Renwick's death last night.

The release followed the standard, first-release format; give the bare facts and follow up with comment and pertinent details later. It stated that a thirty-nine-year-old woman had been found dead at a business premises in the Old Town area of Edinburgh at approximately 9.30pm the previous evening. Her death was, at the moment, being treated as 'suspicious'.

Doug thought back to what Susie said about the stabbing. Damn right it was suspicious. He glanced across to the time the e-mail was sent; just after midnight. Susie, no doubt, making sure the story got out quickly and that Doug didn't have the chance to get the drop on her again. He smiled slightly. Touché.

He skimmed over the rest of the releases and mails he had been sent, flagging up the ones he thought might make stories for the first edition and sending lines on them over to Walter. Spotted one from the Tories, stating that Buchan was taking a leave of absence. No surprise, but he made a note to add it as a line to any future stories he did on Katherine.

Then, noticing that more people were starting to filter in, he ambled across to the picture desk.

'Mornin,' Terry.'

'Good morning, Douglas,' Terry replied, eyes fixing briefly on Doug's bruises and then moving on. None of his business. 'And how did I know I was going to be seeing you so early today?'

Doug shrugged his shoulders. 'You managed to get anything?'

'Well, yes and no,' Terry said, patting his hair down over his bald patch. 'We've managed to clean up the picture a bit, make out some of the faces behind McGinty and that young woman…'

'Katherine,' Doug prompted gently.

'Ah yes, Katherine. However, I can't get that building it the background to sharpen up much. The photo must have been taken from a fixed lens, so it only focused on the forefront of the frame.'

Doug sighed, disappointed. It had been a long shot, anyway. 'Ah well, thanks anyway, Terry.'

'Ah,' Terry said, a smile Doug took as smug spreading across his face. 'So you won't want to hear the good part, then?'

Doug straightened up, felt excitement tingle at the nape of his neck. 'Good part? What good part?'

'Well, I said we had managed to sharpen up the faces of the other people in the photograph. When we did, I recognised one of the people.'

Doug fought back the impulse to give Terry a hug. 'Oh,' he said, trying to keep his voice level. 'And who might that have been, Terry?'

Terry punched up the scan of the photograph he had taken, then hit another button and the enhanced version filled the screen. Doug had to admit, it was good work – the back row of the picture, which Doug hadn't paid much attention to when he'd first seen it, was now made up of clearly defined people rather than amorphous blobs of colour.

'There.' Terry pointed to a thin, pale-looking woman with long, jet-back hair and half-moon glasses similar to his own. 'Ann

Bryant.' he said, nodding his head.

'Ann Bryant,' Doug said. The name rang a bell. 'Where do you know her from?'

'Niddrie,' Terry replied. 'She's a social worker at a community project in Niddrie. I took a photograph of her place about three years ago, when they were having a funding drive. Want to see it?'

He did.

32

Susie usually liked the early-morning CID meetings at Gayfield. They gave her a chance to wake up slowly, getting her first fix of caffeine for the day as she soaked in the latest developments of the case as Burns droned on at the front of the room. He had a habit of scrawling bulletpoints of the big developments across a whiteboard in a garish green pen. Some of the officers had started to call them Burn marks.

But not this morning. She had arrived about half an hour ago, feeling brittle and drained after a night of broken sleep filled with dreams of Lizzie Renwick and blood, only to be told by Burns that she was going to have to stand up and bring everyone up to date on the latest developments in the case.

Not normal procedure, but she got the feeling that Burns saw it as some kind of punishment for her. The Chief Superintendent may have been ready to forgive Doug and the *Tribune* for not letting on about the photograph straightaway, but Burns wasn't. What panicked Susie was why he was picking on her?

She got through the briefing as best she could, filling everyone in about the photograph, the way Buchan had reacted and, of course, Lizzie Renwick's murder. Dr Williams, despite his protests, had carried out the post-mortem examination last night. As he suspected, the cause of death was determined to be the stab wound that had punctured her subclavian artery. She had bled to death. He also found the superficial wounds hadn't been made with the scissors; there had been a single-bladed weapon of some kind used, about six inches long, he guessed from the wounds.

And sharp, very sharp. There were other cuts on her face and chest, and her cheekbone had been fractured. Whoever had killed Lizzie had made sure she suffered first.

After her briefing, Burns took over, leaving Susie standing at the front of the room just long enough to make her squirm. She felt like the class idiot forced to stand up and explain why she had been talking at the same time as the teacher. He assigned workloads to the other detectives and then sent them on their way. Susie was drifting back to her desk when Burns called her into his office.

Oh shit. He knew. He *knew.*

He motioned for her to take a seat as he slurped on his coffee. Fixed her with a cool, appraising stare. Susie tried not to look away.

'Good work with the briefing,' he said finally, rocking back in his chair, folding his hands over his gut.

Susie blinked. Not what she had been expecting. 'Thank you, sir.'

Burns grumbled, leaning forward. 'Look, I know you must have felt like a spare prick yesterday when Buchan got that call, but I want you to have another crack at him and his wife. This photo proves his daughter knew McGinty, I need you to find out what they knew.'

Susie thought back to Buchan's reaction. She didn't think it was going to be easy.

Burns seemed to read her thoughts. 'Take the photograph with you,' he said. 'He'll find it more difficult to ignore the facts with that in front of him.

'Oh, and drop by the lock-up on the way, will you? Williams said he would have the blood work on Renwick ready for us this morning. You might as well get them on the way.'

Susie nodded, got up and made for the door.

'Oh, and one more thing, Drummond,' Burns called as she rested her hand on the door handle.

'Yes, sir?'

'If you find anything interesting, I want to hear about it first, not read about it in the *Tribune*. Understood?'

'Perfectly, sir,' Susie said as neutrally as she could.

Burns nodded and made a show of studying a bundle of reports in front of him. Warning delivered.

33

First edition dragged passed like a slow torture for Doug. He wrote the stories he was asked to, including Lizzie Renwick's death, as quickly as he could, wanting them to be done, wanting to be able to leave his desk and get out of the office.

Usually, Doug loved working on edition. With only an hour to fill four live pages along with any small stories for slots elsewhere in the paper and a round-up of world news, he relished the challenge. On edition, there was no 'I'll chase that up later.' There wasn't time. Sometimes, he had less than ten minutes to research and write a five-hundred-word lead, a task not made easier by the fact that 7am wasn't always the best time of day to get people to talk to him.

But he loved the stress, the feeling of uncontrolled chaos in the newsroom. The cries of the chief sub telling the subs to 'get moving' and get the stories edited and on the page, Walter breathing down his neck as he tried to fill the gaps in the paper. He loved writing with one eye on the clock, knowing he had no time to get it wrong. Not today, though.

He sent his last story, about a mugging on Lothian Road the night before, and leaned back in his chair. Niddrie, he was thinking to himself. What the hell had Katherine Buchan been doing at a community project in Niddrie?

He logged onto the library, punching in Ann Bryant's name to see what they had on her, realising why the name had been familiar when he saw the list of related stories pop up on his screen. One of them was from last year, when fire crews around Edinburgh were being called out to false alarms and ambushed by groups of rock-throwing kids.

One of the worst incidents was in Niddrie when a fireman had been hit in the eye by a rock and hospitalised. Along with the usual outraged quotes from the police and fire brigade, was a comment from the co-ordinator of the newly-formed Niddrie Community Awareness Programme, Ann Bryant. He read her quotes calling for extra funding for anti-social behaviour programmes in the area and better after-school facilities for kids, and wished he could remember more about his conversation with Bryant. He had never met her, only spoken to her on the phone. Would she remember him?

On an impulse, he punched in Katherine's name, cross-referencing it with Ann Bryant and Niddrie to see if there was anything in the library. Nothing. If he was going to get answers on this, he was going to have to speak to Bryant.

He got the address for the project from Terry, who still had that insufferably smug look on his face, then filled Walter in on what he had found and headed for the door. On his way to the car, he dialled Susie's number. After the debacle with the photograph, he wanted to let her know what was happening. Neither of them needed a repeat of yesterday.

After a few rings, he was redirected to her answerphone. Doug left a brief message, asking her to call him as soon as she could. The danger was that she thought he was just calling to see how she got on with his research and would ignore the call, but that was a chance he would have to take. He wasn't going to spill his guts to an answerphone.

Niddrie, and its neighbour, Craigmillar, sat on the east of Edinburgh, buffered from the border with East Lothian and Musselburgh beyond by an outdoor shopping complex and factory outlets.

For years, Niddrie and Craigmillar had been no-go areas for many; high crime, teenage pregnancies, poor health, underage drinking and drug abuse were all common on the streets, which wouldn't have looked out of place in downtown Baghdad, with their rotting, shuttered tenements.

But over the last few years, the council had started pumping cash into the area, which was, after all, only a five-minute drive from the Scottish Parliament at Holyrood. The tenements were replaced by new flats, houses and office complexes. Community outreach projects like Bryant's were being set up and funded, efforts had been made to secure residents retraining and better job prospects.

But the inevitable scarring was still there. The houses may have changed, the streets may have widened and been tidied but many of the problems remained.

Several years ago the body of a baby – no more than a few days old – had been found mutilated, burned and abandoned at the side of a pathway running through Craigmillar. The community had rallied together to bury the child, but the mother had never been found and the origins of the child never discovered.

Despite the developments, the promises and attempts at a new start, Niddrie and Craigmillar still kept their secrets. And some of those secrets could kill.

The NCAP office was housed in one of the newer buildings set off the main road that led through Niddrie. Sitting opposite, a new block of flats – which looked to Doug like a Lego set given a coat of paint and a few balconies – sat isolated in an overgrown field.

A large red banner draped across the office building pronounced NCAP was 'at the heart of Niddrie' in gold lettering. Outside, a minibus with the NCAP logo sat at the kerbside. It looked like it had seen better days.

Doug parked beside the minibus, fished his mobile out of his pocket and tried Susie's number again. No good, still the answering machine. At least she couldn't accuse him of not trying.

Access to the building was via entryphone. He ran a finger down the other businesses – Niddrie and Craigmillar Rejuvenation Project, A&S Legal Services and East Edinburgh Furniture Recycling Project – and pressed the buzzer for NCAP.

'Hello?' a voice said through a wave of static.

'Oh, hi there. My name's Doug McGregor. I'm with the *Capital Tribune*. I'm here to see Ann Bryant.'

A pause, static hissing over the line. 'Do you have an appointment, Mr McGregor?'

'Ah, no. I was given her name by a colleague of mine, Terry Hewson. He suggested I come and speak with her.'

Another pause. Come on, Doug thought. Open the damn door.

Then, just as he thought he was going to be ignored, a sigh on the intercom. 'You better come up, then,' the voice said as the door buzzed open.

• • •

The NCAP office was on the top floor, at the end of a short corridor crammed with cardboard boxes and crates. Someone was moving in or out. He knocked on NCAP's door, heard soft, shuffling steps as someone got out of a seat. Ann Bryant swung the door open and peered up at Doug. She was shorter than the photograph had suggested, only about 5ft 3ins, and her hair was now more white than black and cut almost militarily shot, but it was definitely her.

'Ms Bryant?' Doug said brightly, offering his hand.

Bryant took Doug's hand and shook it. Her grip was warm and weak. 'Mr McGregor. Please, come in.' She stood aside and ushered him into the office, also filled with crates and boxes.

'Moving,' Ann said as she moved past Doug and took a seat at a desk in front of the window. 'We used to be on the first floor, but the previous tenants of this office moved out a couple of weeks ago. More space, so we moved.'

Ann motioned for Doug to take a seat opposite her. 'So, Mr McGregor,' she said, 'what can I do for you?'

'Please, call me Doug. As I said, Terry Hewson gave me your name. He recognised you from this picture.' Doug took out a copy of the picture and the enhanced blow-up Terry had given him, passed them across the table to Bryant. She took them, adjusted her glasses for a better look. 'I was wondering if you could tell me anything about it?' Doug asked.

Ann Bryant's face tensed as she studied the photograph. 'Where did you get this?'

Doug cleared his throat, shifted in his seat slightly. Good question. 'It was sent to me,' he said simply. 'I take it you recognise the people in it?'

'Yes, yes I do,' Bryant said, eyes flitting between the photograph and the blow-up. 'So, tell me Mr McGregor, why am I talking to you instead of the police?'

Doug felt his cheeks burn. 'Ah, well. I'm sure you will be in due course. But, as I said, I was sent that photo first. I guess I'm just a little ahead of the police on the follow-up.'

Bryant handed the photos back to Doug. 'I'm sorry,' she said. 'There's nothing I can tell you.'

'Can't or won't?' Doug asked. 'Look, Ms Bryant, it's you in the photograph, I know that's Katherine Buchan with Derek McGinty. Believe it or not, I'm not just trying to get a story here. I really want to know what's going on.'

'That why you got those bruises, sticking your nose in where it's not wanted?'

The threat echoed in Doug's mind. *You've been asking questions about Derek McGinty. It stops, now.* 'You could say that.'

Bryant studied him for a moment, as if trying to make a decision.

'Look,' Doug said finally, putting aside his notepad and pen. 'Off the record, okay? I promise I won't print anything you tell me here. But please, if there's anything you can tell me about

Katherine or her work here, I'd like to hear it. It might help answer a few questions.'

'Off the record?' Bryant asked, eyes not leaving Doug's. He nodded slowly. Not the way he would have liked it, but if it was the only way to find out what was going on, he would take it. God knows what he was going to tell Walter, though.

'And I take it you're going to publish this anyway, whether or not I talk to you?'

'Unless you can tell me something that's going to change my boss's mind, yes.'

Bryant sighed heavily, stood up and made for a door on the other side of the office. She opened it to reveal a small kitchenette. 'You want a coffee?' she asked.

Doug felt a wave of relief. 'Please. Black.'

Bryant reappeared with two mugs of coffee, placed one in front of Doug and then settled back into her seat. She took her time getting comfortable. 'Firstly, if I see one word of what I tell you in print, I'll sue your paper to the ground.'

'Fair enough,' Doug said, willing her to stop stalling and get to the story. He sampled the coffee. Weak and warm, like her handshake.

'Alright then,' Bryant said, cupping her mug in both hands and looking into it as if she would see her next sentence there. 'The first thing you need to know is that you're wrong on two counts, Mr McGregor.'

Doug raised an eyebrow.

'The woman in that photograph is not Katherine Buchan. And she wasn't a worker here, Mr McGregor, she was a client.'

34

Hal had his phone tucked into the crook of his neck as he packed his case, vaguely aware that Jonathan was hanging around at the door to his room, looking for all the world like a little boy watching Daddy pack for yet another long business trip away from home.

Hal know the look well enough. He had spent his own childhood perfecting it.

In his ear, Eddie Hobbies from Tory HQ in London was asking the same question for about the fifth time. Ever the politician, he had varied his approach each time. He had tried challenging, disbelieving, straightforward and dispassionate so far. Now he was trying for flattery.

'Look, Hal, I trust your judgment – we all do, that's why you got the job in the first place – but are you sure? Isn't it too soon? Surely you should stay there for a few more days, see how it plays out?'

Hal tossed a shirt into his case. Left it unfolded deliberately, looking forward to the rolled eyes and mocking disapproval Colin would subject him to for packing so sloppily. God, he couldn't wait to get home.

'Eddie, I'm sure,' he said. 'The party's involvement in the story is almost tangential now. Buchan has agreed to a leave of absence. He didn't like it, but he's swallowed it now, knows he doesn't need the press interest.

'Anyone asks, they know not to comment any further. If they carry his Bill through parliament, they're doing it in his name because it's what Richard would want. If they decide the Bill's too hot to touch, which is my advice by the way, then they're letting it fall because it wouldn't be right to try and get it through without Buchan being there to be a part of it. Win-win, either way.'

Eddie demurred on the other end of the line, tried his old trick of coughing to stall for time. Hal took advantage.

'Besides,' he said, 'I can monitor the press from home as easily as here now, and if anything does go tits up, Jonathan can be my hands on the wheel here. You should keep an eye on him, Eddie, he's a bright one.'

Jonathan flashed a smile so wide it was almost genuine. Colour crept up into his cheeks as his eyes widened and he gave Hal a silent, overly enthusiastic thumbs up. God help the kid, Hal thought suddenly, he could be a future prime minister.

'Well, if you're sure,' Eddie replied, sounding like a kid being told this was the last story of the night before bed, 'when will you be back?'

Hal glanced at his watch, made a quick calculation. 'Should be later this afternoon. You want to meet up this evening, talk it over then?'

'No, that won't be necessary, Hal. You get home, see your family. We'll talk in a few days, settle your fee. There's also another matter we could use your help on – long-term contract, right up to the next election.'

Hal smiled, fought back the urge to punch the air. 'See you in a few days then, Eddie,' he said.

'Look forward to it, Hal. Oh, and good work.'

'Thanks,' Hal replied. Glanced at Jonathan. 'But it was a team effort.'

35

Susie got in touch just as Doug was drawing into a parking space outside his flat.

'Hey, Doug, it's me. I got your message, what's up?'

'Hey, Susie. Where are you right now?'

A pause on the line. Still wary. 'On my way to an appointment,' was all she said.

'If it's with Richard Buchan, don't bother,' Doug said. 'We need to talk first.'

'What? Oh Christ, Doug, now what have you done?'

Doug closed his eyes. Took a deep breath. There was no way around it, he was going to have to tell her. Now. 'Look, you know that photograph...?'

'Yes?' A pause. Doug could almost see her chewing her lip. 'What about it?'

'Well, I found out a little more about it, found one of the other people in it with McGinty and Ka...' He caught himself. Not yet. 'Katherine.'

'What?' Susie's voice was so sharp Doug had to pull his mobile from his ear. 'You just couldn't leave it, could you? Do you know how much shit you've already stirred up for me?'

'Look, I know. I'm sorry. I tried to call you this morning, but your phone was off.'

'I was at the mortuary,' Susie snapped. Doug imagined the bodies there were warmer than her tone.

'Look,' he said, talking quickly now. 'I'm sorry if I've fucked things up for you. Really, I am. But I've got to speak to you before you talk to Buchan again. I've found some things out that you need to know.'

'Well? Tell me, then.'

'Not on the phone. Meet me at my flat.' He glanced at his watch, worked out routes from Edinburgh to Musselburgh in his head. 'Say twenty minutes?'

'Come on, Doug, cut the crap. If you've got something to tell me, just tell me. Enough of the games, okay?'

Doug chewed on his lip. Tell her now or not? 'No,' he said finally. 'Not on the phone. My flat, Susie, twenty minutes. And believe me, you're going to want to hear this.'

He cut the line before she had a chance to argue.

• • •

Even the buzzer sounded impatient. Doug hit the entry button, heard the door to the tenement bang shut as Susie's footsteps click-clacked up the stairs. He opened his door before she had a chance to knock.

'Look, Doug, I'm not too…' her words trailed off as she caught sight of his face. 'Bloody hell, what happened to you?'

'You should see the car,' Doug said, ushering her in and slamming the door behind her. Taking a moment to check the locks. He saw the confused look on her face. 'Look, I'll get to it. You want a coffee?'

'Yeah, okay,' she said as she made for the living room and took a seat. She wanted to be pissed at him, knew she should be, but seeing him like that made it difficult to stay mad. Damn it, why was she always letting this guy manipulate her?

She heard cupboards clatter in the kitchen, the click of the kettle as it boiled. 'You want any help?'

'Nah, I'll be fine,' Doug said. His voice was tense, anxious. What had he found?

He came through a moment later with two mugs of coffee, set Susie's down on the table in front of the couch and then eased himself into his chair. She saw him wince as he moved.

'You going to tell me what happened to you?' she asked again.

'Got a little warning last night,' he said, sipping his coffee. Too hot. 'Guy jumped me outside, told me not to poke around Derek McGinty any more. Gave me a couple of digs and the car a new sunroof to make sure I got the message.'

Susie leant forward, eyes widening. 'Jesus, Doug, why didn't you call me?'

He smiled slightly. 'Didn't think we were speaking,' he said. Saw her shift uncomfortably in her seat as colour filled her cheeks and added: 'Honestly, it's nothing. I'll be fine.'

'So,' Susie said, breaking the awkward silence, 'what's so important?'

'First, a question,' Doug replied as he tried to get more comfortable in his seat and take the weight off his aching side. 'What was it you found yesterday that you wouldn't tell me?'

Susie scowled at him. 'Don't tell me you got me all the way here so you could try and get another line out of me? Come on, Doug, I really don't need this at the moment, especially with the crap Burns is giving me.'

'It's not like that,' he said. 'Really. But I need to know. I think I know what all this is about. I think you found something that either put McGinty at the Scott Monument or gave him a damn strong motive for being there, right? And I'm guessing he didn't show up on the CCTV. If he did, that image would have been splashed all over the *Tribune* and every news site by now, you'd want every eye in Edinburgh looking for him.

Susie studied him closely, felt a sudden, stupid urge to reach out and take his hand as she saw pain kaleidoscope across his face. How badly had he been beaten last night?

'Maybe,' she said. 'Tell me what you know, Doug. I'll tell you if you're right.'

'Okay,' Doug sighed. It hurt too much to argue. 'Okay. Like I said last night, when I got that photograph of McGinty and Katherine, I had our picture editor scan it into the system.'

Susie nodded. She didn't want to talk about the photograph.

'Anyway, I also asked Terry to see if he could do anything about the picture, maybe give us a clue about where it was taken.'

Susie sat back in the sofa. 'And it did, right?'

'Right. Turns out Terry knew one of the people in the photo, Ann Bryant. She runs a community group in Niddrie.'

Doug saw Susie turn the information over in her mind, trying to see where it fit.

'I spoke to her about an hour ago, right after I called you to let you know what was going on.' Susie shot him an arch look. He shrugged. 'Anyway, after a bit of persuading, she told me a story.' He dug his copy of the photograph out of his pocket and passed it to Susie, ignoring the roll of her eyes. He had been sent the picture, did she seriously think he wasn't going to copy it before handing it over?

'That was taken in April 1992,' he said, 'back when the Niddrie Community Awareness Programme was the East Edinburgh Dependency Care Unit.'

'Dependency care? As in drug abuse?'

Doug nodded slowly. 'Exactly. At the time, the unit was run out of one of the old tenements in Niddrie. It was used as a day-care and hostel centre for recovering drug addicts.'

'So Katherine was working there?'

Doug smiled. 'Not quite. Ann said she was one of the patients.'

Susie's eyes widened as her mouth dropped open. Doug felt a flash of guilty satisfaction. She had recently stunned him into silence with a mind-blowing snippet of information, so it was only fair he repaid the favour.

'Shit,' Susie whispered. 'Katherine Buchan was a drug addict?'

'Yup. Heroin, apparently. Pretty heavy user too, if what Bryant said is true. Oh yeah, and one other thing. You'll never find any of this in her records. Nobody at the unit knew her as Katherine

Buchan. She was registered there as Katie. Katie Milton.'

Susie felt as though the room was beginning to spin as it did after a big night out. Katherine Buchan was a drug user who was at an addicts' clinic under an assumed name. It sounded fantastic, insane… but…

But it also made perfect sense. The daughter of a prominent lawyer and rising political star gets a drug problem and then sorts it out under an assumed name so dearest Daddy's career and image as a wholesome family man is never tarnished.

'H… hold on,' Susie said, glancing down at the photo again. 'So, how does Derek fit into all this?'

He shrugged slowly. 'That's where it falls down,' he said. 'Ann's not sure. He visited from time to time, was always very friendly and helpful, apparently. Seems he and Katherine – sorry, Katie – struck up a bit of a relationship.'

Susie leaned back in the couch, covered her eyes with her hands. Oh yes, Doug had been right. This was certainly going to change the way she was going to talk to Richard Buchan.

It all added up. MSP's daughter see the papers, realises the recently-released rapist everyone is so keen to track down knows her from her days as a drug addict. Said rapist has no job prospects, no cash in the bank, nothing to fall back on…

Except his friend Katie, who would pay anything to keep Daddy's name from being dragged through the mud. £5,000? Susie was surprised McGinty hadn't asked for £5 million.

'You think her parents knew?'

Doug shrugged. 'I don't know, maybe. It wouldn't be the first time a politician has tried to sweep a dirty secret under the carpet. It's worth looking at, anyway.'

'That your next move?'

'Nope,' Doug said, getting out of his seat, wincing as he stretched. 'That's your job. Me, I'm going to take a closer look at Derek McGinty.'

'Huh? Why?'

'Because whoever it was that had a go at me last night wanted to make sure I didn't find something. It might be this, it might not be. McGinty was into a lot of dodgy shit in his time, I want to make sure I'm not missing something. And I get the feeling I am at the moment.'

'Oh, like what?'

'I don't know. Just a…' He turned to stare out of the window, as if looking for the answer. He didn't find it. 'I don't know. But I will when I find it. Anyway, you going to tell me what you found out yesterday, or what?'

Slowly, Susie told him about the £5,000 withdrawn from Katherine's account on the day she died. As she spoke, she could see him adding it to what he already knew, coming to the same conclusions she did. When she had stopped speaking, he pulled a small piece of paper from his shirt pocket and handed it to her.

'What's this?'

'Ann Bryant's phone number. I know you're going to have to see her and go through all this again, officially. She's waiting for your call.'

Susie smiled. 'Thanks, Doug. Look… you sure you're okay?'

'No,' he answered, a crooked smile on his face. 'But I'm a lot better now I know all this.'

Susie got up, drained her coffee. 'I better get going. I've got a few people to see.'

'We okay, then?' The naughty schoolboy act was back.

'Yeah, we're okay. On one condition.'

'Oh, what's that?'

'Next time you get beaten up in the middle of the night, call me, okay?'

'Why, you going to come charging to my rescue?'

'Nah,' she said, opening the front door. 'But I might give the guy a loan of my pepper spray.'

Doug slammed the door in her face. She could hear his laughter as she headed for the stairs.

36

When Doug had first called saying he had to tell her something, Susie had resigned herself to the fact her day was going to be messed up. She phoned Buchan, who was expecting her at his home in Stockbridge and told him she would have to postpone their appointment, apologising profusely and citing 'unavoidable business', which she thought was a fairly accurate description of Doug at times.

Buchan said he understood. His tone of voice said he didn't like it.

Heading back into town from Doug's, Susie phoned Buchan's home. She was just about to hang up when Linda Buchan answered.

'Hello?' Her voice was still blank. Susie wondered if her doctor had doped her up with something.

'Mrs Buchan. It's DS Drummond here. I was wondering if I could have a word with your husband?'

'He's not here.'

'Oh. Can you tell me when he'll be back?'

'No.' The coldness in Linda Buchan's voice made Susie shudder. It was unnerving. 'He said he was going up to the court to pick up some papers.'

'Would that be the High Court on the Royal Mile?'

'Yes.' Voice fading now. She was losing interest in the call. 'It must be.'

Odd, Susie thought. The day he announces he's taking a leave of absence from his political career to focus on his family he abandons his wife to go work at the courts?

Susie made her thanks then ended the call, glad to be away from Linda Buchan's toneless voice. She wondered how much more the woman could take before she had a complete breakdown. Everything Doug had just told her wasn't going to help.

Susie shook off the thought, focusing on the matter at hand. If Buchan wasn't going to wait for her, fine. She would catch him at the court.

• • •

As ever, parking in Edinburgh was a pain in the arse. Susie finally found a space on Market Street, on the steep slope that led on to the Mound. Paying for her ticket, she looked out across Princes Street Gardens at the Scott Monument. An image of Katherine Buchan's ruined body flashed before her mind; Dr Williams picking through the shattered remains, blood and gore streaked across his rubber gloves and surgical gown.

She shuddered, tried to push the thought away, concentrate on the here and now.

The court was only a two-minute walk away. She caught sight of Buchan as he was walking past St Giles' Cathedral, a heavy sheaf of papers cradled under his arm, probably heading for the offices that backed onto the court.

Looking both ways, she jogged across the road to him, calling his name to attract his attention. When she was halfway across the road, something caught the corner of her eye. A familiar face in the steady stream of people moving up and down the street.

Who? Too late, Buchan was in front of her.

'Ah, Detective Drummond. What a surprise, I didn't think you were going to have the time to see me today.' Susie ignored the dig.

'Yes, well, I'm sorry about that, Mr Buchan. However, I have come across some interesting developments. I was wondering if you had time for a quick chat?'

Buchan made a show of checking his watch. 'Well, I do have a meeting in twenty minutes, and I was planning on dropping into my office. But, I suppose, if it's important, I could spare you a few minutes.'

Arrogant bastard, Susie thought as she muttered her thanks. Good to know that discussing his daughter's death wasn't too much of an inconvenience.

• • •

Buchan's office was about the same size as Third Degree's, with institutional decoration lurking behind haphazard attempts to make it liveable. Unlike Burns' office, the walls were crowded with photographs. In most of them, Buchan was smiling for the camera – the perfect PR pose – as he was greeted by various people who Susie assumed meant something in political circles. She recognised one person, though: the Chief Superintendent, standing on what looked like a terrace overlooking a golf course, smiling with glasses raised. Fuck.

There was, as far as she could see, only one picture of Buchan with Katherine and his wife. It was an old shot; Susie guessed Katherine would have been about nine or ten in the photograph, all blonde hair and ruddy cheeks as she stood before her parents, Buchan resting a hand on her shoulder, Linda by his side.

It should have been the perfect family scene, and the picture quality was far better than the squint-eyed effort that hung in Burns' office, but to Susie the photograph looked cold and remote, as staged as the other pictures it shared the wall with.

'Now, DS Drummond,' Buchan said, 'What can I do for you?'

'Well, sir, some new information has come to light regarding the photograph you received a call about yesterday.'

Buchan's brow darkened. 'Ah, yes. I take it those *journalists* involved have been appropriately reprimanded?'

Susie murmured a non-committal reply. If she told him the Chief Superintendent had granted Doug and the *Tribune* a stay of execution, she would never get anything from him.

She saw Buchan glance again at his watch. Time to get on with it.

'Sir, we've managed to ascertain from the photo that Katherine sought treatment for a, ah…' She paused. No easy way to say it. '…a drug problem at a residential programme in the Niddrie area in 1992. While she was there, it seems Derek McGinty was a fairly regular visitor.'

She tried to read Buchan's face, gauge his reaction. Impossible, it was like talking to stone.

'Did you know anything about her problem, Mr Buchan? Was she still using drugs?'

'Of course not!' Buchan snapped, snatching up a pen from the desk, grasping it hard enough to bleed his knuckles white. 'I mean…' He lowered his head, sagged back. 'I'm sorry, DS Drummond. Forgive me. As you can imagine, this is a trying time. No, she wasn't using drugs any more. She had been clean for more than ten years.'

'So you knew about her problem?'

'Of course I knew. When we found out, we got her into the programme, tried to get her the best help we could.'

Susie raised an eyebrow. A residential unit in Niddrie was hardly the best help a QC's money could buy. 'And did you also arrange for Katherine to attend the unit under a false name?'

The colour drained from Buchan's face. He dropped his eyes, suddenly fascinated by the pen he had picked up. 'Yes,' he whispered after a long pause. 'I thought it was for the best.'

For who? Susie thought. Looking at the photographs on the wall, the answer was obvious.

'Mr Buchan,' she began slowly, picking her words carefully, 'regarding the £5,000 we discussed yester…'

The trill of her mobile phone cut her off. Shit. She had meant to turn it off. 'I'm sorry, sir,' she said as she pulled out the phone. 'If I could just have a minute?'

Buchan nodded. He didn't do a very good job of hiding his relief.

Susie answered the phone. Listened to what Burns had to say, felt her jaw tighten.

'Right, sir. Yes, he's here with me now.' Buchan's head shot up. 'Yes, we're on our way, sir. I'll see you there.'

'What is it?' Buchan asked, barely giving Susie the time to finish the call. 'What's wrong?'

Susie took a deep breath. 'Ah… sir, I think you'd better come with me. There's been a break-in at your house. We've got officers there, they're looking after your wife now.'

• • •

A WPc was sitting in the lounge room with Linda Buchan by the time they arrived at the house, rubbing her shoulders gently as she rocked back and forth, tears streaming down her pale face. Her small, thin hands clasped together and released continuously, like two small animals having convulsions as her feet drummed at the floor.

'A doctor's been called to have a look at her,' Burns whispered in Susie's ear as he walked across the room to stand beside her.

'Hmm,' Susie nodded, watching as Buchan sat down beside his wife. He reached out to take her hands in his, trying to calm them in her lap. Linda flinched, as though surprised by his presence, then fell back to studying her hands, ignoring him.

'What happened?' Susie asked.

'We're not sure yet,' Burns replied. 'It was a neighbour who called the police, said she heard screams as she passed the house while walking her dog. When officers got here, they found her like this. No obvious signs of a break-in.'

Susie glanced around the room. Show-home neat, as ever. 'Other than her,' she nodded towards Linda, 'why *are* we calling this a break-in?'

'Two reasons. One, a car was seen driving off at high speed not long before the uniforms arrived. Second, and most important, the dog walker also said she thought she could hear a man's voice over Mrs Buchan's screams.'

Linda Buchan's head whipped in the direction of Burns. 'He said such horrible things!' she screeched in a hitching sob as her hands flew to the sides of her head, as though trying to block out what she had heard. 'About Katherine! Asked for money. Said that she was a drug user, that she... she... was ... was ...'

Her voice dissolved into hysterical, pitched wails that shook her whole body. She dropped her head between her knees and shrieked at the ground. Buchan put his arms around his wife and hugged her fiercely, ignoring the sudden stiffening of her spine as his arms closed around her.

'She didn't know?' Susie asked gently as he looked up at her.

'No,' he said, his face an contortion of anger, distress and... embarrassment? 'She adored Katherine. Telling her would have killed her. I thought if I could... could...' He flailed for words, gave up and bent his head to his wife's back, hiding his face.

Linda shrugged him off, slid off the couch and fell to her knees, her cries becoming even more hysterical.

Buchan sat looking at her, paralysed. He half-reached out, then let his arms drop to his lap. His eyes darted around the room, glare challenging anyone who dared meet his gaze.

'What the fuck are you people doing about this?' he hissed. 'My daughter is dead, my wife has been harassed in our home, my... my...' He stuttered for a moment, face darkening. Linda sat on the floor, sobs now interspersed with pleas to Buchan to stop, just stop, it wasn't their fault.

He shrugged her off. 'What the fuck use are any of you?'

Uncomfortable shuffles around the room as officers busied

themselves with notepads and cameras, studied the floor for vital clues. Burns stepped forward, arms open, voice as gentle as he could make it.

'Mr Buchan, I can understand your distress. But my officers and I…'

Susie walked out of the room. She needed to get away from Linda's sobbing and Buchan's ranting. She stood in the hallway, tried to think.

'What?' Burns asked as he joined her in the hall. 'If you've got something, I'd love to hear it.'

'McGinty,' Susie said, more to herself than Burns. 'When she calms down, I'm betting her description of the intruder matches Derek McGinty. He was here, sir.'

Susie saw understanding dawn in Burns' eyes. 'You think…?'

'Exactly. He took the £5,000 from Katherine, hush money so nobody knew her secret and dropped her dad's career in the shit. Killed her and then decided he wanted more. But he couldn't go back to her, so who else?'

'Go straight to the source,' Burns said.

'Exactly. Why not blackmail Buchan himself? Except when he got here, told Mrs Buchan what he would do unless she coughed up the cash, she flipped out on him. He panicked and left.'

Burns stared at the front door, jaw working slowly as he ground his teeth. To Susie, he looked like a bad-tempered bulldog. He strode to the door, grabbed a uniformed Pc by the arm and spun him round hard enough for the young officer to stagger back.

'Sir, what… I…?'

'Get on to Fettes,' Burns said, ignoring the Pc's stammered confusion. 'Tell them I want the description of Derek McGinty reissued to every uniform, every car and every patrol in the next hour. And this time, I want the cunt found.'

The Pc nodded and hurried outside to radio in Burns' request.

'I'll have that bastard in cells by tonight,' Burns hissed. 'And then we'll have a nice long chat with our Mr McGinty. That sound alright to you, DS Drummond?'

'Yes sir,' Susie replied. 'That sounds just fine.'

37

'... yeah, Carol, that's it. Look, thanks very much. Bye.'

Doug hung up the phone and turned his attention back to the notes and documents spread across his coffee table. He had still been at his flat when Susie called, asking him to see if he could squeeze a story about the break-in at the Buchans' home into second edition. He had glanced at the clock – just after 12.30. It was going to be tight, but he got typing – the chatter of the keyboard only interrupted by the soft flicking of his notepad pages as he paused to check his scrawled notes – and e-mailed the story in, then talked it over with Carol Jones, who was on the desk that day.

That done, he mulled over what Susie had told him about how she suspected McGinty had paid a visit to the Buchans' home. It made sense to Doug, answered most of the questions that he had, but there were still loose ends that he didn't like.

And then there was Lizzie Renwick. Why had she been killed so brutally? Doug guessed that could have been McGinty's handiwork. He briefly thought McGinty had gone to the gallery looking for cash or something he could sell, had run into Lizzie and killed her when she refused to help him, but quickly rejected the idea. If he needed cash, there were a thousand other places he could have gone that would have offered richer pickings without the need to kill someone.

Doug picked through his notes on McGinty and the copy of his record that Susie had supplied him with. From thug to bouncer to rapist. Some career…

Hold on a minute. Bouncer. Doug flicked through the papers in front of him, looking for the notes on the clubs McGinty had worked in, including the place Bethany Miller and her friends had been on the night she was attacked. The club itself was gone now, destroyed by a fire that gutted a section of the city's Old Town, but still, it gave Doug a lead.

In August a couple of years ago, when Edinburgh's night-clubs were allowed to stay open until 5am to cash in on the huge influx of tourists that the Festival brought with it, the council had brought in a scheme to licence all doormen working in the city's pubs and clubs. It was part of a drive to weed out the thugs who were merely looking for an excuse to beat the shit out of people and get away with it.

While working on the story, Doug had come across Rab MacFarlane. Rab ran Capital Events Management, one of the largest security and events companies in the city. Whenever a big star came to Edinburgh to perform, it was a fair bet that you would see a steward wandering around the gig with Rab's company logo emblazoned across his T-shirt. Rab had started the company in the Seventies when he was a young man working on the doors himself, building it up to become one of the biggest doormen-for-hire and private security businesses on the east coast.

There were rumours Rab's phenomenal success was partly down to knowing when to turn a blind eye to some of the more profitable and less legal aspects of the nightclub industry, but Doug had taken to Rab. He had a quick, sarcastic wit and was helpful and articulate when commenting on the story. He had spent a few nights with Rab touring the pubs and clubs in the city where his people worked. Everywhere they went, there were nods of greeting, claps on the shoulder, shaking of hands.

The idea of the tour was to give Doug a better idea of what

doormen in the city had to deal with, get a feel for the need for tighter regulation, but really it was just a pub crawl. Though wherever they went and no matter how much they drank, Rab remained the same; calm and serene, willing to talk and be talked to. He seemed to live by a simple rule: don't fuck with me and I won't fuck with you.

Doug reached for his contact book, flipping through the well-thumbed pages until he found Rab's number. If anyone could help him find out more about Derek's working life in Edinburgh, it was Rab.

• • •

Rab ran his empire from a suite of offices in the basement of a building on Forth Street, only a few minutes' walk from Princes Street. His neighbours were the local radio station on one side and a firm of architects on the other. Doug was met at the door by Janet, Rab's perma-blonde wife, who was always just this side of orange. She and her man had clawed their way up from the gutter to the point where she could afford three sunbed sessions a week, a weekly hair-do and a cacophony of chunky gold jewellery. Janet also drove a two-seater Mazda roadster, which sat gleaming outside their offices.

Personal number plate and flame red, of course.

'Hiya, Doug,' she said, her voice pure Lanarkshire. 'Christ, boy, you bin in the wars or someit? 'Mone in. He's oan the phone, he'll oanlae be wan minute.'

Doug nodded his thanks, complimented Janet on her hair-do. She flashed a row of capped teeth already beginning to stain with nicotine and sat back behind her desk. Whatever her faults, Janet was no fool. She deployed Rab's staff with the military precision of a general at war.

The door to the main office boomed open as Rab steeped through. He was a tall man, dressed in a suit that probably cost more than Doug's last car loan. A gold wrist chain peeked out from underneath the cuff of his shirt. His smile was warm and open, but the eyes shattered that illusion. There was a hardness in his gaze, something that said this was a man who had seen violence, and wasn't afraid to use it if he had to.

'Doug,' he called, taking Doug's hand and pumping it in a vigorous handshake. His eyes strayed over Doug's bruises. 'How are you?' he asked pointedly.

'Going well, Rab,' Doug replied. He could feel pins and needles crawl through his palm. 'Look, thanks for seeing me at such short notice.'

'Ach,' Rab waved a dismissive hand. 'Think nothing of it. You put me across well in that paper of yours, only fair I do you a favour when I can. Come on in, we'll talk.'

Doug followed Rab into his office, which was dominated by a huge oak desk that sat at the far end of the room. Next to the window a large plant with lush green leaves nodded lazily in the draft from the air-conditioning unit overheard. Doug recognised the plant, his mum and dad had one just like it in their home, but he couldn't remember what it was called.

As Doug took a seat, Rab busied himself at a drinks cabinet behind his desk. He didn't ask Doug if he wanted a drink, didn't need to. To Rab, having a drink was as integral a part of doing business as a pen and a contract. Someone visited you, you played the host. It was the way he worked. Doug was glad he'd decided to get a taxi into town instead of bringing the car.

He set a generous whisky in front of Doug and then settled himself into his chair. Held up his own glass. 'Cheers.'

Doug raised his glass, took a sip. The peaty tang of Laphroaig bit into his tastebuds. A little early in the day for him, but not bad. He murmured his thanks.

'So, Doug,' Rab said as he rolled his glass between his fingers. 'What can I do to help you?'

'I was wondering if you had ever heard of a guy who worked

on the doors a few years ago. Derek McGinty?'

Rab turned his head up, studying the ceiling. 'McGinty, McGinty, McGinty,' he said, tasting the name. 'Hold on a minute. Derek McGinty. He no' that bastard who got sent down for raping that wee girl? The one your paper's going doolally for?'

'Yeah, that's him. He ever work for you?'

'No' fuckin' likely. I met him a few times, though, he was always asking around, seeing if there were any jobs going. He worked in a few of the clubs on the West End and down the rougher end of the Grassmarket.'

Doug nodded. 'So how come you never took him on?'

'Loose cannon,' Rab replied. 'Had a monstrous temper on him, by all accounts, could fly off the handle at any moment. Bad for business. And he was a dealer, too.'

Doug's ears pricked up. 'What? Speed, E?'

'Naw, the hard shit. Heroin, crack, that kind of thing. He would deal it in the clubs, wasnae particular about who he sold to either as long as he got his money.'

'You got any idea who he was working for? What clubs he was dealing in?'

Rab's bushy eyebrows met in a deep frown. 'Why the interest, Doug? I thought this guy was yesterday's news.'

Maybe for everyone who hasn't had the shit beaten out of them and their car impaled, Doug thought. 'I'm not sure,' he said. 'But I've been working on a few things recently, and McGinty's name keeps popping up. I was hoping you could fill in some of the gaps.'

Rab gazed at Doug coolly for a moment, as though sizing him up. 'It's important to you, isn't it?'

'Yeah. Yeah, Rab, it is. Anything you could tell me would be really helpful.'

'Well, the truth is I don't know much more than I've already told you,' Rab replied, draining his glass and getting up for another. 'But I can find out for you, if you want.'

'That would be great, Rab, thanks a lot.'

Rab shrugged. It always paid to keep those who could portray you and your business in a good light happy. 'Don't worry about it. I'll make a few calls, let you know what comes up.'

'Great, Rab,' Doug said, draining his whisky. He blinked back tears as it scalded its way down his throat. It felt as if someone had lit a bonfire in his stomach. 'My mobile's on all the time.'

'No problem. But, Doug, one favour?'

Doug froze. Uh-oh. 'Yeah?'

'Don't encourage, Janet. She's bad enough with that fucking hairdresser of hers as it is without young guys like you complimenting her.'

38

'Just what the *fuck* am I paying you for, anyway?'

Charlie sighed. He had been expecting this call since he had seen the afternoon edition of the *Tribune*.

'Look, I...'

'I thought you said you were going to deal with this!' the voice hissed. 'For fuck's sake, I even gave you the cash to buy a gun, and still you can't just get to that bastard!'

Charlie reached for the bottle of whisky at the side of his chair, picked it up and then put it aside again. No. The whisky would dull the pain, but he didn't want it dulled. He wanted it fresh, wanted to remember what he owed McGinty, and why it was so important he had a little face-to-face chat with him.

'Look,' he said slowly, as if trying to explain the rules of the game to a sulking child. 'I'm not psychic. I didn't know the little shit would pull something like that, did I? I thought he would be sticking to you like glue until he could get you alone.'

'Brilliant fucking plan. Follow me around and hope you manage to get to McGinty before he gets to me?'

Nah, Charlie thought. I'll let the bastard have his fun with you first, then I'll deal with him.

'Okay, okay,' Charlie said. His jaw was starting to ache from all the talking. 'I fucked up, I admit it. But I'll get him, don't worry.'

'Oh, and how are you going to do that? If you haven't noticed, his face is splashed all over the papers and television. If he's got any sense, he'll have jumped in that car of yours and headed for the Hebrides.'

'No, he won't,' Charlie said, filing away the dig about his car for future reference. When he had dealt with McGinty, this bastard was going to be next to pay, with interest. Nobody took the piss like that. Nobody.

'He's got scores to settle. He'll still be around.'

'And how are you going to find him now? If he is still in the area, he'll be keeping a low profile.'

'Don't worry,' Charlie said, glancing back down at the *Tribune*. 'I'll make him come to me.'

'And how are you going to do that?'

Beside the main story on how the police were looking for McGinty in connection with the disturbance at Buchans' home there was a side panel, illustrated with a very satisfying photograph of that little twat McGregor sprawled across a garden path, scrambling for a piece of paper like an old wino lunging for a dropped can of beer. The picture made Charlie smile.

'Oh, I'll think of something,' he said.

'Well, make sure you fucking do. Fast. I don't want…'

The phone shattered as it struck the wall. Charlie closed his eyes, took breaths as deep as his ruined nose would allow, forced himself to calm down. Later. He would deal with that arrogant prick later. First, he had to prepare a little surprise for Derek.

39

Back at Gayfield, Susie read through Linda Buchan's statement again, hoping to find some nuance she had missed. There wasn't much to go on. The woman was too hysterical to be of much help.

The neighbour who had reported the screams from the Buchans' home, Margaret Orr – who wore the traditional tartan skirt, silver hair and tweed jacket uniform of Edinburgh's aging gentry with a straight back and a challenging gleam in her eye – had been more help. She had been, she told Susie, out walking her dog, Brandy, when she had heard Linda Buchan's screams.

'I didn't think much of it at first, dear,' Mrs Orr said, fiddling with an ornate silver and jade brooch on her jacket as she spoke. 'After all, the woman has just lost her daughter, and everyone in the area knows she's not coping very well. But then I heard that man's voice, and I knew there was something wrong.'

Susie had asked if she heard anything that had been said, but Mrs Orr just shook her head. Susie could see regret in her eyes. She must have hated not knowing the whole story.

'Not really. All I could hear was his voice; very, very angry, but most of what he was saying was drowned out by Mrs Buchan. I did hear one thing, though, at least I think I did. I think he said something about "being off the leash". Does that make any sense?'

Susie sighed, pushing the report across her desk. It made about as much sense as anything else.

At least there had been one break, it was definitely McGinty who had visited the Buchans' home. Forensics found his fingerprints all over the drawing room door, while witnesses who'd seen 'a dark blue saloon car, expensive looking,' making off at high speed, gave descriptions of a man fitting McGinty's profile at the wheel.

Frustrated, Susie headed to the canteen for a coffee. What she really wanted was to go for a run, relax away from all this, but that would have to wait.

She had arranged to meet up with Doug, compare notes and see if he had managed to find anything that might give them a clue as to where McGinty could be now. *Them?* Careful, Susie, careful.

She knew Burns would have a fit if he found out, and McGinty's background was being pored over by as many bodies as Burns could find, but Susie had learned never to underestimate Doug's ability to get to the juicy facts faster than anyone else. She hoped he was being careful, though. Whoever had given him that beating wasn't joking around.

When she got back to her desk, feeling guilty for the bar of chocolate she had bought to go with her coffee, she saw another file had arrived. 'Shit,' she whispered. More paperwork. Perfect.

Settling into her chair, she reached for the file. It was the information she had requested on Lizzie Renwick. Recalling the way she had reacted when being interviewed, Susie had decided to run a check on her to see if she had had any previous run-ins with the police.

According to the file, she had. Susie began to read faster. She ate the chocolate without noticing. No wonder Lizzie had recovered so quickly when Susie had caught her off-guard with a question: the girl was a pro at dealing with the police. And it explained why she was working with Katherine. The girls had something more than a taste for modern art in common.

What the file didn't do was offer any clue as to why Lizzie had been so brutally murdered. After a thorough search, police had failed to find anything obviously missing from the gallery, and what cash there was, along with the business chequebook, was found among the piles of paperwork tipped from the drawers. So the motive hadn't been robbery. What had the killer been looking for? And was it connected to what was in Lizzie's file?

Susie didn't know. But at least it gave her a damn good place to start looking.

• • •

The pub Rab asked to meet in was a small tavern on the Newhaven shore, not far from where Doug and Susie had compared notes the day of Burns' explosion and Doug's anonymous tip-off. It was a small, low-ceilinged place with tables that had been built from flotsam washed up on the shore and low stools that forced you to adopt the classic drinker's pose: knees hunched up, back bent over the table, one hand hovering near your pint.

Rab was already seated at one of the tables when Doug arrived, a glass of what Doug guessed was Laphroaig in front of him. Across the table, a pint of Guinness waited patiently for Doug. He didn't really feel like a drink, especially since the car was parked outside, but he wasn't going to argue the point with Rab.

'Evening, Rab,' Doug said as he dropped into his stool. 'Not your usual stomping ground, is it?'

'Nah, I fancied a change of scenery,' Rab said, glancing around the bar. From the look on his face, Doug got the feeling he thought it had been a bit of a wasted journey.

Doug lifted the Guinness, nodding his head in thanks and then taking a long drink. Crap décor or not, the pub did a good pint. 'So,' he said, 'I wasn't expecting you to call back so quickly. You managed to find something out for me?'

Rab fixed Doug with a cool gaze. 'That depends.'

'On what?'

'On whether or not you're keen to add to your collection of

bumps and bruises. And don't give me any shit about how you walked into a door or something, I saw you jumping when you sat down. Someone gave you a bit of a going over, didn't they? Made their point with a few digs to the sides, too.'

Doug refused to back away from Rab's stare. 'Yeah, well, it happens.'

'Aye, and usually for a good reason,' Rab replied. He finished his whisky in a gulp, turned and raised his hand to the barman. Message received. Another nip was on its way.

'Look, Doug, let me be straight with you for a minute, okay? I did what you asked, found out a bit more about McGinty and, if you want me to tell you, I will. But this is serious shit, Doug, the people involved are not exactly hungry for publicity, and they don't like nosey reporters very much. They'll talk to you if I ask them to, but they're not going to like it. You've already had one doing over this, Doug, the question is, do you want to risk another one?'

Doug thought it over for a minute, remembering the sound of the knife punching into the car's roof, the way he vomited on the stairs, shaking like a little boy who wanted his mum. The pain in his side when he moved or sat down. No, he didn't want another beating. But there were questions he needed answers to. And if it meant a risk to get them, so be it.

'Tell me what you know.'

Rab sighed, leaning back slightly as the barman placed another whisky in front of him. The measure was a lot bigger than the average bar shot, at least a triple by Doug's guess. The barman retreated. Rab didn't pay.

'Alright then,' he said once he was sure the barman was out of listening range. 'But on yer ain heid be it.'

Doug nodded, felt his stomach twist with a mixture of excitement and fear.

'Your friend McGinty had an interesting time when he worked in Edinburgh,' Rab said. 'Like I told you, he asked me for work and

I always knocked him back, knowing he was a bit of a wildcard when things kicked off. However, not everyone in town is as discerning as I am. And one of the least discerning is Tommy Croal.'

Tommy Croal. Jesus. Croal was one of the biggest drug dealers and muscle men in Edinburgh. Originally from the west coast, Croal had arrived in Edinburgh back in the mid-Eighties, keen to build himself an empire. He had succeeded, but not before sparking off a turf war in the city. For a while, it was common for clubs to be trashed as Croal's men went in and started fights to show the owners that the existing security staff weren't up to the job of controlling trouble.

It worked on a lot of places, the owners deciding it was easier, and cheaper, to just let Croal run the doors than see their clubs trashed every week. Of all the security firms in Edinburgh, Rab's was the only one that hadn't suffered any losses. And the reason for that wasn't Rab, but his general-in-chief, Janet. She doubled security at every club and pub they ran in Edinburgh, always making sure the additional staff were in plain clothes and mingling with the crowd. The men she used – mostly west coast 'friends and family', according to Janet – were under orders: if trouble started, finish it. Hard. Croal didn't pick on Rab's customers for very long.

However, drug dealers were a different story. They were grabbed off the streets and out of bars and given a simple choice: work for Croal and get a better cut of the sales, or stay with their current supplier and see how easy it was to deal from a wheelchair. Doug could see why Croal would have use for somebody like McGinty.

'So, what was he, one of Croal's dealers?'

Rab nodded. 'Partly. But he was also a bit of a co-ordinator for Croal. From what I've heard, he supervised one of Croal's saunas along with another vicious wee shite called Charlie Morris. They made sure the girls and clients were happy, that no one got out of line. Rumour is they also distributed drugs to dealers there.'

'Anything else you can tell me?' Doug asked. 'What clubs he

might have dealt at, if he had regular customers?'

Rab rolled his eyes. 'Fucking typical,' he said with a small smile. 'Never enough, is it? That's as much as I could find out but, like I said, I've had a word, and these people have said they'll talk to you if you want them to.'

'Thanks, Rab,' Doug said as he finished his pint. He glanced at Rab's whisky. Almost gone. 'You want another?'

'Well, it's the least you can do,' Rab replied. Doug made to head for the bar, but Rab placed a hand on his arm, pushing him back into his seat. 'I was being serious, Doug. This is heavy shit. These people will talk to you. But that doesn't mean they're going to just give you a free pass. If you ask something they don't like, I won't be able to help you, understand?'

Doug suddenly felt cold, his mouth dry. Is it worth it? he asked himself. Is it? He pushed the thought away. Too late now.

'I understand, Rab. And thanks for the warning. I'll be on my best behaviour, promise.'

Just make sure you are,' Rab said, draining his whisky. 'Now get me another drink, will you, I hate sitting in a pub with an empty glass in front of me.'

• • •

Half an hour later, Doug was back in his car, heading to meet Susie. They had originally planned to meet up and compare notes, but when he phoned her she suggested getting something to eat instead, saying she couldn't survive on 'a chocolate bar and cups of pish-water coffee'. Doug didn't complain, he was starting to feel hungry himself, so he suggested a little Chinese restaurant he knew in the Tanfield area near to the Botanic Gardens. Susie didn't argue with the thought of Chinese, but was still wary of being seen with him after Burns' bollocking and not-so-subtle warning earlier in the day, so asked if he would pick up takeaway and meet her back at her place, which was only five minutes from the restaurant.

She lived on the fourth floor of a tenement on Broughton Road. Her flat was about the same size as Doug's, and offered outstanding clear views of the industrial estate behind it. She had bought the place when she moved to Edinburgh, before the property market in the capital began demanding that buyers not only pay three times what a home was worth but also sign away their first-born child as part of the deal. She had decorated it with the twenty-first century equivalent of the carpet, laminate flooring, and a few small pieces of furniture to try and make the place feel bigger than it was.

The illusion almost worked, but the 55-inch TV that dominated the corner of the living room – which Doug himself had lugged up the stairs and set up for her – ruined the effect. Susie didn't care. She loved movies and loved watching them on the big screen, whether that was at home or at the cinema.

She took the bags of takeaway from Doug at the door, disappearing into the kitchen as he flopped down onto one of the pair of two-seater couches that sat in the living room.

'So, how'd you get on with Linda Buchan's statement?' Doug called as he pulled off his tie and stuffed it in his jacket pocket.

'Not great,' Susie replied as she carried a tray with the Chinese and a bottle of wine into the room and placed it on a small table that sat between the couches. 'You want a glass of wine?'

Doug thought about it for a second, calculated how much he had already had. 'Just the one,' he said. 'I've got to drive later.'

Susie nodded as she poured. 'Fine with me,' she said, passing him a glass. 'Leaves me more.' She leant forward and heaped rice and sweet and sour chicken into a bowl, then sat back on her couch, curling her legs underneath her.

Doug filled his own bowl with rice and his choice, chilli chicken, then followed Susie's lead and got comfortable. They ate in silence for a few minutes, enjoying the chance to relax, before Susie said: 'Come on, then, how did you get on? Find anything interesting?'

Doug took another swig of his wine and then laid the glass aside.

'You could say that,' he said, then went on to tell her what Rab had told him about McGinty. Susie ate as he talked, but when he mentioned that McGinty had been a dealer for Tommy Croal, her fork stopped halfway to her mouth.

'What?' Doug asked, trying not to laugh. She looked like a kid who had just been told Santa didn't exist. 'Something I said?'

She laid her bowl aside, leant over and dug a file out of her bag then passed it to Doug. 'You never saw that,' she said. 'But I think you may find it interesting.'

Doug flipped the file open, starting reading. Lizzie Renwick's record. He skimmed through it, stopped and then looked up.

'She was a dealer, too?' he said.

'Yup,' Susie replied. 'She was busted dealing at a club in Lothian Road back in '88, when there was a big anti-drugs crackdown.'

Doug did a quick sum in his head. 'So she was eighteen at the time?'

'Yeah,' Susie nodded. 'The judge took pity on her, gave her six months as it was "only" speed and hash she was dealing that time. She went straight back to it, got busted again in '91, then went to work with Katherine at the gallery a while later.'

'Think this is linked to her murder?'

'I wish I knew,' Susie replied. 'It might be, but I don't see how. Unless she was dealing again, she'd been away from that scene for a long time, so anyone who wanted to settle a score with her had plenty of opportunity to do it before now.'

'Unless they hadn't been able to until now?'

'You mean McGinty?' Susie asked. 'Maybe, maybe not. Whoever killed her, they were looking for something. They beat the shit out of her to get something and then tore the gallery apart when she either wouldn't or couldn't tell them, but left the cash and business chequebook behind. Even if McGinty did know her from her days as a dealer, and from what you've said there's a good chance he did, it doesn't explain why he would kill her and just leave the cash. What the hell could he want from an art gallery?'

Doug finished his wine. He wanted another glass. 'I don't know,' he said. 'Hopefully I'll get some answers later.'

'Oh, how's that?'

'Rab MacFarlane,' Doug said cautiously. He didn't think Susie was going to like what he was about to tell her. 'He's set up a meeting for me later tonight with Kevin Tomlin, one of the guys McGinty worked at the Passionata Sauna with.'

Susie sat forward. 'You know it should be me that's going along to speak to him?' she asked.

Doug shook his head. 'If it was you going, he wouldn't even open the door. It's a bloody miracle Rab managed to get me an invite. These guys hate cops, Susie. Sure, you could get a warrant and search the place, but then what? It's been a long time since McGinty worked there, and these guys might develop a case of amnesia just to piss you off.'

Susie sighed huffily, sat back in the couch. Doug could have sworn she was pouting. 'Don't worry,' he said, 'I'll call you first thing in the morning, let you know if I find anything interesting.'

'That before or after you write it up for the *Tribune*?'

Doug remembered Rab's warning. *This is serious shit, the people involved are not exactly hungry for publicity.*

'Before,' he said. 'Definitely before.'

40

'So, Derek, what the fuck are you going to do now?'

There was no answer, only the drone of cars from the street outside. He hadn't expected one though, seeing as he was alone.

He was back in Cairneyhill, standing behind the bar where he had worked until only a few short weeks ago. He had, he thought, been happy here. Comfortably anonymous, getting on with things, biding his time until he could collect what he was due and build a new life. Until his past had caught up with him, and he had been chased out of the village by locals baying for his blood, calling him a monster and a bastard and a rapist.

He didn't blame them.

He thought back, remembering Linda Buchan's reaction when he had told her. It was as though she were a fragile bird he had taken in his hand and crushed. He had never seen a person crumple like that before, face twisted by horror and sorrow. She had fallen to her knees, face a dusky purple as tears streamed down her face. She didn't want to hear what he had to say, didn't want to acknowledge what she was being told. But she believed him. He could see it in her eyes.

And as Linda sat there in the middle of the floor, hugging herself and sobbing as though he had just plunged a knife into her guts, Derek understood. This was what he had put his mother through for the last twelve years. Every time a reporter called at the door, every time he made another headline or the case was featured in the news. This was what she endured.

He fled, driving like a maniac, half-hoping the police would catch him there and then and get it over with.

But they didn't, and he was left aimlessly driving around, trying to think what to do next. They would be guarding Buchan now, there would be no way of getting to him. Unless…

It had taken him less than an hour to get to Fife. It was still daylight when he arrived and, knowing the pub didn't shut till 11pm, he stopped in Dunfermline, the first large town after the Forth Road Bridge. Dunfermline had once been Scotland's capital, a town inhabited by kings and queens. Today, the closest it got to royalty was a shopping centre called the Kingsgate.

He parked at the bottom of the town and headed for Pitreavie Park, a large communal expanse of greenery where families brought their children to enjoy the swings or feed the squirrels and peacocks that made the park their home. He lost himself there for a few hours, trying not to think of anything until it grew dark. By the time he left, the park gates had been shut, but it was simple enough to hop over them. A ten-minute ride later and he was in Cairneyhill. The pub had been ludicrously easy to break into, the stupid bastards hadn't even bothered to change the alarm code since he worked there.

Now he stood behind the bar, the only light in the pub being the glow of streetlights prodding through the windows. He dismantled the rack of spirits that sat on the wall behind the bar, uncorking each of the bottles and sitting them gently on the bar top. Went over to one of the booths opposite the bar, paused, then took down the picture that hung on the wall there. He had put it there himself about three months ago. It might has well have been another lifetime.

He went to the cleaning cupboard in a small alcove behind the bar and found a broom handle and cleaning cloth.

The bottles shattered like movie props when he swung the

broom handle, the noise very loud. He wondered if anyone outside had heard him, found he didn't care. The smell of spilled spirit was cloying, overpowering, and clawed at his eyes and back of his throat. He glanced at the picture, which he had propped next to the door. Tears began to roll slowly down his cheeks. He told himself they were from the fumes.

Heading for the door, he bundled the cloth into a bottle of vodka he had saved, leaving a ragged end popping out so the bottle looked like a crude candle. He lit the wick and threw the bottle at the bar.

The effect was instant. There was a dull whump as the bottle hit the bar and the alcohol ignited, burning shards of cloth spraying out. Bright blue and orange flames leapt from the bar as the spirits ignited. The flames spread quickly, racing across the bar hungrily before spitting out onto the stools, the carpet, the walls. Derek picked up the picture and turned for the door, the heat from the fire baking into his back. He hurried out to the small, deserted car park at the back of the pub and got into the car, watching as the flames danced and capered behind the windows of the bar. When the first window exploded from the heat, he started the engine and drove away, taking his time, not wanting to be too inconspicuous.

He heard the first fire engine screaming to the scene as he drove down the main street and smiled. The police would follow shortly, full of questions and quickly pinning the blaze on him; revenge for being driven out of the village. No doubt the news of what had happened would reach Edinburgh soon enough.

That suited Derek just fine.

41

Kevin Tomlin looked like he had been born in a gym and fed a constant diet of weights and steroids ever since. To Doug he was a six-foot wall of solid muscle. He wore a tight black T-shirt that accentuated every bulge and ripple, while his thick forearms and biceps were riddled with a mapwork of veins. Coupled with the severe military-style cropped hair, dark unblinking eyes and overhanging forehead that would put a Neanderthal to shame, the overall effect wasn't exactly soothing, especially given Doug's situation.

He was sitting in a small back office at the Executive Club, which was in a fairly affluent side street off London Road. It was, Doug supposed, in a prime location to ply its trade; there were four or five hotels nearby that catered to business travellers, while a large assurance company had its offices only a ten-minute walk away. Nobody would raise an eyebrow to anyone walking in the front door, which – with its discreet brass plate saying '*Non-Members welcome*' and brass-set buzzer – could have passed for any other business.

It was only when you heard the heavy bolts slide clear as the door was opened by a man who had obviously been raised in the same gym as Tomlin, you realised the club was something else.

He had been ushered into a large lounge area, complete with plush leather sofas, tasteful decorations and a small bar in the corner. A few men were sitting in the soft-lit lounge, having a drink and talking to each other or the women that were fluttering about, perfect hair and make-up complemented by their fixed smiles.

To Doug, the oldest of them looked to be about twenty-two, if that.

What surprised him most was what the women were wearing; standard issue evening gowns and business suits, with not a negligee or bra strap in sight. But then, Doug thought, that was the whole point of the place – subtlety, discretion. Those who could afford to come to Executive Club valued the privacy of their pleasure. It was a long way from the Passionata Sauna where Derek and Tomlin had worked together, which Rab had described as little more than a three-roomed cupboard in Fountainbridge where the walls shook and you could hear the moans every time a punter asked for 'extras'.

Tomlin had arrived a few moments later. He'd said nothing when he lumbered up to Doug, just beckoned for him to follow and led him to the office. He sat across the table from Doug now, glaring. As Rab had said, he would talk to Doug as a favour, but that didn't mean he had to like it.

'So,' he said finally, his voice surprisingly soft for his massive frame, 'Rab tells me you wanted to ask a few questions about Derek McGinty?'

'Yeah, that's right,' Doug said. His voice was calm and even, his guts anything but. 'I just wanted to see if you could tell me a bit more about him.'

'Like what?' Tomlin asked. Doug could feel the suspicion rolling off him in waves. Christ, what had Rab done to get this guy to speak to him?

Doug took a deep breath, trying to keep calm. No point beating around the bush, he had to ask the question, especially in light of what Susie had told him.

He handed a picture over the table to Tomlin. 'Was this girl ever a dealer for Derek?'

Tomlin studied the picture, eyes flicking between it and Doug. 'Yeah,' he said handing back the picture of Lizzie Renwick that Susie had given to Doug earlier. 'Thin Lizzie, that's what we used to call her. She used to deal for Derek in the clubs on the West End.'

Doug felt like he had won the lottery. So they did know each other. 'Any idea how they met?'

'Yeah, at the Passionata,' Tomlin said. 'Lizzie was already working there when Derek and I started. He was just starting to…' He paused, stretching for the right word. '…to do business for Mr Cr… the boss, and he asked Lizzie to do a bit of trade for him. She jumped at it. Never did think she was much for the sauna business, anyway.'

Doug nodded, Susie's words echoing in his mind. *Why would he kill her and leave the cash?*

'How did they get on, ever any problems?'

Tomlin laughed. The sound made Doug feel like bolting for the door. 'Problems?' he snorted. 'You must be fuckin' joking, pal. There are always problems in this business. Not selling your quota, getting ripped off by customers, other dealers, the pigs. It's not like selling insurance or something, pal. If you don't hit your target here, you're in the shit.'

'And was Lizzie in shit with Derek a lot?'

'No more than any of the other girls,' Tomlin said. 'And besides, Derek was always a little soft on her, anyway.'

Doug looked up. 'Oh, why's that?'

Tomlin looked over at him sharply. *Don't push it, pal*, his gaze said.

'Look, please,' Doug said. 'I really need to know. Rab said you might be able to help me, so help me.' Doug didn't like using Rab's name, but he needed answers.

Tomlin sighed, crossing his arms and rubbing his biceps gently as though they were good luck charms. In his line of work, maybe they were. 'Lizzie looked after someone for him, okay? He never gave a name, but he brought her in once, about six months before he got done for… you know.'

Doug nodded. Bethany Miller. He knew alright.

'Anyway,' Tomlin said, 'Derek said the girl was one of his regulars who'd flipped out in one of the clubs he worked. She was all fucked up on something, puking up and shaking like she was about to have a fit, was in a really bad way. Said the boss of the club wanted her out of the way. Anyway, he put her in one of the rooms in the back, got Lizzie to take care of her. After that, he always looked out for Lizzie, gave her the easy patches to work, always made sure she was covered if she came up short.'

Doug's pulse was roaring in his ears. *Could it be?* He handed over the picture of Derek and Katherine together. 'Was this the girl you saw that night?' Tomlin studied it for a long moment. Doug held his breath, waiting for the answer.

'Yeah, that's her,' he said finally. Doug had to bite back a roar of success. 'Don't know what it was about her, but she got to Derek, that's for sure.'

'Oh, how's that?'

'He was a cold bastard,' Tomlin replied simply, as though it answered all Doug's questions. When he saw that it didn't, he sighed. 'If someone got out of line, he would knock fuck out of them, no questions asked. I saw him beat the shit out of a guy with a coat stand one night, he never even broke a sweat.'

'But how does that…?'

'I'm fuckin' getting to it, okay? Derek did not give a fuck about anyone other than himself. When he first brought the kid in, I thought it was just because he knew that her dying would be bad for business, and he couldn't take the risk of dumping her at the hospital and then blabbing about where she got her drugs.'

'But it was more than that?'

'Not at the time,' Tomlin said, raw impatience in his voice. Doug didn't think he would be sitting in the office for much longer. 'It was afterwards. He kept on calling her to make sure she was okay, told me she had had a hard time and he was going to try and help her. And then he started asking around town, looking for someone.'

'Oh?' Doug's curiosity muffled the growing alarm bells in his mind. Tomlin wanted him out of here. Fine, he would go. Just one more question. 'Any idea who he was looking for?'

Tomlin glared at Doug. It looked as if he were trying to figure out how much shit he would get from Rab if he just beat Doug senseless. 'He never mentioned any names,' he said, his voice icy, 'but he gave me the description of the guy he was looking for, asked me to pass it around the town. We tracked him down to his local about a month later.'

'What did the guy he was after look like?' Doug asked, before he had a chance to stop himself. 'Where did Derek find him?'

Tomlin clenched his fists, knuckles popping. When he started talking again, Doug was getting ready to spring from his chair and dive for the door.

After a minute, he was rooted to the spot, unable to move, pinned to the chair by the shock of what Tomlin was telling him, and the weight of what it meant.

• • •

Susie fumbled for the phone when it started ringing, dragging her from a deep sleep. She glanced at her bedside clock. 3.12am. Doug could pick his times.

'Hello?' she mumbled, not opening her eyes.

'Drummond? Sorry to bother you at this hour. You awake?'

Susie's eyes snapped open. 'Yes, sir,' she said, sitting up in bed. What the hell was Burns doing phoning her at this time in the morning? 'What's up?'

'We've just had a call from Fife. Apparently, the Jamieson Arms in Cairneyhill was torched earlier this evening. Looks like someone used the booze in the pub as an accelerant. There's not much more than a smoking pit left.'

Jamieson Arms? Susie groped for the name, knowing it was familiar. 'Hold on,' she said, 'isn't that the pub McGinty was working at?'

'Exactly,' Burns said. His voice was rough with lack of sleep. 'Witness put a dark blue saloon at the scene at around the time the fire started. Ring any bells?'

Dark blue saloon? Oh yes. 'You mean the same as was seen driving away after McGinty visited Linda Buchan?'

'Right. What we don't know is if this means that he's left Edinburgh and decided to settle a few old scores on the way in lieu of getting his money from Buchan, or whether this is something else. I'm having a staff briefing at 6am to see if we can come up with some answers.'

'Right, sir, no problem.' Susie glanced at her clock again. Less than three hours. 'See you then.'

Susie hung up. She turned over in bed, tried to settle down and not let her racing mind stop her sleeping. On an impulse, she sat back up and pulled the phone from its wall socket, switched her mobile off. If Doug had found out anything of great importance, he could tell her in the morning. Right now, she needed to sleep.

42

Doug sat in the departure lounge, drumming his fingers, waiting. He had a paper open in front of him, and was trying to see how long he could pretend he was reading it before his mind strayed back to last night. His record was forty seconds.

After leaving Tomlin at about 3am, his first impulse had been to just hit the road. It would only have taken about five hours to get there at that time, the roads quiet with only the occasional long-distance lorry or car for company. But five hours there meant five hours or more back, and if his suspicions were confirmed, that was five hours he didn't want to waste.

He had tried to phone Susie to tell her what he had found, but her landline was permanently engaged and her mobile was diverting to her answering service. After the third failed attempt he left a cursory message asking her to phone him as soon was possible, then headed for the *Tribune* and his computer. He logged on, printed off everything he needed, then pulled up the internet and booked a no-frills flight. It wasn't that cheap as he was flying the same day – the first flight he could get was 7am – but he booked it on his credit card without hesitating. He could worry about expenses later.

After getting everything arranged and sending an e-mail to Walter explaining where he had gone, there was nothing to do but wait. Rather than head home he drove to the airport, which was only five minutes from the industrial park that the *Tribune*'s office's were in, parked up in the long-stay car park and headed for the terminal. He checked in then headed for the lounge, snagging a paper on his way in a vain attempt to keep himself from watching the clock.

Doug had never liked flying. He hated the roar of the engines on take-off, the sickening lurch in his stomach as the plane suddenly lifted at a ludicrous angle so the people at the front looked like they were on an escalator about two floors up from the people at the back. But still, there was a morbid curiosity that forced him to look out of the window as the plane took off, wondering what would happen if the engines suddenly spluttered into silence and the plane nose-dived for the ground. But today, he was willing the announcer to call his flight. He wanted, *needed*, to be moving, to get verification for what he now thought he knew. If he was right, it explained a lot, including why he had been beaten up outside his flat and warned off McGinty in the first place.

Giving up on the paper with a frustrated sigh, Doug's eyes drifted to the bar. It was only 5am, but he could get a drink, thanks to the 24-hour licensing of airport premises. You could drink when most people were curled up in their beds.

He headed for the bar, decided against a beer and opted for coffee instead. It was hot, bitter and extravagantly overpriced, but at least the caffeine rush would keep him awake. He could try and sleep on the flight. It was a short up-and-down, but it gave him enough time to grab a nap. Somehow, he didn't think he would.

Susie's number was still engaged when he tried it again, the mobile still switched off.

At 6.10am his flight was finally called and he switched his phone off as he headed for the plane. The flight took off on time, just as cold, watery light was seeping through the dusky purple of the night sky. Doug took a window seat but for once he didn't look out at the ground as it dropped away sickeningly. He kept his eyes straight ahead, willing the plane to get up in the air and carry him to his destination.

• • •

Burns' briefing didn't last long. He handed out copies of the police report from the fire at the Jamieson Arms to the officers, filling in the blanks with what he had managed to glean first hand after talking with the Pcs who were first on the scene.

The most popular opinion was that, after tipping his hand by confronting Linda Buchan, Derek decided to cut his losses and run. He would have known the police would be after him, seen his description and photograph in the newspapers and on the TV. There was a theory that he was heading north or maybe across to Stranraer for the ferry to Belfast and had stopped in on the way to say a little thank you to his former employers and the town that had turned on him. Forces across the UK had been alerted to the fact McGinty could turn up on their doorsteps; descriptions of him and the vehicle he had been seen in circulated.

Susie read over the description of the car. There was something about it that was niggling at her. A dark blue saloon, fairly upmarket. Nothing matching the description seemed to fit the missing car database for the Lothian and Borders region, so where had McGinty got it? It was possible he had bought it with the money he blackmailed out of Katherine, but Susie didn't think he would be stupid enough to blow a large chunk of the only cash he had on a car, especially a flash one, when he had already proved he could steal one.

Assignments were divvied up, Susie volunteering to recheck McGinty's known associates to see if they could think of anyone he might head for. After that, she would head for the McGintys to see if they could think of anyone their son might visit. Normally, she would have just phoned them, but after all the trouble he was getting from the press Sam McGinty had taken to ignoring his phone.

She hoped Doug could help her after his meeting last night, and that he had managed to get away unscathed. She wished she had insisted on going with him, but knew logically that he had been right. If she had tagged along, they would have got nothing. At least this way, they had a chance. All she had to do was trust him to share.

Back at her desk, she switched her mobile back on and it beeped to tell her she had a message. It was from Doug, asking her to call him. Her answerphone told her the message had been received at 3.20am. What could he have found that he thought was important enough to call her at that time? A brief moment of panic at the thought he had been attacked again. But no, couldn't be. If it was that, he wouldn't have sounded so calm.

She hit the redial button and waiting, tutting when she was diverted to Doug's own message service. She left a brief message that she was returning his call then got back to her paperwork.

43

Hal sat at the kitchen table, gently bouncing Jennifer in his arms as he fed her the first bottle of the morning. His phone sat on the table, switched to speaker, waiting for the meeting to start.

Jonathan had called him last night, begging him to take the conference call. 'It's Mr Buchan,' he explained, his tone pitch-perfect worried schoolboy. 'He's demanded a meeting with the parliamentary party, insisted that you were part of it.'

Hal massaged his eyes, sighed. 'But he accepted the statement and agreed the leave of absence, Jonathan, what does he want me involved for? I got the feeling he didn't really like me when we met.'

'I don't know,' Jonathan replied, voice pleading. 'He just insisted we get you on a conference call. So will you? Please?'

In a stupid move for someone in PR, Hal let his conscience get the better of him and agreed. After all, if he and refused and wasn't there, he could imagine Buchan being enough of a shit to take it out on Jonathan.

So now he sat at his kitchen table – his daughter staring at him intently as she suckled on her bottle – waiting for the squabbling to begin.

'Mr Damon, thank you for taking part in this meeting this morning,' Fraser Duncan, the Tory whip, said. 'We appreciate your time this morning.'

'Not a problem,' Hal replied. 'Though to be honest, Fraser, I'm not sure what I can add. I was brought on board purely to advise the party. Now that's done. I don't see what else I can contribute.'

'Well, ah…' Fraser began.

'I'll tell you what you can contribute, Mr Damon,' Buchan said, the anger in his voice seeming to fill Hal's kitchen. 'Now that I've agreed to your leave of absence, you can tell us all how you intend to announce my return to work in a month's time.'

A month? Hal thought. Nice to see he was giving himself and his wife the time they needed to grieve. Wanker.

'Ah, good morning, Mr Buchan,' he said. 'I'm sorry to say, that's not my job, sir. As I said, I was hired purely to advise during this difficult…'

'Not your job?' Buchan sneered. Hal thought he could hear Jonathan squirm in the background. 'You put me in this position. I've agreed for the good of the party. But I will not allow you to leave me or my career adrift like this. Do I make myself clear?'

The good of the party? Hal thought. Typical politician, rewrite history to his own advantage, make himself look like the selfless public servant and Hal the big bad PR man who had heartlessly sacrificed him.

'What is clear, Mr Buchan,' Hal replied, fighting to keep his voice level as the anger spread pins and needles across the back of his head, 'is you agreed to take a back seat at a time when media interest in you and your family would be an unnecessary intrusion. What you choose to do politically from now on is your concern. However, I think a month is a…' Hal struggled for a polite way to put it. Failed. Fuck it. '…an insensitively brief period of time for you and your wife to mourn the loss of your daughter. If you want to return to work before that time, that's a matter for you and your colleagues. Not me.'

'Well?' Buchan snapped. 'What do you say, Fraser? Will you support me? Or are you going to go with this poo… poor judgement.'

Hal smiled in spite of himself.

'Well, ah...' Fraser began. 'I think it's the party's view that Mr Damon's advice has been hugely helpful, and we'd be guided by him on how best to handle this, for the good of everyone concerned.'

'Are you telling me,' Buchan snarled, his voice growing cold, 'that you are siding with this... this... man's opinion over me? After everything I've done for the party?'

Fraser sounded like an old car trying to start as he cleared his throat. 'Now, Richard, please, we're not saying that at all. We're just saying...'

'You're just saying I can go fuck myself. I've lost my daughter, my wife has been terrorised in her own home, and now you're telling me my own party will not support me? Well fuck you, Fraser, we'll see what the party chiefs have to say about this.'

'I can save you the time, Mr Buchan,' Hal cut in. 'I spoke to Edward Hobbes at Tory HQ last night, and explained the whole situation to him.' He paused, allowing the meaning of what he had just said to sink in with Buchan. 'And he agrees with me that, given the situation and the issues that may be raised, an extended absence would be best. What happens after that is between you, the party and your constituency.'

'You little shit,' Buchan snarled. 'You think you've got all the answers, don't you? Well, let me promise you, you haven't heard the last of this, you...'

'I sincerely hope I have,' Hal said, voice hardening. Jennifer was getting to the end of her bottle, he didn't want her to be sucking on air and giving herself wind. 'Otherwise, I might have to discuss the matter in greater detail with interested parties. I wouldn't suggest you make this situation into more of a *car crash* that it already is, Mr Buchan. We wouldn't want anyone else getting caught in the headlights of bad press and knocked down by it.'

On the other end of the line, he heard Buchan snatching in his breath, imagined him gearing up for a rant. Decided to deny him the chance.

'Fraser, pass my regards to Jonathan, will you? If you need anything else, just get in touch.' Before anyone could say anything else, he cut the line.

He got up and walked around the room with Jenifer on his shoulder, patting her back gently to burp her. Turning the conversation over in his head. Was it grief that was driving Buchan to this? He had lost his daughter, was damned if he was going to lose his career. Hal didn't think so. It was more likely that he was a career politician; that his work was his life and his family was an afterthought.

Poor bastard, Hal thought, smiling as Jennifer burped loudly in his ear. He walked back to the table, switched the phone off. Decided he was having a day with Colin and Jennifer. The job could wait.

44

Warehouses and shopping centres passed by, eventually giving way to dense terraces of housing laid out in long, almost military lines that stretched back up the hill. The red-brick and slate-tile architecture reminded Doug of the old mining homes he had seen in Newtongrange in Midlothian, where an entire village and style of home had sprung up around a mine. He supposed it wasn't so different here. Steel or coal, the need for homes was the same.

The taxi driver pulled up in a narrow cobbled street that stretched like a crooked finger up a winding hill. Cars crammed every available parking space in the street on both sides, some bumped up on pavements to squeeze in to even the tightest of spaces. At the end of the terrace two houses had been knocked together and modified to create a pub called the Auckland Arms. It was trying to be a traditional community pub, but the two-for-one meal banners and sign that screamed '*All Premiership matches LIVE on our big screen*' gave it away as another chain pub looking for authenticity.

Doug paid for his taxi then stood for a moment looking at the house. What if it had been a wasted trip? What if there was no one home? It wasn't as if he could take the chance and call ahead. Only one way to find out. He walked to the door, took a deep breath and rung the bell. Waited anxiously for a response, felt his stomach clench when he heard footsteps shuffle to the door.

A bolt slid clear, then the soft clatter of a chain being fumbled away from the door. He was reminded of Sam McGinty the day he had thrown him out. The rage, the sorrow. He didn't blame the man.

The door opened slowly and then she was there, standing right in front of him. She had put on some weight, changed her hair and was wearing glasses, but Doug recognised her, could see the woman she had been peeking out from behind the years.

'Hello, Bethany,' he said.

• • •

Sam was in the kitchen making a cup of tea for Rita when the doorbell rang. He cursed softly, dropped the teabag into the pot and then made for the door, looking out of the window before he opened it. There weren't many reporters there now, most of them had cleared out yesterday when the news broke that Derek had attacked that Buchan woman in her home.

Despite himself, Sam wished Derek would come home, or at least try to get in touch. It was the ferocity of that hug he had given him the other night – the desperation. He knew his son had done terrible things, but he also knew he had paid for them. Now he was alone out there, being hounded like an animal. It was no excuse for terrifying a grieving woman in her home, but, for all Sam knew, all Derek was trying to do was offer his condolences to the mother of a woman he had been in love with. It was a hollow excuse, Sam knew, but it was all he had. And besides, wasn't that what parents did, always believe in the best of their children?

The man at the door had a baseball cap pulled tight over his head, hiding most of his face. But from his build and clothing – a tatty pair of jeans and a battered leather jacket – Sam didn't think he was a reporter. And so what if he was? He would get the same treatment all the rest of them had.

He swung the door open, leaving the chain on. 'Morning. Can I help you?'

'Oh, I hope so, Mr McGinty,' the man said. When he raised his head, Sam gasped. His face was a diseased mess of bruising and cuts. Charlie smiled at Sam's reaction, revealing the jagged, shattered remains of his teeth. He had to fight back the urge to laugh.

'Yes,' he said softly. 'Terrible, isn't it, Mr McGinty? Your son is such a violent man. Now, do me a favour and let me in will you, I'm catching my death out here.'

'Fuck off,' Sam whispered. 'You're not setting a foot in my house.'

'Oh, but I am Mr McGinty, one way or another.' Sam felt his bowels loosen as Charlie raised the gun from his inside jacket pocket, holding it tight against his body so no one behind him could see. 'Now open the door or I'll blow your fuckin' head off and do it myself.'

Sam fumbled for the chain with numb fingers. His eyes darted around the hall desperately, looking for a weapon. That was a joke, what could he use against a gun? What could he do? Oh sweet Jesus, Rita was upstairs. If she saw this, along with everything else... He tried to hold the door closed, staggered back when Charlie shoved it open.

'Thanks,' he said as he stepped into the house, closed the door and raised the gun fully.

'I take it your wife's home? And don't lie or...' Charlie trained the gun on Sam's head.

Sam staggered back, eyes locked on the black void at the centre of the gun barrel. It felt as if there were an invisible finger poking out from it, stabbing him in the forehead where the bullet would enter his skull. He fought to breathe against the overwhelming weight that seemed to have landed on his chest.

'Yuh...' he coughed. His tongue felt thick and dead. 'Yes... she's...'

'Good,' Charlie snapped. 'Let's go and get her. Then you can tell me where the phone is. After all, it would be a shame if Derek missed the party.'

45

The name jumped out of the background reports, snapping Susie from the sleep-deprived stupor she had been lulled into by the heat of the office and boring reading matter.

Charlie Morris.

He and Derek had been doormen together back in the early Nineties, working some of the rougher clubs in town where drinks were usually ridiculously cheap and teeth were swept up at the end of the night along with the plastic pint glasses and used condoms. They had, according to the reports, worked together until McGinty had been jailed for attacking Bethany Miller, at which time Charlie had gone solo. The rumour was that he was now hired muscle with a select clientele, collecting bad debts or dealing with awkward problems for the right price.

Charlie Morris, famed for making off from the scene of the crime in a high-powered car. A dark-blue seven series BMW, just like the one seen screaming away from the Buchans' home the day Derek had paid a visit. The day Susie had seen a familiar face on the Royal Mile when she had met Buchan. A face she hadn't placed at first because of the way it was twisted and swollen, a jigsaw of angry-looking bruises and cuts. She flipped through the file quickly, fishing a mugshot of Charlie. No doubt. It was him.

Had McGinty got in touch with Morris, asking for his help? Were they working together again, trying to blackmail Buchan for a share of the cash? But if that was the case, why would Charlie have been following Buchan while Derek had visited the family home to demand money? A back-up, or was it something else?

Those bruises, the way he had looked… Doug's words: *It's not the first time a politician has tried to sweep a problem under the carpet.*

The thought jolted the last of the exhaustion from her. She brushed the reports aside, lunging for the computer and her contacts file. Found the number she wanted and stabbed it into the phone, willing the person at the other end to pick up.

'Hello, Prestonview police station.'

'Sergeant Allan? Hi. DS Susie Drummond, Gayfield police station. Look, sorry to bother you, but I heard you had a bit of trouble out that way a couple of days ago, something about a car being vandalised and a knife being found?'

Allan mumbled a yes down the phone. From his tone, Susie could tell it wasn't his favourite subject.

'I was just wondering what you could tell me about that?'

'Not much,' he said. 'We found a lot of blood and a member of the public handed in a large knife they said was found at the scene.'

'Let me guess,' Susie said, referring to the reports in front of her, 'Lock knife, heavy brass butt, about ten inches long, immaculate condition?'

'How did you know that?' Allan asked quickly, his voice dropping to a conspiratorial whisper. 'Have you been talking to that damn reporter?'

Doug. Again. Clever wee git.

'No,' she said. 'But it matches the description of one of our familiar faces' preferred weapon. Look, I know you found McGinty's prints on the knife, but did you find anything else?'

Papers rustled at the other end of the line as Allan flicked through the report. 'We did find other prints on the knife, residuals, smudged. Couldn't get a proper look. But we did get lucky with one thing.'

'Oh, what's that?'

'The tyres of the car that was vandalised were slashed. We checked the hubcaps for prints, came up with a couple of good ones.'

Bingo. 'Let me guess, Charlie Morris?'

'Why, yes.' Suspicion shimmered in Allan's voice. 'But how did you...?'

Susie cut the line. Not entirely professional, but she needed to think and Allan's paranoid chattering wasn't helping.

So Derek and Charlie had clashed in Prestonview and, from what Susie had seen, Charlie had come off worse. Old score to settle, or had someone hired Charlie to make sure Derek didn't cause any more trouble or, worse, ask for any money?

Buchan's words now. *I thought it was for the best.*

Jesus, would he be that ruthless? And how the hell did a QC know a lowlife like Morris, anyway? A career was a career, but...

But...

The photographs in his office; only one family picture, a trophy shot, the rest of the walls dominated by images of Richard Buchan, the successful politician. And then there was the way he 'helped' Katherine fight her drug addiction – bundling her off to a community drug programme in one of the rougher areas of town under an assumed name, where no one would blink or ask questions when another young girl came in off the street with a heroin problem. All to make sure the media didn't find out, that nothing touched his spotless reputation.

Had it been Charlie who had visited Doug that night? Had to be. It would be enough to scare Doug off, keep his secret safe. What Buchan hadn't counted on was someone sending Doug the photograph, and Doug being able to track down the people in it.

Susie logged off her computer and headed for her car. She wanted to get to Prestonview, find out if Derek had met with his parents the night he had run into Charlie Morris. And then she was going to have a long chat with Richard Buchan. And she wasn't going to leave until he gave her the answers she wanted.

• • •

At first, Derek couldn't tell where the ringing was coming from. With a dashboard that looked like the control panel for a space shuttle, the BMW didn't offer any obvious clues. But then he noticed a small red LED on the centre console by the sat-nav, and a flashing phone icon in the corner of the screen.

His finger hovered over the screen, unsure what to do. Answer it or ignore it? Ah, fuck it, what harm could it do? He pressed the answer key.

'Yeah?'

'Hello, Derek.'

'Charlie, how nice to hear from you,' Derek said, grip tightening on the wheel of the car. So the bastard had survived. Typical. He always was stubborn. 'Listen, thanks for the loan of the car. It's a beauty.'

'Yeah, well, fuck you, Derek,' Charlie said. His voice had a slight lisp to it. Not surprising really, Derek thought, remembering the feeling of bone splintering against his knuckles.

'Well, Charlie, if there's nothing else…'

'Fine,' Charlie said, his voice filling with a cloying smugness. 'But before you go, someone wants to say hello.'

Derek felt the heat drain from his body as his dad's voice filled his ears. 'Son? Son, stay away from here, he's got a gun and…'

A sickening crack, followed by his mother shrieking. 'Sam, Sam. Oh Jesus, SAM!'

'CHARLIE!' Derek bellowed, the car lurching as he clamped down on the wheel tighter.

'Yes, Derek?'

'You fucking bastard. If you hurt them…'

'Shut the fuck up, you cunt, you don't know anything about hurt. But unless you get here soon, you will, understood?'

Silence.

'Understood, Derek? Do not fuck with me on this.'

'Understood,' Derek hissed. 'I'm on my way.'

'Good,' Charlie drawled. 'Oh, and Derek? Drive carefully, I'd hate you to damage that car of mine.'

Screaming, Derek smashed his fist into the sat-nav screen.

46

Toys were strewn across the floor of Bethany Miller's living room like rubble. A teddy bear sat propped up at a small table under the window, an Action Man and a doll in a flowery pink dress keeping it company. Beside the table was a bucket of Lego bricks and what looked like the parts from a child's model railway. Cartoon characters smiled down at Doug from the shelves: Bugs Bunny and Wile E Coyote rubbing shoulders with Spider-Man and some oversized blue stuffed toy clutching a red blanket. At the small steps that led off the living room and down to the kitchen, Doug saw a child's safety rail.

So she had a family now. It should have comforted Doug. Instead, it made him feel worse. 'Now, Mr McGregor, was it? You say you've come all the way from Edinburgh to see me.' She glanced at the large clock on the wall. 'I've got things to do today, so I think you'd better get to it.'

Doug nodded, clearing his throat, stalling for time. Now that he was actually here, he realised he had no idea how to talk to this woman.

'It's about your time in Edinburgh,' he said slowly, 'about your work at the Shore Thing Sauna.'

Bethany's face darkened. Doug had half-expected her to cry out, scream at him to get out of her home, but she didn't. She took off her glasses, wiped the lenses on her blouse, then set them back on her face and glared at Doug. He couldn't read her expression.

'How did you find out?' she asked. Her voice was as cold as a headstone.

'I asked around,' Doug said, lying. He didn't want her to know the whole truth, wasn't sure she could handle it.

'So what do you want to know? Why I was working there? Simple answer, Mr McGregor: money. I needed the money. It wasn't easy being a student in Edinburgh, you know. There are a lot of toffs at Edinburgh uni, kids whose parents have more than enough money to make sure they can have the best of everything. My parents were well off, but they couldn't run to that, so I had to find a way to make my own cash.'

With her looks, it wasn't a surprise that Bethany went to work in a sauna. Clients would pay big money for her services. Especially one client.

He thought back to Tomlin's words. *We tracked him down to his local.* At first Doug had thought that was a pub. It didn't take long to realise what Tomlin really meant.

'You had a special client, didn't you, Bethany? Someone who would ask exclusively for you and paid a lot of money for the privilege.'

Anger flashed in Bethany's eyes. 'So what if I did?' she whispered. 'Look, Mr McGregor, I think you should be...'

Doug held up his hand. 'Please, just give me a minute. It's important. Your special customer, did he ever give you his name?'

Bethany stared at Doug for a minute, hand playing restlessly with a loose strand of hair that had fallen down at the side of her ear. 'He only ever called himself Roger,' she said slowly. 'Look, what is this all about?' She glanced across at the mantelpiece, a picture of her and a man – older-looking, tall, the first hints of a double chin being pulled tight by an open smile that narrowed his eyes to slits. 'My husband's only gone out to drop the kids at nursery, he'll be home soon. And I don't want him knowing about this, okay?'

Doug looked around the room. Nothing in here chimed with the impression of Bethany he had built up in his mind. There was no graduation picture on the wall, and draped over the ironing board was a cleaner's tunic in the washed-out blue you only ever see in hospitals. So she had never returned to study. So much for his idea that she had completed her degree, taken a job as a teacher.

The beige sofa was tired and old, sagging in the middle, decorated with felt-tip pen marks on the arms and various stains, no doubt from children spilling drinks. But the room itself was clean, the shelves were neatly ordered and there wasn't a spot of dust anywhere. Bethany obviously took great pride in taking care of her home and family, despite a lack of spare cash.

Next to the tunic on the large pile of ironing was a pair of overalls, their original colour masked by splotches and smears of paint. Doug glanced back at the photograph, noticed the man's hand that hung loosely over Bethany's shoulder looked rough and accustomed to hard work.

And the house, despite its careworn feel, was meticulously painted and wallpapered in a way he didn't think this family could have afforded. A painter, then. Or a tradesman, at least.

There was a family portrait on the wall above the electric fireplace – the kind taken in a professional studio. One of the children was just a babe-in-arms so it must have been taken at least a couple of years back. Bethany was still an attractive woman, but not the way she had once been. She looked genuinely happy in the photo. Holding a baby – in blue, so a boy, he assumed – and an angelic girl of around two or three maybe, with a mischievous grin and tight blonde curls.

Her husband with cropped hair, broad shoulders, confident grin, tattoo just peeking out from under the sleeve of his striped polo shirt. A military insignia?

Next to the fireplace was a widescreen TV and an eclectic DVD collection. *Peppa Pig* and *Fireman Sam* were scattered over the floor, but on the shelves was a disparate collection, from *Ross Kemp in Afghanistan* and *Top Gear* to box sets of the kind of costume drama his mother loved. Doug never understood the appeal.

He shrugged off his thoughts. Knew he was stalling for time. 'Is this the man who visited you?' he asked, handing over one of the photo print-outs he had brought with him.

Bethany took the print, stared at it. Her face went slack as the colour drained out of it. She gave one, hitching sob then dropped her head, her shoulders shaking as she tried to hold in the tears. She didn't give Doug an answer, but he didn't need one. He had known since Tomlin had told him about the man who McGinty had been searching for all those years ago. A bit under six-foot tall with the stocky body of a rugby player, jet black hair, wore glasses.

Richard Buchan.

McGinty would never say why he wanted that guy, Tomlin had told him. *Just that he needed to find him, had a score to settle.*

'Bethany, I'm sorry,' Doug said as gently as he could. He felt like shit for upsetting her like this. What right had he to drag all this up, anyway? It wasn't as if he was a police officer, wasn't as if anything she told him was going to put away the bad guy. No, it was all to satisfy his own bloated sense of curiosity, the hunger, the desire to get to the scoop first. It was, he knew, an addiction. For others it was alcohol, drugs, sex. For Doug, it was the story.

'Is there anything you can tell me about him?' he asked. 'Anything that he told you about himself, about what he did?'

Bethany looked up at him, eyes red rimmed with tears. 'Please, Mr McGregor, this is in my past. I'm happy now.' He believed her. She would have needed to move on, to rebuild her life. And the only way to do that, would be to forget completely. To blot out the horror she endured.

'Rory doesn't know anything about this.' She wiped a tear away. Closed her eyes, took a deep breath. 'I haven't thought about any of this for years,' she said, fixing him with a cold glare. 'I've tried not to remember it. Why should I now? For you?'

‘Because I think he’s still hurting people,’ Doug said quietly, still holding her gaze.

‘And you’re going to stop him?’ she asked, just enough emphasis on the ‘you’ to make him uncomfortable. ‘And who exactly are you?’

‘I’m a reporter with the…’

‘Yes,’ she cut him off, ‘I know *who* you are, Mr McGregor. But who are *you*?’ He’d barely started to say ‘Bethany, please, I…’ when she interrupted him again.

‘Let’s be clear, Mr McGregor. This is a very powerful, well-connected man. Why do you think I moved so far away? He might as well *be* the police for all the good they did me. This isn’t the kind of man to which shit sticks.’

It was the first time she had sworn and it threw him slightly. ‘He has people to take the shit for him. Do his dirty work. And he doesn’t take kindly to people like me getting too uppity. I learned that to my cost, Mr McGregor, and I’m not prepared to pay any more. Just why *are* you here and what do you want from me?’

She sat very still, not flinching, her steady eyes still fixed on his. He felt they were drilling into him. Accusing. And then, slowly, realisation spread across her face.

‘You’re not really interested in him,’ she said, brandishing the photo. ‘This is about… about him, isn’t it?’

Doug nodded slowly.

‘Yes, I think it’s linked to who attacked you,’ he said. He couldn’t bring himself to speak Derek’s name in front of her. ‘I think you might have been targeted because of the man in that photograph.’

‘But why?’ Bethany cried, tears streaming down her cheeks, her self-control lost again.

‘I don’t know,’ Doug said, hating how hollow the words sounded. ‘Is there anything you can tell me about Buc… about Roger? Anything that might help me understand?’

‘Nuh… no, I don’t think so,’ Bethany said, wiping at her eyes angrily. 'He was always a perfect gentleman. Came in, asked for me, tipped generously when he left.'

Doug felt heat rise in his cheeks. 'And there was nothing... odd… about what he asked for when he visited?'

Bethany's head snapped up, defiance behind the tears.

'There was an incident.' She paused again, looking over his shoulder, into the past.

Doug waited. Any good interviewer knew you gave people space and time if you wanted to hear what they had to say.

She sucked in her breath and diverted her gaze to a spot on the floor to his right. She was ready to tell him, but shame wouldn't allow her to look him in the eye.

'Like many powerful men, when he liked to relax, he liked to let go of responsibility. Of power, of control. To pass it on to someone else. There were other girls who specialised in that. But not me. That wasn't my thing. But that's what he wanted and he didn't want them. He wanted me. And he was prepared to pay. A lot. So I gave it a go. It began with a playful spank, a bit of ordering around. But it got out of hand.'

Again she paused, her eyes firmly fixed on the past now. Barely aware that Doug was still in the room with her.

'He asked for more, wanted to be tied up, humiliated. I borrowed some gear from the other girls, a gag, whip, manacles. I started to improvise and that's where… it started to go wrong.

'I… well, let's just say I couldn't hear the safety word… the gag, you see… so I didn't know. I thought… Well, anyway. I thought wrong, didn't I?'

She finally looked Doug in the eye and there was a wild-eyed fear about her as she recalled Buchan's reaction.

'He was furious. Said I'd made a grave mistake. That I'd regret it. How was I to know?' she implored Doug. But he had no answer for her.

'He said I'd pay for it. But I never saw him again. But that was it for me. I quit the sauna the next night, and then… then…'

She trailed off, eyes dropping again. She didn't say anything else. Didn't need to. Doug know what came next. All too well.

But what did it all mean? So Buchan liked the saunas, got a bit more than he bargained for one night when he asked to be tied up. Was McGinty blackmailing Buchan, not Katherine, because he knew about his dirty little secret. From what Susie had said, Katherine didn't seem close enough to her father to pay off a blackmailer for him, but it was possible.

It was…

He stood up. He was still missing something. He could feel it. But he wouldn't find it here. Not in a room with a woman who he had forced to revisit her worst nightmare.

'Bethany…' He paused, not sure what to say next. 'Thank you. I…'

Bethany stared up at him, tears glistening behind her glasses. 'Thank you?' she whispered. 'I don't want your thanks, Mr McGregor. I want this done. If you think that bastard is doing something he shouldn't be, I want you to get him for me. I want you to make him pay. You owe me that much, at least. Don't you?'

Doug nodded. Headed for the door. He wanted, needed, to get out of here. Now.

He waited as she undid the door latch, swung the door open onto a day that seemed too bright. He stepped out, turned to say goodbye. Saw a frown he knew from countless other interviews.

'What?' he asked as gently as he could. 'Bethany, if there's something else. Anything…'

'It's nothing,' she said, shaking her head. 'It's just Buchan. When the kinky stuff started, he always made me wear a wig. A blonde one. And he always called me Katie. But there's nothing really weird in that, is there?'

47

As usual, the curtains were drawn tight at the McGintys' home. Susie walked up the path briskly, keen to get this out of the way. After talking with Allan, she was convinced Derek had been in touch with his parents, but if they hadn't come forward so far, she didn't think there was anything she could say to change their minds and get them to talk now. But then, what parent would give up their child to the police?

The moment she left the McGintys she was going to find Richard Buchan and have a talk with him about Charlie Morris. He could hide behind meetings and parliamentary business if he wanted, Susie didn't care. She would ask her questions in front of the First Minister if she had to.

Sam McGinty opened the door when she rang the bell, keeping the chain on. The strain of everything that had happened was getting to him, she thought. His eyes had the dark, twitchy look of a man who hadn't sleep for weeks and his skin was a sickly white that glistened with sour sweat. When he spoke, his voice trembled.

'Yes?'

Susie showed her warrant card. 'Mr McGinty? I'm DS Susie Drummond. I was wondering if I could have a quick word with you about your son?

'No, not today,' McGinty said, his words coming in quick,

clipped barks. 'My… ah, my wife isn't well. Tomorrow, come back tomorrow.' He began to shut the door.

Susie put her hand out, stopping him from shutting the door fully. 'Look, Mr McGinty,' she said, aiming for her best we're-all-friends tone. 'I'm sorry. I realise this has been quite an ordeal for you and your wife, but this is important. I'll be as brief as I can, promise.'

'Go *away*!' McGinty hissed, slamming the door. Susie staggered back, then strode forward and banged on the door with her fist. Fuck this. No one slammed a door in her face.

'Mr McGinty,' she shouted, 'open the door, sir. I have to talk to you. Now. If you don't talk to me, I can charge you with obstructing a police officer. Is that what you want? To put your wife through that?' It was a cheap shot but she was sick of being given the run-around.

The door swung open. Sam McGinty stood there, shoulders hunched. His eyes found Susie's and glared into them desperately. Susie stepped into the hall. The door slammed shut behind her. But how could that be if Sam was…?

There was a sickening crack as Charlie pistol-whipped her from behind, blood exploding from the wound and gushing down her neck and back. Susie fell forward, her knees unlocking from the explosive pain and confusion. She hit the floor heavily, heard herself grunt as the air was driven from her lungs. Tried to get up, tried to speak. Couldn't. Too much effort, anyway. The world was getting dark. From far away, she heard Sam McGinty cry out, first when she was hit, then when he was folded over by a vicious punch. She was dimly aware of being flipped over, and then a nightmare leered down at her. A nightmare with a blue-green face, jagged teeth. A monster pointing a gun between her eyes.

A monster named Charlie Morris.

• • •

Doug arrived back in Edinburgh at just after 11am, having paid a taxi driver a stupid amount of money to get him back to East Midlands Airport as soon as possible and then persuading the desk clerks in the terminal to change his return ticket for the next available flight.

Striding, almost running, back to the car, he tried Susie's number. Still diverting to answer machine. Shit. He hung up, tried her at Gayfield and was told she was out. The officer taking the call, who Doug could have sworn was that officious little prick Eddie King, asked if he wanted to leave a message. Doug declined.

He drove back to the *Tribune* offices, ready to fill Walter and Greig in on what he had found out. As Bethany wouldn't be named officially, he wasn't sure how much they could print yet, but he was damned if he was going to let Buchan stay quiet and get away with everything he had done. Again.

He got to the newsroom, slightly out of breath from bounding up the stairs to the editorial floor three at a time, and headed for Walter. He was expecting to have to talk Walter out of giving him a bollocking for just flying down to England at the drop of a hat, but he thought his findings would grant him a stay of execution.

But when Walter saw him, he merely nodded, his face a carefully composed mask of calm. He held a hand up as Doug opened his mouth to speak, calming him and pointing to his desk.

'You got another package,' he said, making sure Doug understood. Walter couldn't remember a time when he had seen McGregor so wound up. 'It arrived this morning.'

Walter said something else, but Doug didn't hear it. It felt as though he floated to his desk, his legs were so numb.

It was a small jiffy bag, about A4-size. Doug sat in his chair heavily, ripped it open. It felt as though everyone in the newsroom was watching him. He pulled the contents of the bag out, which were accompanied by a note. It was one line, but it spoke volumes to Doug. '*This is what Lizzie Renwick died for*,' it read.

Doug turned his attention back to the contents of the bag. After a few moments, he understood. In journalism, he had been taught that a story should always answer six basic questions: who, what, when, where, how and, most importantly, why. He knew all of it now. It was obvious, really. He should have seen it sooner. The first phone call had been the key. And he would have seen it sooner, if he hadn't been so caught up with his obsession in finding Derek McGinty.

• • •

Susie came round slowly, a monstrous, grinding pain pounding in her head in time with her pulse. She looked round, her neck feeling stiff and brittle and took in her surroundings. Moving her eyes was agony.

She was slumped on the living room couch, Sam and Rita McGinty beside her. She tried to move her hands to her head, realised they were bound tight behind her. She tried to move her legs, found they were also tied at the ankles. Shit, what…?

'Ah, so you're awake,' Charlie Morris said as he turned from the window and looked at her. 'About fucking time, too.'

'Morris,' Susie said. Her voice sounded like a stranger's to her ringing ears. 'Don't do this, I know that…'

'SHUT UP!' Charlie bellowed, levelling the gun at Susie's face. She whimpered, screwed here eyes shut and winced away. She didn't want to die.

'That's better,' he said, his voice bubbling with amusement at her terror. 'This is all your own fault, you know. If you'd done what old Sam there had asked and just left like a good little pig, you wouldn't be here right now.'

Susie hitched in her breath, biting back the scream that was clawing at the back of her throat. She refused to give this bastard the satisfaction. 'Charlie,' she said slowly, 'I know about Buchan. If you just talk to me, I…'

The sound of a door rattling cut her off. Charlie's head whipped towards the kitchen as he smiled his ruined smile. He stalked towards the kitchen, paused and turned round. 'Any of you peep and I'll blow his fucking head off,' he whispered.

Rita McGinty squirmed beside Susie, trying to bite back her sobs. 'Shh,' Sam said softly. 'Shh. It'll be alright, love.'

From the kitchen, Susie heard the back door opening. And then Charlie's voice again, more smug than ever. 'Ah, Derek. Nice of you to come. Come on in. Now the party can really get started.'

• • •

Doug had the accelerator to the floor all the way to Stockbridge, ignoring speed limits and, where possible, traffic lights. He screeched to a halt outside the Buchans' home, drawing a harsh look from the Pc stationed at the front door. He looked about ten years old to Doug, his uniform about a size too big for him.

'Morning, sir,' the Pc said as Doug walked up to him. 'You looking to break a speed record or just lose your licence?'

Doug flashed a smile he hoped was sheepish. 'Sorry, running late for a meeting with Mr Buchan.'

'And you are…?'

'Doug,' he replied, offering the officer a hand. He didn't take it. 'I'm one of Mr Buchan's assistants. I've got to deliver these,' he lifted a bundle of papers and folders for the Pc to see, 'to him for a briefing. But you know how Edinburgh traffic is, I'm running late.'

The Pc looked him over, expression set; the wee boy playing polisman. 'Go on, then,' he said, 'but lay off the loud pedal the next time, okay? That's not a toy car you've got there.'

Doug bowed his head in thanks and hurried for the front door. When Buchan answered it, Doug felt a wave of rage so strong it was almost uncontrollable.

'Who the hell are you?' Buchan hissed. His tie was yanked down, and Doug thought he caught a whiff of whisky on his breath. His hair, so perfect in all the press shots Doug had seen, was unkempt, as though raked with his fingers.

'Doug McGregor.'

He saw recognition crawl over Buchan's face, disgust and outrage twisting his mouth into a savage sneer. 'I suggest you don't make a scene, Dick, unless of course you want me to show this', he lifted the package from the folders and papers, 'to that nice policeman there.'

Buchan's eyes flicked between Doug and what he was carrying, torn. Could he grab it before Doug had time to pull away, could he explain the commotion to the policeman?

No.

'Come in,' he said, swinging the door wide. He watched Doug as he stepped into the house, eyes burning with hate. Doug didn't mind. The feeling was mutual.

Buchan moved across the living room to a large cabinet, tried to block Doug's view of the whisky with his back as he cleared a glass away. Took a moment to smooth his hair, straighten his tie. To this man, image, control, was everything. But Doug saw through the façade now, knew the real man that lurked beneath the surface.

He was a worse monster than McGinty ever was.

'So,' Buchan said, 'what do you want?'

'Nothing, really,' he said. 'Just to tell you that I know. At first, I couldn't figure it out – why you would set a thug on me just for finding out about Katherine's drug problem? Seemed like a bit of an overreaction. After all, the public loves a good sob story. Spin that the right way, you've got a guaranteed vote winner. So it didn't add up, until I looked a little deeper, and found out about your… arrangement… with Bethany Miller.'

From the corridor, Doug thought he heard soft footsteps coming down the stairs. Probably just the old floorboards in the house settling.

Buchan's eyes were chips of ice behind his glasses. 'Just get to the point, Mr McGregor. I'm sure we could come to a mutually beneficial arrangement.'

Doug laughed. He couldn't help it. 'Mutually beneficial? Oh, you mean like the one you had with Katherine.' He watched Buchan's eyes go wide. Tried not to enjoy it too much. 'Oh yes, I know about it all, Dick, it's all right here.' He slid a small A5-sized book from the folder and thumbed through the pages.

'Oh yes, Katherine kept a diary of what you did to her. From the first time you assaulted her when she was twelve. Every single time.' Doug's voice was hoarse with rage now.

'How DARE you!' Buchan roared, his face contorted into an almost feral snarl. 'She was my daughter, I would never….'

'Forget the act, Dick,' Doug said. 'It's all in there. But it wasn't about sex for you, was it? Never was. That's why you went to Bethany when Katherine couldn't take any more and ran away. Your money, your say, your humiliation. Tell me, Dick, is that what it was? The control? The power?'

He paused, heard Bethany's voice whisper in his ear. *You get him for me.* Took a deep breath, drove the knife home.

'Is that why you had Bethany raped after she took things too far? To show her who was boss? Who was in charge?'

Buchan's face flushed. A muscle twitched in his jaw, as though he was chewing on something bitter. Maybe he was.

Buchan opened his mouth to speak, took a step forward, hands bunched into fists. As he did, the door creaked open and a haggard-looking woman with lank hair and dead eyes shuffled into the room.

'Richard,' she said, her voice as dead as her eyes. 'I heard voices, what…?'

'Get out, Linda,' Buchan hissed, voice so full of rage that his wife flinched away from him. 'Can't you see I'm busy here?'

'Oh, don't worry about it,' Doug said, forcing his eyes from Buchan's clenched fists. 'We're done, Dick. I'll assume you won't want to make an official comment?'

With a roar, Buchan lashed out, grabbing for the folder and the diary. Doug span away, but Buchan knocked his arm up, the folder and papers spraying into the air. Doug lunged forward for them, was grabbed by Buchan and slammed against the wall, making his wounded side scream in protest. Was vaguely aware of Linda Buchan falling to her knees where the folder and diary had landed.

Don't let her see them, Doug thought. *Oh please, Jesus, don't let her see…*

'You bastard,' Buchan whispered, his breath sour in Doug's face. 'Who do you think you are to…?'

'Let me go, you sick fuck,' Doug bellowed, thrashing against Buchan's grip. No use, the bastard was strong, fuelled by rage.

'You little shit,' Buchan hissed, spittle peppering Doug's face. 'I'm going to…'

A scream filled the room and Buchan suddenly lurched forward, pinning Doug to the wall. The he fell to the side, hands falling from Doug's shirt as his wife's hands snaked around his neck, fingers sinking into his cheeks.

'BASTARD!' she shrieked, clawing and biting at him. 'You bastard! She was your daughter, your *daughter,* and you raped her. Abused her and drove her to drugs. Bastard!'

Doug lunged for Linda, pulling her off Buchan with all his strength. She lashed out wildly, swinging her arms back and grabbing his head. Doug roared as he felt hair being ripped from his scalp, and threw Linda clear. She landed heavily and slid across the polished wood floor.

Buchan staggered to his feet, using the back of his hand to wipe away the blood gushing from the welts his wife had clawed into his face. He charged into Doug, catching him off balance and driving him to the ground, where he landed on top of him.

'CUNT!' he bawled into Doug's face. 'I'll kill you!' He rocked back and punched Doug in the face as hard as he could. Doug's head whipped to the side with the impact. His vision blurred, then doubled. His ears rang. Blindly, he flailed out with his hands and grabbed Buchan's head, driving his fingers into his eyes.

Buchan screeched and fell back. Doug rolled to the side, gasping for breath. Dimly, he could hear the policeman battering at the door, demanding to be let in.

Just kick it down, you stupid little shit, Doug thought as he backed away. Buchan was on his feet again now, wielding a poker from the fireplace. He raised it over his head, eyes burning into Doug's as he braced himself to bring it down.

Somewhere there was the sound of breaking glass. Maybe the Pc had decided to break in, after all. Too late. Buchan took a step forward.

Doug looked around desperately for a way out, his breath great gasping gulps, searching for something, anything, he could use as a defence, but there was nothing; it was over…

Buchan screamed and staggered backwards, blood spraying from his mouth. The poker dropped to the floor with a heavy clang as he clawed for his back. He crashed into the display cabinet, the crystal inside shattering musically under his weight as wicked shards of the glass dug into his face and arms.

Doug looked around, saw Linda Buchan standing there, her husband's blood plastering her blouse to her body. She looked down at the jagged shards of the whisky bottle in her bloodied hands, as if reminding herself it was there. Glanced over at Doug and then back at her husband, who was whimpering like a beaten dog, legs prodding out of the ruined cabinet at odd angles. She dropped the bottle to the floor, stared at it for a moment, then fell to her hands and knees, scrambling over the shards of glass. Doug could never decide if she was looking for something to finish her husband off, or to use on herself. He managed to find his feet and leapt forward, pushing her clear of the glass. She wailed and lashed out at him, beating at his chest with her small, bloodied fists.

He could feel her hot tears soak into his shirt. Slowly, the screams gave way to bitter, body-wrenching sobs. Doug lay on the ground in a pool of blood and shattered glass, rocking her gently, holding her face tightly to his chest. She had seen Katherine's diary. Learned the truth. That was enough. He didn't want her to see the pictures that were scattered across the floor. The pictures of a young woman tied to a bed, naked, humiliated. Broken. The pictures Buchan had insisted McGinty take of the night he raped Bethany Miller.

He closed his eyes tightly, told himself he wasn't going to cry. Lost the battle long before the ten-year-old policeman charged into the room.

48

Charlie led Derek into the living room, gun trained on his back. When Derek looked to his left, saw his parents tied up on the couch beside Susie, he whirled on Charlie. 'You fuck!' he spat. 'Let them go, they're just…'

Charlie drove a fist into Derek's stomach, doubling him over. He gasped and fell to his knees, Charlie following up with a vicious boot to the face. Susie felt bile scald the back of her throat as she heard bone crunch when Charlie kicked Derek in the face again.

'Leave him alone!' Rita McGinty shrieked. 'Just leave him alone, you…'

Charlie pushed the gun into Rita's face. 'Shut the fuck up, you stupid old bitch,' he sneered. 'I'll get back to you in a minute, but first…' He turned back to Derek, swung back his foot and drove it into his stomach. Derek rolled over and wretched, coughing as he fought for breath.

'You think you can just leave me lying in the street?' Charlie yelled. 'Nobody does that, you bastard. Nobody!' He kicked Derek one final time then leant forward, levelling the gun at his head. Rita screamed again as Charlie's finger tightened on the trigger. Susie felt adrenalin sear through her veins. If she was going to do something, it had to be now. She had to…

Before Susie could move, Sam McGinty drove himself forward, using his head as a battering ram on Charlie's side. Charlie staggered, the roar of the gun deafening in the small room as Sam fell on top of him.

Susie lunged forward, trying to keep her balance. She lashed out as hard as she could, shoulder-barging the hand that held the gun. Charlie bellowed in frustrated rage and kicked out, driving Sam aside and thudding him into Susie. She staggered, hit the corner of the coffee table and crashed into it, the table collapsing like cheap kindling under her.

Charlie staggered to his feet, loomed over her. 'You fucking bitch. You fucking little CUNT! I'm going to…'

Susie drove her feet up as hard as she could into Charlie's crotch. He fell backwards, bouncing off the fireplace and crumpling to the floor. Susie wriggled out of the ruin of the table, moving as fast as she could. She got to her feet, lurched over towards Charlie, desperate to get to the gun before he could, could…

She was grabbed from behind and hurled back onto the couch. Looked up and saw Derek towering over Charlie like an angry, bloodied god. He kicked out, stamping down onto Charlie's hand, the sound of bones snapping rising above the scream. He bent over and scooped up the gun, seemed to study it for a moment as though it were a toy he had never seen before, then dropped to his knees and rammed the gun into Charlie's mouth.

'How's that, Charlie?' he whispered. 'You like that? Not as good as terrifying my folks, but not bad, huh?' His arms trembled with rage. 'It was him, wasn't it, Charlie? He sent you, Buchan.'

Charlie nodded slowly. Tears were leaking from his huge, terrified eyes.

Derek nodded, satisfied. 'I knew it. That fucking bastard. Don't worry though, Charlie, I'll give him your regards with this.' He pushed the gun forward slightly, smiled as a dark patch spread across Charlie's crotch.

'Bye, Charlie,' he said, turning his head away, preparing for the blast.

'Derek.' The voice was so calm and controlled, it took Susie a moment to recognise it as Rita's. 'Derek, that's enough, son. Put it down, please.'

Derek spun, confusion in his eyes. 'Mum, I...'

'No, Derek, enough. Put the gun down, son.'

Derek looked back at Charlie then to Rita. After what seemed an eternity, he leant away, dropping the gun onto the floor and pushing it towards Susie.

Rita McGinty smiled. She was crying again, but, to Susie, her tears seemed different. Clearer. Derek got up and untied his parents, gave them rough hugs before he did. Maybe it was the only way he thought he could.

'You're a copper, aren't you?' he asked Susie as he stood in front of her.

'Yeah,' she said, struggling to keep her voice even. 'And I'll tell people what you did here, how you helped me stop Charlie. But I need to ask you a few questions, Derek. You seem to be the man with a lot of answers.'

Derek snorted. 'Nah, I don't think I'll stick around for that,' he said, checking Susie was still securely tied before heading for the back door.

Sam stood up, placed a hand on his son's shoulder. 'No more running, son,' he said.

Derek whirled round. 'Dad, I can't. After everything that's happened, everything I did, there's nothing here.'

'There's us,' Sam said. 'I'm not saying what you did was right, son, but at least tell us why you did it. Make us understand why you thought it was the right thing to do.'

And there it was. Finally. That one, simple question. Why, Derek?

Why?

His eyes flitted between his father and Susie. Stay or go? Run or face the past? He sighed finally, shoulders sagging. The illusion of the angry god was gone, replaced by a confused and lost man.

He walked over to Susie. 'You better fucking tell them what I did,' he said and then untied her.

She nodded her thanks, picked up the gun and ejected the clip. Then she reached for her phone to call everything in. She was very careful. No one saw her hands shake.

49

It was just after 10pm when Susie walked into the pub, eyes roaming across the room for Doug. She saw him sitting at a corner booth, pint of Guinness in front of him, a glass she knew was a double vodka and lemonade sitting opposite, waiting for her.

She took her seat, not saying a word but merely reaching for her drink. She hoped it would dampen the throbbing in the back of her head, a little memento of her encounter with Charlie Morris.

She looked tired, Doug thought, but that was no surprise. Being held at gunpoint by a psychopath could do that to you.

'You look like shit, Doug,' she said, setting her drink back down on the table.

Doug laughed, touched the growing bruise on his cheek. His face felt like it did when the dentist gave him anaesthetic before a filling; numb and foreign, full of strange contours and alien curves. He planned to be drunk long before the numbness wore off.

'So,' he said slowly, 'how did it go?'

Susie shook her head. She had spent the last ten hours being poked and prodded by doctors, filling out reports, writing up statements and, of course, being interviewed by fellow officers about what had happened at the McGintys' home.

In the films, the cops beat up the bad guys and went home.

In reality, they went to do paperwork, especially when a gun was involved.

'Well, we got what we were looking for,' she said. 'Morris admitted he was the man that beat you up outside your flat. Turns out he had a wee scrote named Mark Kirk following you for quite some time; finding out what you were doing, where you were going, who you were with.' Her eyes fell on Doug, making sure he understood what she had just said.

'You mean like me and you?' He paused, took another drink of Guinness. 'Shit. I take it Burns found out?'

Susie nodded. 'Oh yes. Hauled me into his office, gave me a real bollocking about not going to the press, jeopardising an investigation, not going through proper procedures, that sort of thing.'

'He going to report you to the Chief Superintendent?'

'Actually, no,' Susie said, a small smile at the corners of her mouth. 'He wanted to, but said he refused to give Buchan the satisfaction of seeing the Chief jump through hoops and claim a scalp.'

'What about Buchan?' Doug asked, remembering the way he had loomed over him with the poker. He shivered. 'He regained consciousness yet?'

'No, he's still at the Infirmary. Most of his wounds were superficial, but his wife did a fair bit of damage when she stabbed him in the back.' She watched Doug's face go pale, his eyes fall to his pint. 'She's going to be okay, Doug. Really. They've got her sedated at the moment, and she's going to be evaluated in a couple of days. If there's a way to help her, the doctors will.'

Doug wasn't so sure. He remembered the desperation on Linda Buchan's face as she scrambled around the floor looking for a shard of glass, the howl of frustration when he stopped her. He wondered if he had done the right thing.

'...what the fiscal says.'

Doug looked up from his glass, Susie's voice dragging him from his thoughts. 'I'm sorry, what?'

Susie smiled slightly. 'I said, we'll have to see what the fiscal says about the case against Buchan. We've got him for trying to kill you, and of course there's what's in the diary, but the rest of it is all fairly circumstantial.'

Doug gave a frustrated grunt. She was right. According to what he had managed to find out, there had been no specific forensic evidence linking Buchan to Lizzie Renwick's murder. Anything that was found, such as clothing fibres or fingerprints, could be explained away by any half-decent lawyer easily. After all, it had been his daughter's gallery, and what father didn't visit his daughter?

But he had done it, Doug was sure he had. He had gone to the gallery, thinking Lizzie had the diary and the pictures of Bethany, tortured her to try and find them and, when she had told him she didn't know where they were, he had killed her. He was capable of it, Doug had seen that much in Buchan's eyes when he loomed over him with the poker. No fear, no doubt, no hesitation; only hatred and intent.

Doug had discovered his secret and, as a result, had to die. Lizzie would have been no different to him. Just another threat to his reputation and what was left of his career.

According to Katherine's diary, her father had begun abusing her when she was twelve. She had written about her confusion as to why 'Daddy wanted to touch me in his secret way today' and how he had taught her 'new ways to show that she loved him.' The diary was a catalogue of abuse stretching over the years, building to the sickeningly inevitable rape.

'*It hurt so much*,' she wrote. Doug couldn't be sure, but he thought he could see tear stains on the page. '*He was on top of me, pinning me down, panting in my ear like a bull. I tried to tell him to stop, tried to push him away, but he was too strong, forcing it into me again and again and again. When it was over, he collapsed on top of me and burst into tears, telling me how sorry he was, how much he loved me. I hate him.*'

Shortly after that, she began to head out at the weekends, finding drugs and booze were an easy way to blot out the horrors she endured at home. The horrors she was too ashamed and afraid to share with her mother. Reading the diary revealed she lasted for a year in a drug-addled haze before, after one attack had turned violent, with Katherine left bleeding and bruised after Buchan had tried to bugger her, she had fled.

Not long after, she ran into Derek at a nightclub. What attracted him to her? Doug wondered. Her dependence, her vulnerability? Whatever it was, they had developed a bond, began a relationship. And, somewhere along the way, she had told him about what her father had done to her.

'You want another drink?' Susie asked, draining the last of her vodka and heading for the bar. Doug nodded and she returned a few moments later with a fresh pint for him and another vodka – a double – for herself.

'So, does it explain what happened when she met McGinty?' Susie asked. She knew Doug had read the diary, but she hadn't been able to get to it herself yet. And, with McGinty in hospital for observation after the beating Charlie had given him, she hadn't been able to get his side of the story, either. For that, she would have to rely on Doug.

Doug nodded. 'Yeah, from what the diary says, after she overdosed, she tried to sort herself out. She says that she and Derek were spending more and more time together, and she wanted to get herself off heroin. But she couldn't do that on her own, so she went to her dad and demanded money for a rehab programme.'

He laughed sadly. 'The poor bitch. After everything she went through, to have to go back to him and ask for help to kick a habit he drove her to. But he helped her all right, gave her the cash, checked her into the programme in Niddrie and put her under an assumed name then abandoned her. All to protect his precious career.'

'But how does Bethany Miller fit into all this?' Susie asked. 'And how did you find out about her link to Buchan?'

Doug explained what Tomlin had told him about McGinty's hunt for a man who had hurt Katherine, how he had traced that man to the Shore Thing Sauna in Leith. He paused when Susie's mouth fell open.

'What?'

'Something the woman who heard Linda Buchan and McGinty arguing said. She said she heard McGinty say "off the leash", but thought she could have misheard it. I bet it was "off to Leith".'

'It's possible,' Doug said. 'He must have told her exactly what Buchan had done to Katherine, and how, when she ran away, he found other ways to get his… thrills.' Bethany's words: *He always made me wear a wig. A blonde one. And he always called me Katie. But there's nothing too weird in that, is there?*

'And that's when it all went wrong?' Susie asked. 'When he started to get kinky with Bethany?'

'Yeah,' Doug nodded, taking a gulp of his pint to kill the pain. He felt a twist of discomfort talking about this. He had promised to keep Bethany's name out of it. But after everything, Susie deserved to know it all. And besides, he knew she would keep quiet once she understood.

'So, what happened?' she asked, rubbing a hand across her forehead as though trying to massage away the frustration of not knowing what Doug did.

'Bethany wouldn't tell me the details, but you can probably guess. She had Buchan tied up one night, it all got a little out of hand. He lashed out, promised he'd make her pay, then…' He shook his head as the thought occurred to him.

Jesus, it really was all about control.

'Then,' Susie said, fingers subconsciously drumming Morse Code for frustration on her glass, 'he gets McGinty to attack Bethany. But why? And how?'

'Katherine,' Doug said simply. The thoughts were coming too fast now. If he wanted to outrun them, he would have to switch to whisky soon. Not the worst idea.

He glanced at Susie, saw the confusion on her face.

'It's all in Katherine's diary,' he said, remembering what he had read. Wished he couldn't, knew he always would.

I don't know how to write this. What happened this morning. It still doesn't feel true. I wish it wasn't. Not any of it. Perhaps it isn't. Perhaps I've gone mad. But that's just wishful thinking. But I have to write it down. Record it. Because if I don't, I'll begin to doubt all of it. Because I want to – more than anything in the world. To believe this isn't true.

I'm sitting here, pen in hand, and I feel numb. Like the world has been picked up, shaken and put back down again. But now everything's in the wrong place.

I loved him so much. I love him. But do I? I don't know how I feel.

It was just after 9, I know because I was running late for work. I opened the door and he was just standing there. I've never understood when people say someone looks like death warmed up, but I did after seeing Derek.

He barely said a word, looked in shock. I was so startled to see him I didn't say anything for a few seconds so we just stood there saying nothing, looking at each other. I felt my heart skip. His look was so dark I knew we were over. That he was going to end it. End us.

I was the first to speak, I don't remember what I said, something breezy probably. But I wasn't going to let him in. Not if he was going to end it. He could bloody stand on the step and see if I cared. But when he spoke his voice sounded so empty and strange that I agreed to let him in.

He sat on the couch for a while, like a statue. Just staring at his hands. Then he asked if he could take a shower.

I remember feeling irritated but his eyes turned on me and there was a look I hadn't seen before and for the first time I felt afraid. But I dismissed that idea. Foolish, I thought. This is Derek. Lovely sweet devoted Derek.

'I've done something...' he said and held my gaze for the first time. There was something in his voice that made me believe him. But what he told me was so sickening I still can't believe it. How could he? Derek, so gentle and loving, considerate when we were together. How could he do something so... so violent, so degrading to another human being? Something so like my father? I felt a creeping over my skin that I didn't actually know this person. This man who I thought I loved. He explained to me in great detail. What he had done to that poor girl. Like I was his priest hearing his confession. I wanted him to stop. Begged him to stop. Tell me it's not true I begged. Please just stop.

But he didn't. Not even when I couldn't breathe through the tears. He kept going. How he'd hurt her. How he'd humiliated her. And all for me?! How could he blame me for this? My fault.

Was it? Had I driven Daddy to it, then Derek? I just don't know anymore. He collapsed onto his knees at my feet. Wouldn't take his eyes from mine. Begged for forgiveness. Begged for me to understand. To know I loved him. What could I give him? A dozen Hail Mary's?

I needed to get away from him. I went to the bathroom to wash my face. And I saw my reflection. How could he love me? How could anyone love me? Red, blotchy. I tried to calm my skin. To look normal again. But there would be no normal again. And suddenly felt a wave of relief. He wasn't breaking up with me, he DID still love me.

'I had to do it, don't you see?' he said. 'Tommy said that if I didn't do this, didn't... take the pictures, they'd find you. Hurt you. And I couldn't bear that, Katie. I just couldn't.'

Doug shook his head. Buchan must have loved it. Get the man who was hunting him to attack the prostitute who humiliated him and take the pictures to prove it. He used people like chess pieces.

Susie drained her glass, crunched hard on the ice. 'So she forgives him? But they know there's no way he can run, so she keeps the pictures as what? Insurance?'

'Maybe,' Doug said. 'Or maybe they were trying to blackmail Buchan all along. She mentions in the diary that they wanted to make a life together. Maybe that's what they were asking Buchan for. The money for the pictures. Remember what Lizzie heard her say on the phone? "It's the price we agreed?"'

'Jesus,' Susie said. 'So that's why he hired Charlie to track Derek down as soon as he resurfaced. But how the hell did he even know how to get in touch with someone like Charlie, anyway?'

'The saunas,' Doug replied, remembering what Tomlin had told him about Charlie and Derek working together. 'Charlie must have recognised him as someone with money, Buchan must have recognised him as someone he could use. Especially when it came to satisfying some of his... requests.'

'What I don't get though is why wait until Katherine was dead? Why not try to kill him sooner?'

Doug rubbed at his eyes. They felt grainy with exhaustion. 'Control,' he muttered, more to himself than Susie. 'With Katherine alive, Buchan knew he had a way to keep Derek at bay, string them both along and pretend to pay for their silence. But the moment Katherine died, Buchan knew Derek had nothing left to lose, that he would be coming to him for money, or worse.'

'But why did she die, then?' Susie asked, feeling like she was on the wrong page. She hated playing catch-up. 'Why, if she was about to disappear with the man she loved, did she end up at the bottom of the Scott Monument?'

'To let Derek be free,' Doug said, feeling tears behind his eyes. What a fucking mess. 'It's all in the diary. She loved Derek. She really did. But this man made himself a rapist for her, a monster, an animal. He basically became her father. And she knew that he – they – would never be free of Buchan's influence. So the only way to escape for both of them was to take away the control he had over them. It's the last line in her diary: "*This is my choice. Not my father's, not Derek's. Mine. Derek always told me to have faith. Believe. And I do. I believe he's a good man. And I have faith that he will do the right thing.*"'

'Jesus Christ,' Susie whispered. What would it be like, knowing death was your only option, that it was better than the life you had endured? 'If Lizzie didn't have the diary, then who did? Who sent it, and the photo, to you?'

'McGinty,' Doug said simply. 'Think about it, whatever we might think of him, he's not stupid. He knows that the moment Katherine is dead, Buchan has no reason to keep him alive. So fuck it, why not try to hurt the bastard? But no one is going to believe him if he just rings up and tells his story. No, he needs someone to figure it out for themselves, find the truth on their own. With Bethany, he already showed that he could use people like chess pieces to get what he wanted. So he decided to use me to get at Buchan.'

'You sure it was him?'

'Check when you speak to him, but yeah, it was him,' Doug said. 'I should have seen it when he first called me. It was the way he spoke, what he said. "Derek McGinty pushed Katherine Buchan to her death." Not Derek killed Katherine, but pushed her. He blamed himself for putting her in a position where she thought the only way out was to kill herself. And how would she feel, knowing he raped another woman for her? So he phoned me and put me onto his trail, giving me a juicy little titbit to make sure I was interested.'

'You mean the photo?'

'Yeah,' Doug said. 'A shot like that, Terry says it was most probably taken on a timer from his camera.'

They sat for a moment, alone with their thoughts, silence hanging between them. Doug was turning it over in his mind, how easily he had been played and manipulated by McGinty. And something occurred to him. Being played. Was that it? He thought back to how easily Mike Granger had let him in to the Halfway House, how he was always happy to answer questions. Mike Granger, who, he had once told Doug, moved to Prestonview after working in Edinburgh pubs where 'he saw some crazy shit'.

Doug thought he was using Mike, but was it the other way round? Was Mike another piece of the puzzle? Did he know Charlie – or Croal or Tomlin? Had he been using Doug the entire time to get to Derek?

A quick call to Rab would answer the question. But later. Not now. He glanced over at Susie.

'Right, get your jacket,' Doug said, draining his pint and standing.

Susie's mind was filled with Charlie's gun, the impotent terror she felt when he pointed it at her face, the sound it made when it went off, the feel of it when it was smashed over the back of her head. She had thought she was going to die, that…

She blinked back the tears that had been welling in her eyes. 'Wh… where are we going?'

'My place,' Doug said, not taking his eyes off her, hoping she hadn't misread what he'd said. Her eyes told him she had. 'Look, we've both had an utterly shit day. If you're like me, you've seen a few things that you probably don't want to sleep with in your head. So, we're going to my place. We'll watch a crappy film, get shitfaced and talk until we're ready to sleep.' He paused, added: 'And no arguments, you get the couch. I insist.'

Susie laughed. It hurt her head, but it felt good anyway. 'Fair enough,' she said. 'But how about my place instead? I've seen your TV. I've got enough of a headache as it is without trying to watch a film on it.'

Doug tried to look hurt. It didn't work. 'Fair enough,' he said, heading for the door and holding it open for her. 'After you, ma'am.'

They walked out into a typical Edinburgh night; cold and wet. Susie didn't mind, the chill helped her head.

'Want to get a taxi?' Doug asked.

'Nah, let's walk a bit,' she said, pulling her jacket tight against the cold.

They set off down the street. As they walked, Susie felt a flicker of panic. She was playing a dangerous game, she knew it. Burns wouldn't be happy about the amount of time she was spending with the reporter that had caused him – and her – so much trouble. Weighed it up, found she didn't care. She could worry about it tomorrow.

Tonight, she needed a friend. Someone who understood what she had been through, who would see her as more than the stupid bitch at the office who fucked her boss, ended his marriage and kept her job. Someone to talk to, confide in.

Off the record, of course.

• • •

Hal stood in the kitchen, lights off, the TV on the wall muted as the news ticker crawled across the screen and a presenter with too-perfect teeth and hair so styled it looked painful silently spoke in front of a picture of Richard Buchan.

The story had begun to break just after 6pm. There weren't many details, the official line was that Richard Buchan, the Tory MSP who recently lost his daughter, had been hospitalised following an incident believed to involve a member of the press at his Stockbridge home. It hadn't taken Hal long to get the rest of the story. All it took was a call and a few flattering words to Jonathan.

So now he stood, listening to the gentle hum of the fridge, adding what Jonathan had told him to what he knew. Thinking about the woman involved in the hit-and-run that Buchan covered up with a little help from the then Chief Constable. Was she just an innocent bystander, someone who was in the wrong place at the wrong time? Or was she something more? Another hooker he decided to use and abuse? Who fought back and paid the price?

Maybe. And even if she was, so what? It wasn't Hal's business. Buchan wasn't his client. He had been hired to do a job, had done it. End of story.

Except…

Except, every time Hal thought about it, about what Buchan had done to his own daughter, he thought of Jennifer. Lying in his arms, helpless, defenceless, relying on him – her *father* – to protect her from the world. And he would. He knew that.

His phone was in his hand before he realised it, the text written. '*You might want to have a look at Buchan's car crash from a few years ago. Ask the Chief Superintendent about the girl who wasn't there and absolutely wasn't hurt. Call me if you want to know more.*'

Hit send, switched the phone off. If McGregor was going to reply, Hal didn't want to deal with it.

Not tonight. Not when he had a daughter to kiss goodnight and a husband to hold in the dark.

• • •

Sam found the picture two days later, wedged between the shed and fence at the bottom of the garden, roughly wrapped in an old jacket. It was a portrait photograph of a woman on a beach, arms wrapped around herself, smiling against the wind that whipped her hair into long blonde streamers around her head. She was beautiful, but she looked tired to Sam.

There was nothing with the photo, but when he flipped it over, he found '*Eric Mullard Studios*' printed on the back of the frame, along with a handwritten scrawl: '*So I can watch you while you work,*' it read. '*I have faith, Derek, thanks to you. Love you, Kx*'

Sam rewrapped the picture in the jacket and took it back to the house. He would hang it in Derek's room. It would be there for him when he came home.

Acknowledgements

With huge thanks to Bob McDevitt for his unstinting support of my work, Craig and Sara at Saraband for putting me on a bookshelf, Joe Farquharson for the brilliant cover design and the sprints between streetlamps, and my Mum and Dad for (almost) never complaining about the printer churning out yet another story at 2am when I was growing up.

And, of course, to my wife, Fiona, who encouraged me every step of the way and remains the best decision I ever made. Love you, B – always.

About the author

Bob McDevitt

Neil Broadfoot worked as a journalist for fifteen years at both national and local newspapers, covering some of the biggest stories of the day. A poacher turned gamekeeper, he has since moved into communications: providing media relations advice for a variety of organisations, from Strathclyde Fire & Rescue Service to high-profile sporting clubs in Scotland. He's now working as a communications officer for the Scottish Government.

Neil is married to Fiona and a father to two girls, meaning he's completely outnumbered in his own home. He lives in Dunfermline, the setting for his first job as a local reporter. *Falling Fast* is his first novel.